I0549207

In the Light
of the Eclipse

A Novel

Bryan Caron

Divine Trinity Films
Publication

In the Light of the Eclipse
Published by Divine Trinity Films
©2013 Divine Trinity Films
http://publications.divinetrinityfilms.com
www.divinetrinityfilms.com

Text Copyright ©2013 Bryan Caron

Original Cover Art
Designed by Bryan Caron
©2013 Bryan Caron

I would like to thank the dreamers who
challenged me to write this tale:

Amber, Sammi, Rebecca, Dustin and Heather.

Your inspiration is everlasting.

Contents

For Paula

In the Light
of the Eclipse

1

Zoe and Kayla

Zoe met Kayla by accident on the bridge overlooking Lover's Pond. It was a brisk, slightly foggy morning and Zoe was out on her usual jog around the lake (something she did to keep herself busy between waking in the morning and heading off for schooling, more so than staying fit or healthy). As she crossed the bridge at just past six fifteen (she remembered the time well because it was ten minutes earlier than when she would normally cross the pond; her feet felt so much lighter that day), Zoe stopped to take in the sounds and smells of the morning, which on a day like this—as the dew dripped off the flowers and the soft hint of moisture caressed her face—was just delightful. She leaned up against the rail to let the rays of the sun breaking through the thinning fog warm her face and noticed something peculiar in the water. It wasn't a duck or a fish as one might expect to see in the early morning, but a family of pearls dancing just above the water. Zoe slid her head between the lowest rails to get a better look and the pearls disappeared under the water. She strained to see where they might have gone, but it was still too dark to get a real good look into the normally crystal clear water. Maybe she had imagined it.

Then Kayla was there. The splash of her hair pushed Zoe back in surprise. She hit the bridge tremendously hard, splintering not just the rail but her head just the same. She slipped down to lay on the boards, halfway between complete awareness and passing out. For the briefest of moments, Zoe swore she saw a pair of fins splash up from under the water, but that was just silly—mermaids (along with dozens of other such supernatural creatures like ghosts, witches, demons and angels) only existed in fairytale stories, like the fairest of them all, *Little Snow-White*, read to her every night before bed when she was just a babe learning to walk. It turns out that what Zoe thought was a fin was simply the eccentric cut of the sea-green towel that Kayla now wrapped around her brilliantly tan, flawless skin (though these attributes could simply have been figments of the blur in Zoe's eyes).

"Are you okay?" Kayla asked. Her voice was kind and sweet—maybe a little too sweet—as was her touch. The towel felt comfortably familiar against her skin, soft and pleasant, as if she was back home playing with her family's sheep. It felt good to know that the fleece she sheared didn't actually go to waste, though she knew it was most likely mixed with Gail and Timber's cotton to make it ever so softer.

Zoe pressed her hand to the back of her head where warm blood trickled down her neck. "I think so," she said, her voice gruff and a little groggy, though it was completely understandable why.

"I'm sorry for scaring you," Kayla said as she helped sit Zoe up against the rails. "I thought you were a caretaker."

"I thought you were a mermaid."

Kayla laughed. "I wish to Heather I was. That would be awesome. I love swimming."

"Me, too. But not enough to break the rules." A standing rule of Quorum Circle nobles was that no one shall ever go swimming without a noble present, to be both lifeguard and watch tower. Zoe and Kayla were both still much too young to understand exactly why.

"You aren't going to tell anyone, are you?" Kayla was fraught with anxiety, which made Zoe wonder if Kayla had been caught before. Was the punishment for such an act that bad? Perhaps it was for a second (or third, or maybe even fourth) offense.

"I won't say anything," Zoe said.

"It'll be our secret?"

"Yeah."

Kayla wrapped her arms around Zoe with delightful fervor. "Thank you thank you thank you thank you thank you."

Zoe hissed as Kayla's appreciation bit at her wound.

"Sorry," Kayla said.

"It's okay. Just promise you won't do it anymore."

Kayla stood and held her pinkie high in the air. "I swear on the heart of Heather, I will never again swim alone." It was a promise Zoe accepted as truth, but one that wasn't about to be honored. Kayla would return to the pond at the crack of sunrise at least once a week, and though Zoe suspected as such, she never confronted Kayla about it, or ever told anyone. She wouldn't have been much of a friend if she did.

Zoe smiled and slipped back to the boards, quite dizzy and sick.

"We better get you back home," Kayla said. She helped Zoe to her feet, resting the patient's arm around her neck for balance the way she saw her caretaker, Daniel, do for Thomas after celebrating the start of his seventeenth year of breath, though that was for other reasons altogether—reasons Kayla wasn't allowed to find out about for another few years. "Where do you live?"

"Pasture Ranch," Zoe said. "Near the back winds."

"Feather my tail," Kayla chirped. "How'd you get so lucky?"

"Lucky? Why? Where do you live?"

"Just outside the hub in industry squalors."

Zoe laughed, not because Kayla lived there (though the only time she was ever allowed to spend there was when she helped Francis drop off the newest crop of fleece for production), but because of what she called it. Kayla still seemed to take offense. "I'm sorry," Zoe said to rectify the misunderstanding. "I've never heard it called that before."

"Yeah."

Zoe wasn't quite sure what that meant, but she let it go. For all she knew, she'd never again see Kayla. They may have been a part of the same community, but they were from two very different worlds. Where Pasture Ranch, with its peaceful ambiance and extravagant views, was believed by most to be an Eden, Industry Quarters (even with its complete lack of crime, decent standard of living and the decadent aroma of bread and other fine, delicious scents that filled the air) was considered a slum—what with the absurd amounts of lumber art and the near-constant holler of machines. In the scheme of it all, Industry Quarters was a far better place to live than even the best place in the rest of the world— or so the students were taught—but it was still a small, overly crowded burg compared to the vastness of farms that stretched for miles along the eastern edge of the Horizon Desert (which itself stretched west as far as the eye could see and then some). Only a dozen cultivators were allowed to raise animals and till the land. Everyone else was otherwise banned from stepping foot upon it (unless it was your turn to study and learn pertinent farming methods)—not because of any old quorum rule, mind you, but because the caretakers believed the farms were sacred and had to be treated as such. So it was with Kayla, a free spirit unafraid to break the rules set by man, but unwilling to break the unwritten rules set by her god.

"What's wrong?" Zoe said, knowing full well of her reticence.

"Can you make it back from here?" Kayla asked.

"Come on, scaredy-cat. It doesn't hurt." Zoe pulled Kayla across the imaginary line separating the exceptional from the ordinary. Within that first step, Kayla cried out and jumped back, shaking. It wasn't long at all before Kayla was running back down the path toward the Grand Hub, obviously heading home to Industry Quarters. Zoe lowered her head with a little bit of shame and a little bit offended. She wondered if there was anything she could do or say that would change this ridiculous mindset that residents of Pasture Ranch were somehow better—more revered—than everyone else. It wasn't true; in fact, if anything, Zoe was more like Kayla than any of her fellow cultivators.

When she got back home, Frances and Maisy, Zoe's caretakers and a lively pair of hoodwinks, stood on the porch watching her walk from the edge of the cornfield to the warping steps. To her surprise, instead of being angry and upset about being late for her morning studies, Maisy hugged and kissed her.

"Thank Heather," Maisy said. "I've been worried sick. Where have you been?"

"I was on my run and I fell and hit my head." Zoe revealed her bloody palm.

"Frances, hurry. Get the physician."

"I'm okay," Zoe assured her.

But Maisy was her caretaker, thus obligated to care for her. She pulled at Zoe's hair, searching for the wound to see how bad it actually was. "What were you doing?"

"I was playing with my friend," Zoe said, careful not to reveal Kayla's indiscretion. She may have insulted her by running off the way she did but she still wouldn't tattle on her.

"Which friend?"

Zoe opened her mouth to say and then realized she didn't even know her name. How odd and rude was that?

"Why is everyone scared of us?" Zoe asked instead.

Maisy smiled and hugged her. "Come on," she said, shuffling Zoe into the house. "Let's clean you up."

The physician, Nestor, arrived about an hour later. By then, the wound had all but congealed. He cut it back open anyway, not only to make sure that it hadn't gotten infected, but to allow his ward, JD, to learn the fine art of sutures. JD's hands were shaky and he apologized each time he poked Zoe with the needle (which was a lot). Zoe giggled every time he did, hoping it would make JD more comfortable. When he finally finished (taking much longer than it should have, especially with Zoe only receiving three stitches), Zoe smiled and shook his hand.

"Thank you," she said and kissed him on the cheek. He blushed; it was so cute.

None of it, though, healed the real wound Zoe obtained that day. In fact, there wasn't any medicine or cure in the world, much less inside Nestor's bag of tricks, that could. Zoe knew of only one way to do that, an opportunity that presented itself the very next morning. Frances was to go into Industry Quarters to collect orders for the fresh crop of corn that was about ready to harvest, and Zoe, with her fluttering eyes and cherub smile, talked him into skipping her morning studies to go with him.

The day started with a stop at the Milk Wagon, home to the most superb French toast she had ever eaten. They took a seat near the back—the booth in the corner that allowed her the perfect view of the mountains, and at the same time, sight of anyone and everyone who came in to eat. When Greta, the owner of the Milk Wagon (and a delight in any conversation) served their breakfast, she pinched Zoe's cheek with the affection of a caretaker, a habit that lasted for many years, and one Zoe would never tire of. She even joined them at one point to discuss the merits of a book Zoe was tasked to read—and one she didn't understand in the least (unlike many others, which she understood with great aplomb). It was hard to leave, and not just because her stomach was so weighted down by the sugary and syrupy and buttery sweetness of her breakfast. Greta was very insightful, genuine and caring—qualities that weren't always present in everyone she met (and had yet the pleasure of meeting). But Zoe was on a mission; finding Kayla had to remain her top priority. She pulled at Frances' arm and begged for his cooperation, ending his conversation prematurely. His apologies weren't necessary as Zoe all but dragged him out the door.

Once in Industry Quarters, Zoe snuck away to find Kayla. Little did she know that Kayla had training in the Palisade Mines and wouldn't return until sunset. To stall, Zoe asked Frances to show her how to take orders; something she would eventually have to learn anyway. Problem was, it ended up making the work go faster. Once she proved she could do it without any help, Frances had them split up—cover more ground in a shorter amount of time. Zoe thought about "losing" her order sheets so that they would have to retake them, but that would be ethically wrong; she couldn't do that. With an hour before sunset, and all orders taken, Frances collected them up and they headed for the Grand Hub. Lucky for Zoe, Frances ran into Victor, a shopkeeper in the Quarters, to gather the next week's worth of stock. The two fell into a long discussion, yammering on about fishing at Fallen Island and how good the crop was this year. Zoe couldn't believe they could talk so long and so much about the same boring topics, but it did keep them there long enough for Kayla and her study group to return. Zoe immediately apologized for trying to force her to do something she didn't want to do.

"Can we be friends?" Zoe asked.

"Yeah," Kayla said, hugging Zoe with a bear hug so tight it popped her shoulders.

"Who's your friend, Zoe?" Frances said, resting his hand on Zoe's shoulder.

"Kayla," Kayla said, stretching her hand out for Frances to shake.

"Nice to meet you Kayla," Frances said. "Where'd you two meet?"

"I told you yesterday," Zoe said. "She helped me when I hit my head, remember?"

"Of course. How soon I forget. Thank you for your help, Kayla. Now, we better be getting back."

"Can I stay here tonight?"

"Not tonight, Zoe."

"Please," Kayla said. "I'd really like her to stay."

"Please," Zoe added.

Both of their faces were cuter than a newborn bunny, as their little baby teeth (Kayla's front teeth, having already been replaced by fully grown adult teeth, actually made her look a little bit like a rabbit) sparkled bright in the setting sun under their constant pleas, their folded hands and adorable eyes. How could he not give in to that?

"Thank you," Zoe said and hugged Kayla again. They jumped up and down together.

"This is going to be the best," Kayla said.

The two of them ran off hand in hand, leaving Frances with nothing but a smile and the satisfaction of having made the right choice.

From that day on—and for the next eight years—Zoe and Kayla were nearly inseparable. They spent all of their free time together running, swimming, homework, chores, rock climbing, cooking and even sometimes sleep (though whenever they had a midnight sleepover, it was always at Kayla's, as there was no way Zoe was ever going to talk her into staying the night in Pasture

Ranch). Whatever it was, they loved each other's company, possibly because the secret they shared bound them in a trust that only came around once every eclipse.

It really was something special.

2

A Secret Morning Swim

On the morning that marked the beginning of Kayla's eighteenth year of breath, Zoe got up an hour before the rooster's crow and headed into Industry Quarters. She had never walked the streets at night before so it was a bit scary, but also quite amazing. The smell of baking bread was at its strongest and the bright glow of the full moon turned the artwork all around her into a fluorescent wonderland. It made it all the more brilliant to lie back in the shadows and watch a couple of kids turn paint into such beautiful pictures. She almost wanted to join them in taking brush in hand but she had something much more pressing to do, and time was of the essence.

Zoe inched her way through the slightly wilted bushes surrounding Kayla's house and pressed her hands firmly on the glass of her bedroom window. Kayla never locked her window so it was quite easy to open and crawl in without rousing her, though she hoped the change in noise level from the roar of the machines didn't do it for her. Thankfully, Kayla was still asleep when the room returned to silence. Zoe snuck up to Kayla's bureau and shoveled her swimming suit, towel and a change of clothes into her pack, a task that took longer than expected (it couldn't just be any old clothes; it had to at least look good together). When she was happy with what she had chosen, Zoe tiptoed back to Kayla's bed and kissed her cheek.

"Wake up, sleepy," she whispered into Kayla's ear.

Kayla groaned and rolled over. "Go away."

"Kayla, wake up," Zoe said, shaking her shoulder.

When Kayla finally realized who it was, she sat up quickly and looked around as if her caretakers were hiding in the walls, waiting for just the right reason to take her to Quorum Circle for punishment. "Zoe," she whispered. "What in Heather's name are you doing here? What time is it?"

"It's time to give you my gift."

Each year, to mark the day of a person's first breath, caretakers and friends would do something special for that person, from taking over that day's chores to whisking them off to Serenity Lake for a grand snorkel, so long as it was something that was unique to the presenter of the gift. For this, the last gift Zoe would ever give Kayla, she wanted to do something more amazing than life. She pulled Kayla out of bed.

"What are you doing?"

"It's a secret. Come on."

Kayla felt a little blushed walking the streets of Industry Quarters in her sleeping gown, especially when they passed Henry (who had a not-so-secret crush on Kayla) sweeping flour out of his caretaker's factory.

"Where are you two lovely ladies headed off to so early?" Henry said.

"No time to chat," Zoe said, keeping from making eye contact.

If she had, she would have felt obligated to stop, and Zoe was in far too much a hurry to do that. Henry did it for her.

"Just wait, I'll come with." Henry set the broom against the inside of the door and jogged after them. "Wait up."

Now Zoe had to stop. "You can't come, Henry." Her hand was outstretched, keeping him from coming any closer. Kayla was pulled in behind her.

"Why? What's the big deal?"

"I'm giving Kayla her gift. This is for her and I alone. So if you don't mind…"

"Her gift? What could you possibly be giving her this early?"

"None of your business," Kayla interjected. She stepped around Zoe, who felt a little honored and shocked (though she didn't know why). "Now be a good little boy and get back to work. Go on." She waved her hand. How Kayla could get away with that was beyond Zoe, even if Henry was a year younger than her (and no more than a couple of months older than Zoe, for that matter). Maybe she was using his infatuation against him.

Then again, maybe not.

"No. I want to see what this is."

"We aren't moving until you leave," Kayla said.

"That's fine. I have all day."

"We don't," Zoe whispered to Kayla. She acknowledged her, but with only the slightest turn of her head so that Henry might not notice.

"I don't want to have to get physical," Kayla said. Her voice was strong, commanding. "But I will if I have to."

"Do you promise?" Henry said, which disgusted Kayla to no end.

"Just leave us alone."

"Tell me where you're off to and maybe I will."

"No."

Henry shrugged. Zoe grew ever more irritated. The sun would be up soon; once it was, her gift would be ruined. If she weren't such a lady (or had been taught to be such by her caretakers), she probably would have popped him one (or urged Kayla to, in the very least) just to make her point. Luckily, she didn't have to.

"Is there a problem here?" Luke said as he slowly sauntered up to them. In tow behind him were a few others, including Alan and Harper—a group dubbed the Heather Biters (so known because of their tendency to bite the hand that fed them), for which Kayla was a supportive member. Zoe didn't know them well, but she was fully aware of the group (as was almost everyone in Heather), which was comprised mostly of folks from Industry Quarters—though recruitment also spanned to the Palisade Mines and Fishers Wharf—who didn't care much for the laws of Heather. They avoided the teachings of the church and fought for a longer, more fulfilling life, even if that meant living in fear of becoming destitute. They were small, often detested, but were loyal to a fault; something Zoe was proud to believe came from her via Kayla.

Henry shifted back as the three of them stepped between him and Kayla. "No problem," he said.

"We need to go," Zoe said, this time louder, hoping the Heather Biters would hear.

"You go ahead," Luke said. He crossed his arms, never once taking his eyes from Henry. "We'll make sure he doesn't follow you."

"Thank you." Zoe pulled Kayla away, looking back a couple of times to make sure the Heather Biters didn't go and do anything drastic. She didn't want Henry to follow (and if she had a choice, she wouldn't ever have to lay eyes on him again), but at the same time, she didn't believe he deserved to get hurt.

Kayla's attention, though, remained on Zoe, excited to find out where exactly they were going, which as it turned out, just so happened to be where they first met—Lover's Pond.

"What are we doing here?" Kayla asked. The crisp air nipped at her skin.

"What else?" Zoe tossed Kayla her summing suit.

Kayla was a bit confused until Zoe stripped down to her very own suit. "Are you crazy?" Kayla said.

"No more crazy than you've ever been." With a smile, Zoe leapt into the water.

Kayla huffed a laugh. Knowing how much Zoe hated her for swimming off hours, to see her at the center of those dark ripples verified what a truly great friend she was. She couldn't have asked for a better gift.

"What are you waiting for," Zoe said, "a noble? Get your tiny little behind in this pond already."

Kayla quickly changed out of her sleeping gown and was swimming alongside Zoe in no time flat. As the rising sun warmed the water, Kayla caught Zoe by surprise and dunked her. When Zoe was able to rise (coughing up a fit after swallowing some water), she sprinted after Kayla to return the favor. This type of horseplay, as well as challenging each other to see who could hold their breath the longest, who could throw a rock the farthest, and how straight they could do a handstand under water, lasted until the sun had risen well past the tip of the mountain peak. A noble would arrive shortly to check that the pond life was fed and that no extraneous trash had found its way in from the ocean.

"Time to get back, I guess," Kayla said. She was disappointed, and understandably so.

"What's the hurry?" Zoe rose from the pond and pulled the towels from her pack. She set them out at the edge of the pond and lied down. "It's too nice a day to rush back."

Kayla quickly joined her, soaking it all in. "You are amazing," she said finally. "Thank you for this."

"Anything for my best friend," Zoe said. "I'll be honest, though. I never thought it would be this much fun. I totally get why you do it now."

"Let that be a lesson to you. Listen to me more often."

"Consider me schooled."

They laughed, interrupted only by the arrival of the noble (Jonas, if Zoe wasn't mistaken).

"What are you two doing out here this early?" Jonas asked. "You haven't been swimming, have you?"

"Of course not," Zoe said quickly, shocking Kayla. "It's Kayla's day of breath and I thought it would be nice to join her in getting a good tan for her party tonight. That's all."

Jonas eyed them carefully. Zoe smiled, almost reaching complete flirtation. It wasn't that hard to do. With his height, his chiseled jaw and what could have only been rock-solid abs, if Jonas had been ten years younger, Zoe would have had no problem coupling with him if he asked. Kayla added a wink for good measure. Jonas hinted at his own smile before crossing the bridge to go about his work.

Kayla tried hard to keep it quiet, but there was no chance of hiding her laughter. "I never would have guessed you to be this devious," she said.

"I learn," Zoe said, laughing along with her.

The rest of the morning was spent tanning in between cool dips under the supervision (and flirtatious twinkle) of Jonas, talking about Kayla's upcoming party, what others may gift her with this year, and which boys they'd like to companion with (and some they'd just like to companion). The physician's ward, JD, who had just celebrated his seventeenth breath a month before and looked hotter and studlier than any other boy their age, was the only one they agreed on (and one they swore never to pursue lest the other live through a horribly degrading embarrassment). It was all a much needed breath of fresh air, especially for Kayla, who hadn't had a carefree day for quite some time. But as the sun hit its peak at midday, Kayla spun their light and airy chats into a topic that Zoe wasn't at all comfortable discussing.

"I'm not going to the lottery tomorrow."

Saying such a thing felt almost blasphemous. Zoe really didn't know how to respond. "But you have to," she ended up saying. "It's mandatory."

"Yeah, but I'll be dead in a matter of weeks anyway. So what's the point?"

She was right, and Zoe had nothing but compassion for that fact. Where God so loved the world, Heather, for whom the very few dared to dub "the goddess of condemnation," held a much crueler hand over her inhabitants. Every seventeen years, under her ever-watchful eye, an eclipse would render the entire land dark, and in its wake, Heather herself would remove the soul of every man and woman who had surpassed the age of seventeen years and take them home to the land of the unknown nothing. Why Heather required such an excessive sacrifice for the special bounty of riches she so graciously provided (which included ever flourishing crops and an abundance of shops and eateries) was uncertain, but some believed that it was a way to keep the land pure of evil and disease—a wrath of cleansing, if you will—that probably went back as far as the beginning of life itself. Not even the act of prayer or surrender could keep someone from living past the age of thirty-four, or as in Kayla's case, the ripe young age of eighteen. Zoe completely understood what Kayla was feeling and couldn't fault her for opening up to her. "It doesn't seem fair, does it?"

"You're damn right, it's *not* fair. In what just world is a little girl forced to suffer the heartbreak of losing her entire family in one snap of the finger?" She, of course, was speaking of her little sister, Lenoire (or as most everyone called her, Lenny), who was given breath by Kayla's caretakers nine years after the last eclipse. Lenny was a rare breed, branded with a sickness at birth, rendering her mute and unable to relate to anyone except those she was familiar. It was especially hard for her to accept change. If anything ever became out of place, or if someone touched her the wrong way (as Zoe found out once, stealing her nose was *not* a good idea), she would go into a fit that couldn't be quelled for anything. It was a hard life to begin with, but Kayla loved Lenny more than the sun and the stars, and having to leave her with strangers at this stage in her life was unforgivable. "What kind of heartless god would do such a thing?"

"I don't know," Zoe said. "But Heather is our god, and she has her reasons."

"She has no right." Kayla wrapped her arms around her knees and stared out at the horizon

"Maybe. But we have to believe that her reasons are pure."

"We aren't all special like you, little miss child of the eclipse."

Zoe turned away. As a final gift for her people's sacrifice, Heather would bestow a child, born with the eclipse, upon the land. Some believed this child held special powers (though that has never been proven); still others believed that the child inhabited every soul that was taken under the eclipse. No matter the belief, one thing was certain—the child of the eclipse was Heather's voice, without whom crops would die, people would rise up and the land would crumble. The child gave the residents hope that one day her wrath would end. To use this status in a derogatory way did hurt, but Zoe couldn't take it personally. Kayla was just as hurt by what was approaching and she needed to vent.

"Lenny doesn't understand this whole game," Kayla continued, "and yet, tomorrow she's going to be handed to some new, unknown face just like that. And there's nothing I can do about it. So the way I see it, it's better I don't know who picks her."

"You don't really believe that, do you? Whoever it is that picks her, you can help them. You can help Lenny."

"The only way I can help Lenny is to steal her away. Just take her and leave this place once and for all."

"You can't do that."

"Why not? All we'd have to do is take your father's boat out to sea and let the winds carry us where they may. At least then we might have a fighting chance."

"A chance at what, exactly?"

"A long life. The most Lenny can hope for here is seventeen more years. What kind of life is that? Really?"

"That's the draw."

"It's a load of feathers is what it is."

"Maybe," Zoe said, "but I have to believe that all life is a gift and we have to accept the time we're given." She rubbed Kayla's back lightly. "No matter what."

"I know."

"Besides, you don't even know if leaving will do anything."

"Just because no one has ever come back doesn't mean anything."

"You may be right. But what happens when you're out at sea and the eclipse takes your life anyway? What happens to Lenny then? Instead of another seventeen fruitful years, she'll die, just like you. How can you possibly take that chance?"

This time Kayla had no answer. She fought back tears. "You don't get it," she finally said. "You can't possibly understand. You've been blessed by Heather's own hand. You were born on the eclipse. You were picked by Maisy to live on the ranch. You were given the chance at a full, complete life. And here I am, born two weeks too early. How am I supposed to react to that?"

"Live." Zoe held Kayla for another hour in silence before they left to return to her home, which had been dressed in streamers and banners and giant lights that lit up the entire street.

"I can't stay for the party," Zoe said, a bit guilty. "I have to harvest the north side of the field this afternoon. But I hope you'll give some thought to coming to the lottery tomorrow. It won't feel right without you there."

"I will," Kayla said, though it felt more polite than sincere. Zoe squeezed the back of Kayla's neck before departing. When she was gone from view, Kayla went inside, drew Lenny a bath and then took a nap before everyone arrived for her day of breath party—one she couldn't enjoy in the least. It was meant to be a celebration, with cake and treats piled as high as the sky, but this year it felt like nothing more than a living wake. The only thing on her mind all night—and into the rise of the next morning— was what would happen to Lenny after Heather stole Kayla away from her. It was enough to curse the heavens and weep for the possibility that she might, in a generous act of kindness, be spared from her inevitable fate.

3

The Lottery

Zoe was up early, dressed in her best gown. A child would be betrothed to her today, branding her an official caretaker and blossoming her into a woman under the eyes of Heather, so she wanted to look her absolute best. After all, it was a day to be remembered; it was a day to be honored; it was a day to be proud.

It was a day Zoe wanted so badly to share with her best friend.

Maisy walked into Zoe's bedroom with her hands cupped around her mouth. "You look beautiful."

Zoe blushed brighter than the rose in her hair. It was a rare occasion when she would doll herself up like this (church didn't count, as she never put this much makeup on for that, or wore anything quite as fancy), and when she did, all of the admiration that came with it embarrassed her to no end. "Thank you," she said anyway to appease Maisy, who fixed the light curls of Zoe's hair a bit, bringing some forward across her chest.

"You nervous?"

"Not really," Zoe said, though she wasn't exactly sure what she was feeling. "I'd feel better if I knew for sure Kayla was going to be there."

"She'll be there," Maisy assured. Zoe still couldn't fully believe that. "We better go if we want to make it on time."

Zoe brushed her gown to make sure any errant creases were knocked out and walked with Maisy and Frances to the Grand Hub, where everyone was gathered around the fountain in the main square. The statue at the center, allowing water to fall from one hand, flowers and plant life from the other, was the human representation of Heather. No one knew for sure what Heather actually looked like or whether she was even half as beautiful as the creators believed her to be, so it was actually more of a representation of the purity and sanctity of the land itself than of the woman who had become the goddess.

To the north of the fountain, facing Industry Quarters (so as to have the mountains of Palisade Mines as the backdrop of the event), was a large stage with banners and flags in several different colors flapping about in the wind. Each flag represented a different community of Heather, one of which would be given to each individual between the ages of fifteen and seventeen to announce where each one would live for the next seventeen years. Zoe wasn't at all worried, as she would undoubtedly inherit her caretaker's farm, just as every other ward would inherit their caretaker's homes in their own communities. To those who did not have a ward that would survive the eclipse, or was over the age of eighteen—like Zoe's neighbors, Georgia and Leland, whose ward, Mason, was ten at the time of the last lottery, or Carlton of Palisade Mines, who was fourteen at the last lottery and never coupled— were obligated to give their homes up to wards of multiple child families, based upon the scores they received in their schooling exams. That meant that Kayla's home was one that would be given to a new family this year, adding to the burden of whoever selected Lenny as their new ward.

Zoe looked for Kayla as everyone muddled around, talking mostly about what age they wanted their wards to be or where they hoped to be placed. Henry, being one of the eldest males to participate in the lottery, was confident that he'd be given a home in Pasture Ranch, due to his higher than high marks on his butchering skills (which meant he was looking to take Raynor's house, where all the cattle was raised). By the time Terry, the quorum headmaster, took to the stage, Kayla was still nowhere to be found.

"To all residents of Heather," Terry said with a booming voice that traveled beyond the mountain pass, "let me declare a good day to you all and welcome you to the lottery of the forthcoming eclipse."

Everyone applauded except for a very few, including Zoe. A day ago, she would have been right there with them all, but thanks to Kayla, she had become quite indifferent about the entire thing. Was it right for Heather to do what she did, even if it was for a pure or just reason? Zoe finally did start clapping, though only when Frances and Maisy urged her to do so.

"Thank you," Terry continued. "Now, to begin the festivities, I would like to invite my ward and soon-to-be quorum headmaster, Susanna, to speak to you all."

This time Zoe did applaud alongside everyone else. No matter what she felt about the impending events, there was no cause for rudeness when dealing with the nobles. And Susanna, as far as Zoe knew, was a nice girl and would make a very good headmaster.

"Thank you all," Susanna said as she waved for her people to close their applause. Her voice was far from as loud as Terry's, but she still presented a clear and commanding presence. "Thank you. You are all wonderful and I appreciate your kindness. You know, I was just an infant when Terry selected me to be his ward. And though I would never come to truly know my birthrights, I am very gracious for all that Terry has provided me and taught me over my sixteen years. I can only hope and pray upon Heather's gracious heart and kind hand that I am able to provide my ward with the same amount of love that I was given, and that those of you who will be watching over this land from Heather's abode will be proud of me and my rule."

Zoe couldn't help but be moved by the sentiment. It was everything she ever wanted to say to her own caretakers.

"I also hope," Susanna continued as the cheers died into the wind, "that I can make all of you who will continue on with me here in Heather as proud as I am of Terry and the love and generosity he gave to all of you in Heather's name. Praise be to Heather and praise be to our continued love and charity as we pass through the light of the eclipse. Glory be to Heather."

"Glory be to Heather," the crowd repeated. Terry hugged Susanna as the crowd applauded. Zoe knew this pause in the festivities would be longer, so she took the time to once again look for Kayla. She didn't want to leave Frances or Maisy's side, so she had to scan with just her eyes, a decision of no help whatsoever. The streets were far too crowded and Zoe was far too short to see over everyone. What did catch her eye, though, as the headmaster called out for quiet and took to announcing the rules of the lottery itself (something that wasn't really necessary, as everyone already knew what was to come, but a tradition nonetheless), was a girl she didn't recognize and swore she hadn't ever seen before—which was odd because she looked no more older than sixteen. She wore a dark brown cloak with a hood that looked as if it would fall from her head at any second, but stayed stationary and firm against the back of her head, under which was a tapestry of rich black hair (a deep ebony, if she wasn't mistaken) that bounced with curls that never ended. What was most striking about her, though, were her lips—bright red amongst a pale white skin.

"Snow White," Zoe whispered and smiled.

"Zoe, ward of Frances and Maisy," Terry called.

"Zoe," Maisy said, pushing her toward the stage. It took a second, but Zoe finally understood what was happening.

"Here," she called out. "I'm here." Terry called out another name, Bailey, followed by Justine, as Zoe made her way up onto the stage. Being the first child to be given breath at the last eclipse, she would get to choose her ward first, followed by the next to be given breath and so on until all of the females aged no less than fifteen had their picks. This would, of course, be followed by all of the males that were fifteen years or older (some of which would not be able to participate in the lottery because the amount of wards to the number of caretakers was always quite a bit less). Because of the eclipse, there was usually a pretty large gap between the last of the seventeen-year-olds (of which this year, there were eight, including Susanna) and the first to be born after the eclipse. In this case, Ressa and Christopher didn't give their daughter, Kelly, breath for almost a year after, which meant that she had only just turned sixteen. But she was only the first of about five-dozen girls born during those first two years after the eclipse.

Once all of the girls were lined up on the stage according to their date of breath, Susanna spoke again to the crowd. "These represent the young girls who will select among the lottery. Before they do so, we will designate their home. First up is Zoe, the daughter of the eclipse, and in Heather's good graces, she will have the opportunity to choose her new home."

Zoe was a little shocked. She didn't expect to be able to choose her home, and though for a second she thought about the possibility of living in Industry Quarters, if nothing more than to prove it wasn't as bad a place as most believed it to be, she thought first of the child she was about to inherit. Her current home was the best place to raise a child, not to mention that farming was what Zoe loved to do most.

"I choose to remain at my current residence," Zoe said, but had to repeat it a second time, as the first was too quiet for most near the back of the crowd to hear.

"Praise, Heather," Susanna said and handed Zoe a red flag. She raised it high in the air, even though she didn't want to, as it was just a way to flaunt her presumed preeminence. She lowered it quickly and smiled graciously, if not entirely genuine. Susanna then held up a small, gold cauldron with a sparkling handle that held the names of all the children under fifteen to the crowd for a warm reception. When she lowered it down in front of Zoe, she said in a clear command, "Select your ward."

Zoe took a breath. For the first time all day, she was nervous. She didn't think she would be, but as she looked out at the crowd, she still couldn't see the most familiar face among dozens of familiar faces, and that was devastating. What calmed her nerves was the most unfamiliar of them all, Snow White, a face she chose to keep her focus on as she reached into the cauldron, praying to Heather that she would pull Lenny's name. Lenny knew Zoe more than anyone else that would survive the eclipse and she believed that her acclimation into her new environment would be much easier if she was there to guide her. She selected a small metal plate that felt as lucky as any other and handed it to Susanna. Turning her focus to Heather and all of her glory, Zoe closed her eyes and lowered her head, repeating Lenny's name over and over in the lightest of whispers.

"Janette, blood ward of Christian and Gertrude," Susanna announced.

Zoe's shoulders dropped in disappointment. She recomposed herself quickly, knowing all eyes were on her. Letting anyone know of her discontent was rude and unbecoming of the child of the eclipse. She smiled bright (no matter how fake it might have been) as Gertrude and Christian walked Janette, a young four-year-old from the Grand Hub, up to the stage to meet Zoe. Her smile became quite genuine quite fast as she realized Janette was just as precious a gift as any other, including Lenny. At this point, it was custom to return to the new caretaker's home, or at the very least go off someplace quiet and get to know each other. But Zoe wasn't in the right state of mind to do that just yet. She would be spending plenty of time with Janette over the next two weeks to acclimate her from her old lifestyle to her new lifestyle. Right now, Zoe was much more interested in finding out who would pull Lenny's name from the cauldron. Christian and Gertrude were very understanding and took Janette down to Lover's Pond.

Zoe sat at the edge of the fountain. The light spray of water the wind picked up hit the back of her neck as she waited for Lenny's name to be announced. Sometimes a loud cheer roared through the crowd as a caretaker from Pasture Ranch chose a ward from Industry Quarters, or when one of the caretakers from the Grand Hub or the Quarters was granted a new home in Palisade Mines, Fishers Wharf, Pasture Ranch, or even in Quorum Circle. Elisa was granted the farm just down the path from Zoe's, but when she pulled the name Paul from the cauldron, Zoe grew even more frustrated. If there was anyone she hoped would get Lenny, it would be a new caretaker in Pasture Ranch, a prospect that quickly became less of a possibility with the disappearance of each new red flag. By the time the last girl chose her ward (little two-year-old Tommy from Palisade Mines, who would now grow up in Industry Quarters), Zoe had lost all hope.

The boys were called up to the stage next (numbering some-where in the three dozen range, though it might have been more; Zoe didn't really care). After the first half a dozen were through (the second of which was JD, who chose Connor, an infant from Palisade Mines), Henry inherited the last of the red flags. Zoe lowered her head into her hands. Prayer was now all she had left.

"Lenoire, blood ward of Daniel and Catherine."

Zoe started to cry. Henry wasn't her ideal choice but it was much better than the multitude of alternatives she could think of. At least it was comforting to know that Lenny was going to be closer, able to live a quiet life where she would be able to get to her quickly if and when necessary. Zoe stayed put to quell the shake that had erupted across her body as the rest of the boys chose their homes and wards. Surprisingly, each of the boys ended up receiving a ward, something that caught Zoe completely off guard, not to mention the rest of the crowd—no more so than Susanna and Terry, who were both completely shell-shocked. In the end, it didn't really matter. Zoe was happy enough with the results and had her own ward to meet.

"Excuse me," Terry said quite frantically. "May I have your attention?"

Zoe stopped short of leaving the main square to listen to this new (and in some ways unprecedented) announcement.

"I am surprised to say that, unlike any year before, we have one last ward to attribute, and no further caretakers." Susanna and Terry conversed in secret, then, "Is there anyone still out there willing to accept a second ward?"

Zoe scanned the crowd, all of whom were doing the exact same thing, all of whom were just as confused and stunned as everyone else.

"Anyone, please," Terry said, growing more distraught with each passing second.

Zoe was a bit confused why Susanna didn't take on the responsibility, what with being the new quorum headmaster of Heather and all. It went to show Susanna's true character, one of which Zoe didn't admire in the least. Then again, she was no better, thinking it best to sneak away herself. But after spotting Snow White behind the crowd (and the only person not looking about for anyone to do the right thing), Zoe sucked up her own trepidation and called out, "I will. I'll accept the final ward."

Susanna and Terry sighed relief and invited Zoe back to the stage. "The child of the eclipse," Susanna called out. She pulled the final metal plate from the cauldron and handed it to Zoe. "I'll give you the honors."

"The unborn blood ward of Jack and Winter," Zoe called out. With Jack's help, Winter waddled to the stage. Zoe looked out to the crowd again, catching sight of Frances and Maisy, who blew kisses of admiration her way. Who she no longer saw was Snow White, no matter how hard she looked (and it really wasn't that hard anymore, seeing as how the majority of the crowd had gone). It was odd, to be sure, but wasn't a priority. There was a lot she still had to do, especially now that she had not one, but two wards to familiarize herself with.

Taking notice of Winter's condition (which could only be considered, "ready to explode"), Zoe blew a quick kiss of her own to Maisy and trotted off the stage to greet Jack and Winter, keeping them from having to climb up to her.

"Thank you, Zoe," Jack said immediately. "We appreciate your selflessness."

"It was meant to be, I guess," Zoe said, blushing slightly.

"Praise Heather," Winter added.

Zoe rested her hand on Winter's belly. "Praise the child of the eclipse," she whispered with a warm and heartfelt smile.

4

Zoe, the Caretaker

I t took a little extra time for Zoe to make her way to Lover's Pond, but she didn't want Jack and Winter to feel unwanted. Along the way, they enjoyed a hearty talk, which included a story or two about Zoe's time schooling in Jack and Winter's residence of Palisade Mines. One such story went a little like this:

"After I had collected the coal that was designated for my body weight, I picked the barrow up and started wheeling out. I did okay at first, but there was this short rough patch that you had to go through and when I hit that spot, I mean, gone. I was in the pile of coal. It was in my mouth and my nose and just… everywhere. I spent the rest of the day this black mess and couldn't eat anything for days without that charred taste in my mouth. It was awful. Let me just say, if I didn't have my choice, I would definitely not have been sent to live in Palisade Mines. My exam scores were horrendous. I really respect what you all have to put up with, I really do."

Janette was asleep along the line of lilies when Zoe, Winter and Jack finally reached the pond. She took the first few minutes to apologize profusely to Christian and Gertrude for her absence, and then introduced them to Jack and Winter. Of course the four of them already knew each other from trips to the Hub and mineral runs, but Zoe kind of liked the formality of it all... it just felt right.

"That was a very admirable thing to do," Gertrude said upon hearing what Zoe had done at the lottery. "I'm not sure if I would have wanted to take on a second ward at seventeen. I was hardly ready for this little blessing. But after Maylene blossomed, it felt like the right time."

"Well, you know, I figured that's probably what everyone else was thinking, too. It didn't seem right for everyone to shy away from the opportunity just because it might be hard. I mean, what's life without a few challenges?"

"Except when it comes to mining," Jack threw in for good measure.

"Exactly," Zoe said. And they laughed.

"Did you know it was the child of the eclipse when you volunteered?" Christian asked.

"Not really. I wasn't even thinking about that at the time. But I'm glad it was. It's almost as if fate was calling, you know?"

"Heather was watching over you," Gertrude said.

"Completely," Zoe said. "Though..." Her demeanor fell inward at that point.

Gertrude knew exactly what was running through her mind. "You would have rather Heather gave you the other girl," she said. "Your friend's sister."

Zoe wanted to burrow her head into the ground. It wasn't that she wouldn't love Janette with all her heart, but how could she possibly convey both without looking like a complete ass.

"You don't have to feel bad, Zoe," Gertrude said. "I completely understand."

Zoe smiled, but the reassurance wasn't all it was cracked up to be.

"Did she at least find a good home?"

"Yeah," Zoe said, feeling good about the response. "She'll be a couple miles away, but at least she'll be in Pasture Ranch, close enough in case she needs me for anything."

"You're a good person. I couldn't ask for anyone better to take care of Janette." Gertrude hugged Zoe. It was kind and compassionate, warming Zoe's heart.

Before Gertrude woke Janette, Zoe took a moment of formality to discuss her caretaking style, something a lot of caretakers never wanted to reveal unless they had to because it might cause friction between the old and the new. What if, for example, the current caretaker's style was one of the administer, having laid down an exorbitant amount of rules that would be obeyed or else be punished, but the new caretaker was more of a careful friend, setting few rules, only to apply punishment when the ward did something that could seriously hurt them? What if a ward of a sturdy hand (mostly an overprotective caretaker who didn't let the ward do hardly anything without their supervision) was passed on to an eye in the sky (a caretaker that lets them do whatever they want, until it leads to hurting someone else)? But Zoe wasn't one to turn away from a confrontation. She felt it better they know.

"I've always been of the mind that you have to be firm with them," Zoe said, "but give them room to breathe and explore.

My caretakers were playful rulers. I have rules and restrictions, but Maisy and Frances always listened to my side of why I might have broken a rule, or give me enough freedom that I don't feel suffocated. I can't think of a better way to raise a ward. I hope that's all right."

Winter was the first to respond. "It's always how I felt."

"I think I'd have tried to be more an administer," Jack said, "but you're a good kid. I trust you wholeheartedly."

"Me too," Gertrude said. "It doesn't matter what type of caretaker you are, so long as you love and care for the child the best you can." Christian was also in agreement, even though he himself was more a careful friend. Janette would just have to learn to follow the rules a bit more.

"Thank you," Zoe said, partially blushing. Her mouth was dry and her hands were sweaty. She must have been much more nervous than she thought.

It was then that Gertrude introduced Zoe to Janette as "the kindest young woman," which instantly turned Zoe red all over. Janette was shy at first (though that could have been because she was still half-asleep), but the more Zoe talked about Pasture Ranch, her sheep, and what games she liked to play, Janette started to warm up to her. By the time Zoe pretended like she couldn't stop from rolling down the hill and fell into the pond, Janette was all smiles and laughter, even more so when Zoe asked for help in getting out of the pond and pulled Janette in with her (well, after the shock from the cool water wore off anyway). The two of them played for quite some time, Janette taking Zoe all around the pond and over the hillsides, up to the point of utter exhaustion. When they finally did sit (at Zoe's request; Janette wanted to keep playing), the five of them enjoyed a nice little lunch and talked some more about what Janette liked most (hamburgers and kitties, it turned out) and a little about the punishments Zoe had received (anywhere from a slap on the back of the hand for touching an electrical outlet to sitting on her knees in the corner of the kitchen for climbing—and almost falling off—a large, thick oak near Timber and Gail's front walk that had been there for millennia, and one she was told not to climb on numerous occasions). It wasn't until Zoe set off a round-robin of yawns did it occur to them that Janette had grown weary, practically collapsing over, her yawn was so big. A rollicking laugh ensued but didn't last long, at least for Zoe.

Kayla (or who appeared to be Kayla, as the level of the sun and the distance from Zoe shadowed most of her features) sat on the uppermost point of the hillside that rolled away from Lover's Pond (a small cliff most everyone called the tongue), her back turned to Zoe. Gertrude looked to see what had caught Zoe's attention.

"Go to her," she said, knowing exactly who it was.

"I should," Zoe said. Her eyes never left Kayla. "But this is our time."

"It's best we go anyway," Gertrude said, pulling Janette into her arms. "Janette should really take a nap."

Winter took Gertrude's cue. "And we best be getting back as well. I have an appointment with Nestor soon and I would hate to be late."

"Are you sure?" Zoe said, helping Winter up (which was no easy task).

"She needs you more than we do right now, I'm sure," Gertrude said.

"She looks like she could use a friend," Winter added.

Zoe bid farewell to them all with a kiss. She waited some time (making sure they were all out of sight) and then walked slowly up the hill.

"They're good people, Gertrude and Christian," Kayla said when Zoe was just feet away. Even though her back was turned, and Zoe thought she was being quieter than a cloud, Kayla still heard her. It must have been her heavier than usual breaths.

"Extremely," Zoe said. She sat next to Kayla and looked out at the mountains, which were gloriously green on this fine summer day. Occasionally, during the winters, the peaks of the mountains would whiten with snow. But that was rare; this was a much more familiar view.

"Janette's a little wild thing, though. You'll need to watch out for her, especially now that she'll have plenty of land to run around on."

"Really? I never would have guessed."

Kayla laughed, a chuckle that was subdued quickly with, "Who were the others? I don't think I've ever met them."

"Winter and Jack. They're going to have the child of the eclipse."

"Is that why they were with you and not their other caretaker?"

"I am their blood ward's caretaker."

Kayla finally looked to Zoe, confused as all get out.

Zoe smiled. "I volunteered to take her... or him... Nobody else was willing to."

"You volunteered? Okay, that's just weird. Are you telling me we ran out of caretakers this year?"

Zoe nodded. So did Kayla.

"You want to know something even weirder? I saw someone today…"

"Yeah, that's the weirdest thing I've heard all day."

Zoe could have killed Kayla with her eyes. "Funny."

"I thought so."

"No, but seriously, this girl… she couldn't have been more than sixteen, seventeen, but I've never seen her before."

"What did she look like? Maybe she's a rat from the squalors."

"Honestly? Have you ever heard the tale of 'Little Snow-White'?"

"Snow White? You're serious?"

Zoe answered with the pierce in her lips.

"Okay. Well, if that's the case, I can definitely say I've never seen her in the squalors. You check the magic castle or the dwarf hut in the woods?"

"Those were the first places I checked and they were completely empty."

Kayla chuckled. "Then I don't know what else to say except, if it *was* Snow White, that is definitely top points on the bizarro scale."

"Right? And she kind of creeped me out a little, you know. She kept staring at me like I was a piece of meat. I was going to go and talk to her when the lottery was over, but she disappeared after I volunteered. I couldn't find her anywhere."

Instead of the snarky comment Zoe was expecting, all Kayla came back with was, "Hm."

"That's all you have to say?"

"Double hm?" Kayla smiled bright, an infectious little smirk.

"Yeah." The two giggled for a brief, somewhat awkward moment before Zoe said, "I stayed to find out about Lenny."

"I don't want to know."

"How come? You have to be wondering where she got placed? And with whom."

"It doesn't matter. I won't be around for her, so where she lives and who cares for her isn't important."

Zoe wanted so bad to tell her who it was, but she knew that unless Kayla spent the next two weeks in the mountains (which wasn't completely out of the question if it weren't for the fact that Kayla wouldn't dare leave Lenny), she'd find out soon enough anyway. If her caretakers didn't tell her, it would be Henry himself. What better way to get close to Kayla than telling her he was Lenny's new caretaker? "Okay… but if it was me, not knowing would kill me. I'd hate for that to be my only thought over my last few days."

"Well, that's where we're different. It doesn't bother me one bit."

With the tone in her voice, Zoe knew Kayla was lying, but she let the subject rest. They spent the rest of the day (until the sun kissed the tip of the desert) sitting in silence, neither wanting to leave the other, neither wanting to disturb their unspoken serenity. When they returned to Kayla's, Lenny was asleep. Kayla kissed her goodnight anyway and Zoe left to get home to finally accept the congratulatory praise her caretakers were no doubt eager to bestow upon her. The kisses, hugs and lively chatter wasn't something she was looking all that forward to, though; it had been a really long day and she wanted to have a nice, quiet meal and get some sleep. On the other hand, it felt good to do something so unselfish and kind, and something that no other caretaker had ever had the foresight (or opportunity) to do.

Her lips curled upward as she walked through the front door of her house, already feeling the aura of admiration before she ever heard a single word.

5

Chess Moves

Zoe moved her king's pawn to e4 in a typical opening of what would begin another inevitable loss to Lenny. It wasn't that Zoe was bad at chess, far from it. Zoe was the reigning champion of the Falcon Club's annual chess tournament. It just so happened that Lenny was a master savant of the game who, Zoe was convinced, could literally see the entire game in her head before Zoe even made her first move. That couldn't be entirely true, as Zoe always tried to throw the little genius off her game by mixing things up with the most off-the-wall move she could think of, but every time she did, Lenny would make her move just as fast and with as much confidence as any other. *Just amazing.*

Lenny's move, of course, was her typical counter (pawn to e5), so Zoe grabbed her king's rook pawn and shifted it to h4. Just like any other odd move, Lenny had her piece moving before Zoe even had her fingertip off the pawn. In retrospect, it wasn't the smartest move; the game was over in less than ten. And as always, Lenny didn't say anything, scribbling down every move (in the old English descriptive notation, no less) of every game into her little journal as if she was keeping some kind of historical record. Zoe, on the other hand, couldn't keep her mouth shut, coaxing Lenny with silly quick one-liners about the moves she made, hoping to get a tiny inkling of a smile. "Game on, little sister," she said as she set up the next game, or "Oh, you think you're so smart, huh?" as Lenny placed her in check after only two moves (*mate in five*, Zoe was sure). None of it worked. Lenny won the next game in seven moves (smart one, moving all the pawns up first) and the one after that in twenty (when Zoe tried to at least play straight, in all seriousness). After the fourth game, Zoe wanted more than anything for Henry to finally arrive, just so she might have a chance to try a new game—that wasn't chess. But that was beyond her. All she knew was that Kayla was supposed to be the one watching Lenny so that she would be forced to meet Henry (who, it must be mentioned, her caretakers believed to be an obvious companion for Kayla) as punishment for not attending the lottery. It was a brilliant move on the part of Daniel and Catherine if you really thought about it, but one which Kayla countered by asking Zoe to stay instead, heading out to who knows where for who knows how long.

Zoe was in the kitchen fixing a snack for Lenny when the front door opened.

"Praise Heather, you are not going to believe this."

"Kayla?" Zoe was dumbfounded.

"Zoe."

"What are you doing here?" When Zoe returned to the living room, Kayla was slumped in the chair behind Lenny. It seemed as if she had just run the entire circumference of Heather in less than a minute, which is to say, she was totally out of breath and could barely say what she had to say. "You all right?"

Kayla bent over and grasped her chest as if she were trying to grab her lungs and pump some air into them. For a second, she thought Kayla would simply keel over and die—or cough up a hairball, an image that cracked Zoe up into a fit that challenged the intensity of Kayla's breaths.

"It's not funny," Kayla said through uneven huffs.

"I know, I'm sorry. Are you okay?"

"Yeah, of course." Kayla sat erect, pretending (and poorly at that, what with her hands clutching her sides as if something might tear through her skin at any second) that everything was normal. "I've got some crazy outstanding news to tell you."

"Let me get you some water."

"Thank you," Kayla said and dropped the act. She rested her head in her arms until Zoe brought the water, which was gone in less than a gulp. "Zoe," Kayla said, still wheezing slightly, "if I ever have to run like that again, please pray for Heather to strike me down once and for all."

"With the blaze of Heather's fingernails, I swear it. Now," Zoe said, with the curiosity of a kitten in a sewer, "tell me what's so important you'd risk coming back here like this."

"Okay, so, I was up near the ridge, taking a hike through the breasts, and guess who I caught following me?"

"Henry?" Zoe said, half-joking.

"Good guess, but, yeah, no. That's just… no."

Zoe chuckled. "Well, I thought maybe that might've been why you had to run so fast to get back here."

"No, this was something much better."

"Tell me."

"It was JD."

"JD was stalking you?"

"I wish, but sadly, no."

"Then why was he following you?"

"I'm getting to that. Just wait. So, I call him out for being a blatant creeper, you know, trying to get him to confess, and he totally plays it off, claiming he saw me heading out there and thought it would be the best time to ask me something. Let me tell you, my heart was racing and I have no idea how red I might have been."

"No redder than you are now," Zoe quipped with a laugh.

"Stop," Kayla said, smacking Zoe playfully across the arm. "Just listen. I asked him what he wanted to talk about, hoping to high Heather he was going to ask me to be his companion."

"Did he?"

"No." Kayla confused Zoe by being so excited by the response. "Remember, I am far from being the lucky one in this story."

"So what did he say?"

"He wanted to know if *you* had a companion."

Zoe's hands covered her mouth, failing to hide the shock that melted from her eyes.

"I know, right?" Kayla said cheerfully. "I couldn't believe it either."

This time Zoe slapped Kayla. She was a little hurt by the comment but knew it was all in jest. "What did you say?"

Kayla smiled brighter than a lightning bolt at midnight. "He wants to meet you at Lover's Pond. Today. Like, right now."

Zoe let out a squeal usually reserved for a six-year-old. It made Lenny curl her arms over her head. Neither of them took notice.

"Are you serious?" Zoe said.

"Why would I lie about something like that?"

"JD? The physician's ward?" Zoe wanted to make absolutely sure they were talking about the same person.

"Yes." Kayla was getting slightly irritated.

Zoe's shocked excitement shifted quickly into confused doubt. "Why now?"

"I don't know. Maybe your little stunt at the lottery finally knocked some sense into the guy."

"You think?"

"Who cares? He wants to meet you. Isn't that enough?"

"And he wants to meet right now?"

"He's probably already there."

"And you're okay with this?"

"Yes, now go already, before I lie and tell him you're not interested."

Zoe was frazzled, unable to think clearly. "Okay, yeah, right. Good." When she finally made sense enough to get to the door, she stopped and wiped her hands across her clothes, which not only made her look like a frumpy digger, but it left nothing to stimulate the imagination. "I can't go like this," she said.

Kayla agreed. "Let's check my closet. Heck, you might even find something of yours in there."

Indeed, she did. It was a dress she had left there the previous summer when she went directly to Kayla's after church so they could go swimming, after which she went straight home. She always meant to take the dress back but it always slipped her mind, which now worked out perfectly. Of course, the dress alone wasn't enough, especially for Kayla, who threw a cotton ribbon around Zoe's waist and supplied her one of Catherine's sashes. Makeup was also needed and it took nearly a half hour for that to be perfected. By then, Kayla had decided she would go with her, and though Zoe argued about taking Lenny, Kayla wasn't about to be deterred. Zoe left to get a head start as Kayla collected Lenny, her journal and a couple of pens. By the time Kayla caught up, Zoe was standing at the edge of the Grand Hub, looking down the path at the pond. For a second, Kayla was afraid JD might have thought Zoe had stood him up.

Lo and behold, there he was, sitting on the rail of the bridge. His hands were crossed over his lap and the squint in his eyes was just heart-meltingly adorable.

"What are you waiting for?" Kayla said, pushing Zoe a step forward. "Get your ass down there already so he can have it." Zoe punched Kayla, disgusted (but oddly excited) by the innuendo. Kayla laughed heartily in response.

There was no greater smile than the one on Zoe's lips as she made her way to the bridge. Kayla quickly stole Lenny around and up the hill to get the best, unobstructed view of the encounter, hiding just under the tongue. Lenny sat a few feet down the hill and scrawled in her book—an endless stream of nonsense.

"JD," Zoe said as she lightly stepped up to him. He turned and smiled. Zoe blushed and turned her head down, unable to keep from giggling.

JD slid off the rail. "Zoe. I was afraid maybe Kayla didn't tell you."

"She wouldn't do that," Zoe said.

"I thought as much. You look beautiful, by the way."

"Stop." Zoe blushed even brighter.

Kayla couldn't help but laugh. Even though she couldn't hear them, Zoe's body language was enough to set her off.

"So, what did you want to see me about?" Zoe finally said.

"I wanted you to know that I thought what you did at the lottery was amazing. I wouldn't have had the guts to do it."

"You heard about that?" As if anyone hadn't heard.

"Who hasn't? Susanna doesn't have the best lock on her lips, you know."

"Not really. I don't know her very well."

"I do, and let me just say, she may be suited to be headmaster, but she's lousy with secrets."

"I'm sorry," Zoe said, but was unsure why.

"Anyway, I really do respect what you did, and…" JD turned away slightly.

"And what?" Zoe asked, her spirit light and airy.

"Here it comes," Kayla giggled to Lenny, though she was oblivious.

"I've always been attracted to you, Zoe," he said, "ever since that first day when I sutured your head." JD's hand on the back of Zoe's head chilled her skin with exhilaration. "But it was always more a physical attraction. After what happened yesterday, I know now that your beauty isn't just skin deep."

Oh. My. God.

If an apple could get any redder, that would be the color of Zoe's entire body at that very moment. "Thank you," she squeaked out, "very much. I've always felt the same about you."

JD smiled. "I don't know," he said. "You may not like what you see on the inside. But I'd like to show you otherwise, if I may."

"I look forward to it." Zoe then climbed up onto the rail, an odd act given the length and the splendor of the dress she had on. It didn't perturb her from straddling the rail as if she were wearing an ordinary pair of jeans. She tapped the rail and rocked back and forth as she waited for him to join her.

"That's it, Zoe. Reel him in," Kayla said giddily.

"Precious moments," a voice chimed from behind her.

Kayla was shocked at first, thinking Lenny had finally said something, but was even more shocked when she saw an extremely attractive young girl with pure white skin and glowing red lips reading Lenny's notebook.

"Snow White," Kayla whispered.

The stranger looked past Kayla to Zoe and JD, who laughed graciously with one another. "Are they your friends? They look happy."

"They are, so don't even think about screwing it up for them."

"I wouldn't dare."

"Good."

Snow White smiled and looked back to Lenny's notebook. Kayla suddenly turned protective. She stepped between them, having to push Snow White away slightly to do so. "Who are you, anyway?"

"I'm just visiting."

"Just visiting. Right. So what's your fascination with Zoe?"

Snow White looked a bit stunned.

"Yeah, she told me you were at the lottery, *Snow White*."

Snow White smiled. Mesmerizing. "She's a very sweet girl."

Kayla was now confused. Was she talking about Zoe or Lenny? It didn't matter; Snow White gave her the creeps. "What are you doing here?"

"I was coming down off the mountain and saw you climb up here. I was just curious." Snow White picked a flower from the ground near Lenny.

"I mean, what's your business in Heather?"

Snow White sniffed the flower and handed it to Lenny.

"She won't take it," Kayla said. "She doesn't know you." To her surprise, Lenny did take the flower, lingering her hand against Snow White's a little longer than Kayla thought was even possible. "What in Heather's name?"

"You should be more optimistic," Snow White said. "You never know what the future may bring when you believe in the impossible."

"You don't know me," Kayla said. "Don't tell me what I should and shouldn't be."

"I'm sorry. I didn't mean any disrespect."

"Too late. You can go now."

Snow White nodded and walked away without another word.

Kayla knelt down next to Lenny and took the flower away. "We don't want this," she said, and though Lenny didn't object, her shoulders tightened slightly. Kayla tossed the flower away and returned to her spot, but Zoe and JD were gone. *Feather my tail!*

When Kayla and Lenny returned home (as the sun painted the sky in a beautiful rainbow of colors), Daniel had moved the couch right in front of the door and sat waiting with Catherine.

And Henry.

"Where have you been?" Catherine said. Her arms were folded across her chest; her eyes were flamed like a wildfire.

"I had something I had to do," Kayla said. She knelt down and whispered to Lenny to go to her room. She did as ordered.

"We told you to wait here for Lenny's new caretaker."

"I know."

"What do you have to say to him?"

Kayla fought rolling her eyes. Of course it was Henry. *Thanks a lot, Heather. You're a real crack-up.* "Sorry."

"I'm not pleased with you right now," Catherine said. "I thought I raised you better than this."

"I said I was sorry. Can we eat?"

"No," Daniel said.

"What?"

"We've been generous with you, Kayla. We didn't push you to go to church and turned a blind eye for swimming off hours at the pond."

"You knew about that?"

"But ditching your sister's caretaker..." Daniel threw his arms up and walked from the room—a true-blue eye in the sky.

Kayla lowered her head. She felt bad.

Catherine stood and rested her hand on Kayla's shoulder. "What you did was wrong, and I think you owe it to Henry to make it up to him. But we're going to leave that up to you." Catherine squeezed the back of Kayla's neck and left the room.

There was a bit of an awkward few minutes where the house was so silent, you could actually hear the hum of the factories.

Finally, Henry stood and said, "You don't have to do anything for me. I get it."

He left. Kayla now felt even worse.

That night, she realized her caretakers were right. She was being an ass and she would eventually have to make it up to him. Over the next few days, Kayla was there whenever Henry came to see Lenny, even helping him understand her tics and nuances. She made sure to give him advice on how to handle her tantrums and what made her the happiest, even going as far as to (try and) teach him how to play chess. And though Kayla said it was for Lenny, in the end, she had to admit—if only to herself—that she was actually having fun with him. If anything, it at least took her mind off of Zoe and JD, and what fun they must have been having.

6

A First Kiss

Maisy adored JD.

She was so happy that he had finally asked to court Zoe that she pushed them to spend as much free time together as humanly possible, going so far as to coax them into spending their nights together as well, if nothing more than to continue to get to know each other—which turned out wasn't hard at all. Conversation came so naturally to them both, it was a wonder they hadn't become friends years before. Maisy saw sparks ignite between them as they cozied up under the stars—that same sense of bliss she and Frances had when they courted twelve years earlier.

It was necessary to spend time with their new wards over the days that followed, and though they still weren't quite at the stage of holding hands or public displays of affection, it was extremely difficult for Zoe to think of anything but JD when they were apart. She had to push herself to focus on Janette and care for her as any good caretaker would. But in the end, the only thing she looked forward to was the sunset (which, under these circumstances, took longer to arrive than a dying snail) so that she could meet back up with him, at which point they would hike up Gentle Pass (one of two small hiking trails that wrapped around the edge of Fallen Mountain Pass—or the "left breast" as most would say—that ended at the bottleneck of a large waterfall), or take a stroll around the lake and talk about their wards, their thoughts, dreams and desires; but most importantly, about each other.

On the fourth day of their courtship, JD suggested they take Janette and Connor on a private boat ride out to Fallen Island. None of the caretakers had an issue with that; it gave them some well-deserved alone time. The trip started out rough, as Janette got sick over the edge of the boat on the way out and Connor wouldn't stop crying (Caleb and Barbara had given JD some tips, none of which seemed to work at all), but when they reached the island, things settled quickly. Zoe sat down with Connor and hummed a lullaby in hopes of settling his nerves as JD walked the edge of the island with Janette, showing off all of the neat little fish that couldn't be seen at the pond. As Zoe brushed her hand over the peach fuzz Connor had on his head, she came to realize why he was being so ornery—the little tyke was teething. She checked for little white divots in his gums and gently pressed the tip of her pinkie against them, an act that not only gave Connor something to gnaw on, but calmed him right down, as if he hadn't ever been crying.

"Is that all I have to do?" JD joked.

Zoe took care of Connor for most of the day. JD, meanwhile, became fast friends with Janette, running around the island playing tag and hide and seek. When JD grabbed a ball he found in the brush and started playing catch with Janette, Zoe couldn't help but claim it was because he was tired of running. The two little ones finally went to sleep at the same time a few hours later (a miracle in and of itself), which gave Zoe and JD a chance to sit with their feet in the water and dream about what else might be out there in the far reaches of the horizon.

"I believe there's magic," Zoe said, thinking of Kayla, the mermaid that wasn't.

"What kind of magic?" JD asked.

"The kind where anything and everything is possible, where no limitations exist; where you can live forever."

"Isn't that what we already have here?"

Zoe smiled. "Yeah," she said. "Glory be to Heather."

That was when Zoe took hold of JD's hand for the first time. There wasn't any moment in Zoe's life that she could remember being any better than this one right here.

When they got back to the mainland, the four of them went to grab a bite to eat at Patty's Burger, home of the most scrumptious chocolate velvet milkshake around. One cup, two straws. When Zoe's nose touched JD's while going for a drink at the same time, the lightning that ignited in Zoe's gut was numbing—in the best way possible. Janette just cracked up hysterically.

The next day, Zoe and JD took a day away from their wards to hike up The Peak, a ten-mile path that led to the tip of the second highest mountain, which oversaw everything to the far-reaching edges of all three seas that surrounded Heather. The air was thinner at the tip and the last mile or so was rockier and steeper than anything Zoe had ever hiked before. Suffice it to say, it took a much longer time to hike and was much harder than she was expecting. But it was well worth it. As the sun licked the edge of the Horizon Desert, the sky became the most beautiful painting she had ever seen, or ever would see. She sat with JD for hours in complete bliss, oblivious to the storm clouds rolling in. It wasn't until the air chilled past what was comfortable that Zoe suggested they head back down.

"We'll never make it before dark," JD said.

"We have to try. There isn't any shelter up here, is there?" Zoe was getting a bit apprehensive.

"I actually think there might be a small cave about a mile that way."

"Let's hurry."

JD and Zoe walked (hand in hand, of course) west across the thin-cut ledge of The Peak until they saw the cave that JD had been referring to.

"How did you know that was there?"

"I've hiked this trail before," he said. "With Nestor."

"Nestor hikes?"

"Yeah. I think he brought a couple of girls up here when he was younger."

Zoe wasn't quite sure what to make of that statement. "Oh, really?"

"It's not like that," JD said.

Light raindrops were already hitting her head, so Zoe took him at his word. "Let's just get there."

JD helped her cross a spiky ledge that dipped into a crevice between the edges of the steep walls. About halfway across, Zoe stopped to fix her footing. That's when she saw someone on the other side of the gorge at the backside of The Peak. At least she thought it was a person; with the clouds shadowing what was left of the sun, it could very well have been a simple rock.

"Hey," Zoe called out. She waved but got no response.

"What's wrong?" JD asked. He then saw the figure. "Who is that?"

"I don't know," Zoe said, but her gut said otherwise. From what she could see, the figure was wearing a cloak, and there was only one person she knew of who wore one of those.

"Hey," she called out again, waving even harder, as if that would actually change anything. "It's about to rain. Come with us."

"No time," JD said.

"We can't just leave her out there."

"She'll have to travel around the edge to get here. That's a half hour, tops. I'm sorry."

Zoe didn't much care about that, but at the same time, the rain was getting heavy. They would be soaked by the time they reached the cave as it was.

"You need to find shelter," she called out. With that, JD pulled Zoe deeper into the crevice. By the time they reached the outer ledge of the cave, the figure was gone. "Where'd she go?"

"We can't worry about that now," JD said. Zoe agreed, but held out hope that the stranger was able to find shelter.

Zoe stumbled into the cave, tripping over a harsh lip at the opening. She laughed as JD steadied her and tried (to no avail) to wipe away the rain, which had by now reached an utter downpour. They both wound up using the water dripping off their clothes and hair to spray each other. Zoe screamed as JD hit her with what felt like a bucket of water to the face and JD grunted as he dodged her attempts to spray him. It all coalesced into a wild tussle when Zoe tackled JD to the ground in fits of laughter. After a few moments in each other's arms (and locking eyes for what felt like forever), the magnetism of their attraction bounced across them like lightning. There was only one thing left for Zoe to do.

She kissed him.

They kissed with an electricity that could light up the moon; they kissed with a passion that could burn the mountain to ash; they kissed as if it were the very first kiss of mankind, which to Zoe, it truly was. Little did she know that they had a witness—a young woman, pale and cold.

Zoe didn't find much rest that night, and not just because the wind and rain had frozen her all but solid. She couldn't sleep because that kiss lingered on her lips far past the time of expiration. It melted into her mind and her body, making her dream, wish and pray for another, no matter how long or short it might be.

The urge to tell Kayla about it, though, far outweighed any of that.

7

Snow White

The rain had subdued quite a bit when Zoe woke to a loud crash of thunder. She shivered; her hair and clothes were still pretty damp, but at least the wind had gone away. In her best attempt to get warm, she shifted closer to JD and pulled his arm across her body. It didn't help in the way she had hoped (the dampness in his own clothes just made it even worse). A noise from outside caught her attention just then and Zoe's curiosity (and a little bit of fear) got the best of her. She tried to shake JD awake, but he was out; there was no waking him. Plus, she really didn't want to—he looked so sweet. She wouldn't have to go far to investigate the noise; he'd be okay alone for a bit.

The noise, a lot like someone—or something—disrupting the rocks on the hillside, occurred again as she climbed up over the outer edge of the cave. She hoped it was simply the wind knocking at a nearby tree and not some monstrous mountain lion or cougar prancing around outside. If that were the case, she would no doubt be cat food. Her heart twittered in rapid succession as she looked around. What she saw calmed her at the same time it excited and confused her. Climbing away from the cave (rather quickly at that for the amount of water, mud and rock that covered the slightly steep ascent) was Snow White. Zoe's first instinct to call out to her almost ended in devastation.

With a quick glance up at Zoe, Snow White lost her footing and slid uncontrollably over a small rocky ledge. Zoe clasped her hand across her mouth. The guilt of having killed Snow White got the better of her and she could barely move a muscle without trembling.

"Help," Snow White yelled.

You don't know how relieved Zoe was to hear that single word. She wasn't sure what she should do, though, so she called out for JD. He still didn't wake up.

"I'm slipping," Snow White called out. "Please, somebody."

Zoe checked the cave once more, hoping against Heather that JD was coming to help. When he didn't, Zoe asked herself what Kayla might do, then made the bravest choice she ever had to make and slid down the mountain. It was a treacherous descent, to be sure, and one slight misstep would put her in the same predicament as Snow White. Luckily, she reached the ledge without much trouble (now absolutely sure that if she hadn't have said anything, Snow White would have made it quite easily as well— yes, this *was* her fault).

Snow White dangled about two feet below her, hanging on to a sliver of a cut inside the rock face. How she was able to grab hold of that was beyond Zoe, as was how she was going to help her back up.

"Are you okay?" Zoe said. Yeah, like that would help.

"Hurry," Snow White said—a bit more calmly than Zoe was expecting. "I don't know if I can hold on."

"Okay, give me a second to find something to pull you up."

"No time. You're going to have to catch me."

"Catch you? How?"

"Climb down to the ledge below me."

"What ledge?" Zoe couldn't see anything below Snow White and wasn't about to take her word for it. If there was a ledge there, why didn't she just let go?

"It's too far for me to jump. I need you to help break my fall."

"I can't do that."

"You have to. Please."

Snow White was right about one thing—there wasn't anything Zoe could do from where she was. Her only choice was to trust that Snow White was telling the truth about the ledge. The only thing left to do now was find a way down.

After a quick inspection, Zoe saw the rainwater sliding down around the curvature of the rock. It was steep, and there weren't a whole lot of rocks to grasp, but it was the only possible choice. She took all the time she could to settle in, choosing to slide down on her back rather than her stomach, believing it would be easier to grab a foothold or catch a rock with her palm if she were facing this way. It ended up being the right choice, especially after she slipped and slid down a quarter of the way. She was able to maneuver her legs just enough to land the ball of her heel on a rock, but only because she was able to see it clearly. By this time, Zoe was able to see the ledge that Snow White was talking about. It only extended some three feet from the face of the mountain and was another few feet below her, disconnected from her current path. She wasn't going to be able to climb back up and continuing down the trail would eventually force her off another ledge. There was only one way across and that was to jump. There was no room for error, that was for sure, but at the same time, she had to hurry, or else Snow White might miss the ledge completely and crumble to her death (her chants to hurry didn't help).

With no other options that she could see, Zoe slid down to a good-sized rock sitting about a foot above Snow White's ledge, placed the center of her foot against the flattest point on the rock and steadied herself against the mountain. After a deep breath (and a quick prayer), she pushed herself away from the rock, using her upper body for momentum. She landed in the direct center of the ledge but instantly lost her footing and stumbled forward. Tucking as best she could, she fell to the ground and rolled, almost falling off the other side. Luckily, she was able to slam her foot against the opposite cliff side. Her butt dangled just off the ledge, her elbows locked against it. She was able to use them to crawl her way back up and settle safely just under Snow White.

"I'm slipping."

"Yeah," Zoe said. "One more second." *Give me some time to collect myself, for Heather's sake.*

"I'm slipping." The pitch in Snow White's voice was much higher now. There was no time. She was coming, ready or not. Zoe stood as erect as she could, preparing to catch Snow White's weight and keep her from going over the edge at the same time. Snow White was some eight feet above her, so even the smallest of reservations would doom them both.

That all flashed away in an instant.

Snow White was in Zoe's arms in mere seconds. Her legs

clipped Zoe's arms, knocking them away as her body fell forward against her. Zoe struck the back of her head against the rocks but still had enough adrenaline to grasp Snow White's arms and keep her from falling off the ledge. Snow White knelt down to steady herself. Zoe, blood trickling down the back of her neck (what is with that?), sat against the mountainside. And with Snow White's ankle swelling like a balloon, there was no better option than for her to join Zoe.

"Are you okay?" Snow White said. She winced slightly, feeling a sharp pain course her body.

"I'll be fine. You?"

"I twisted my ankle."

The two sat in silence for a little while to let the adrenaline and fear wash away with the final drizzle of rain. Zoe spent most of it looking for a way back up the mountain.

"We can't get back up. Not that way."

"But I have someone waiting."

"I'm sorry."

Zoe was far too frustrated. "What were you doing out here, anyway?"

"I was looking for you."

"Why?"

"You offered me shelter."

"I knew that was you on the other side of the break. Why didn't you say anything when I called out?"

"I don't know. Honestly, I wasn't even sure if you were real."

"I know the feeling," Zoe mumbled.

"When I realized you were heading for a cave, I worked my

way around the cliffs. You two were fast asleep when I finally got here. It wasn't my place to bother you."

Zoe felt utterly foolish. She looked for a way down and, with the help of the rising sun, found a path a few feet from where they were. It would take a bit of time (and some creative maneuvering on Zoe's part to help Snow White), but it was definitely possible. Snow White hissed a bit when she put weight on her swollen ankle for the first time, but the more they traveled (Snow White using Zoe as a nice, soft crutch), the easier it got, more than likely because her ankle steadily grew numb.

Once on the trail and several feet down the mountain, Zoe finally asked, "Where do you live?"

"At triangle point."

"Triangle point?"

"You've never heard of triangle point?"

"No. Should I have?"

"I only assumed so because it's where the Horizon Desert, Pasture Ranch and the Fallen Mountains meet."

"Yeah, okay," Zoe said as if she had known all along. "Near the north side of the back winds prairie."

"Right. You do know it."

"I know of it. It's off the edge of Timber and Gail's farm, so I've never actually been there."

"That's a shame. It's a beautiful place."

"Why do you live there?"

"It's the best place I could find."

"I don't get it. Why not stay with your caretakers?"

"I don't have any caretakers. Not since the last eclipse."

"Wait, what? You were alive during the last eclipse? How is that possible? You can't be more than sixteen."

"Thank you." Snow White produced a bright, winning sunshine of a smile. "As a matter of fact, in a weeks time, I will come upon my thirty-fourth day of breath."

"Thirty-four? Are you kidding me?"

Snow White shook her head. It suddenly clicked with Zoe. "Wait. If that's true, then that would make you—"

"The child of the eclipse."

Stunned solid, Zoe had to stop.

"What's wrong?" Snow White asked.

"Give me a minute," Zoe said. She rested Snow White against the mountain and sat on a nearby stone. Snow White massaged her ankle until Zoe was again ready to speak.

"You're a child of the eclipse?"

"Yes."

"How come I've never met you before?"

"I left Heather two weeks before the last eclipse."

"You left? Why?"

"Trust me, I didn't want to. I was chased out."

"By who?"

"By someone who thought that my death was the key to breaking Heather's curse."

"Really? Why would anyone think that?"

"I don't know. But I came back to find out."

"Is that why you've been following me?"

Snow White looked away from Zoe. "You are the child of the eclipse. If anyone can connect all of this, it's you."

"Why would you think that?"

"I thought if my attacker had passed on what he knew to his ward, they might be following you, which would give me a chance to find out exactly what it is they know, and why they thought killing me was the only option."

"No one's been following me… except you."

"I know that now. But I have a feeling you still may be able to help me figure this out."

Zoe took a breath. If Snow White was correct, this could be the chance to save not only Kayla, but everyone in Heather. It was an opportunity she couldn't pass up. Not now. Not if it was even remotely possible.

"I'm Zoe," she said, holding out her hand to formally introduce herself.

"Yes, I know. I'm Snow White." She shook Zoe's hand.

Zoe's eyes were huge. "Really?"

Snow White was unable to control her laugh. "Your friend called me that. My non-fairytale name is Brittany, though I kind of like Snow White. It fits."

It wasn't clear if it was relief or disappointment, but Zoe's body relaxed.

"Does this mean you'll help me?"

"Let me think about it," Zoe said, not wanting to look too eager just in case Brittany was lying through her teeth, which was still a definite possibility.

Shortly after, Zoe and Brittany reached triangle point—a beautiful place indeed. Long, delicate vines traced their way around the mountain like a tapestry of hand-woven cloth, and dripped with the light glow of rainwater coming from the mountain. A small stream that connected all three edges of the lands together flowed across its lip, culminating in a small, but no less magnificent waterfall, which itself stepped up every few feet until it hid within a hole that had worn away just enough to create several stalagmite teeth inside the mountain.

Brittany led Zoe to a small crevice that turned back into the mountain. It was also covered by several vines and, upon first look, wasn't very wide and didn't look as if it went anywhere. But Brittany insisted they go inside. To Zoe's surprise, once she was a few steps in, the crevice opened up into a lovely cave, lit generously by several torches hugging the walls.

"Praise Heather," Zoe said. "How did you find this place?"

"I explored every corner of Heather when I was a kid. You'd be surprised at what you can find when you take some risks."

"I guess so."

Zoe sat Brittany down on a small ledge toward the back of the cave (which she figured Brittany used as a not so comfortable bed). Brittany then picked up a cloth at the foot of the ledge and opened it, revealing a stockpile of wild berries. "Would you like some?"

Zoe was hesitant; she didn't recognize the type. "I'd better not."

"They're not poisonous, if that's what you're afraid of."

It was, and as Brittany tossed a couple into her mouth to prove just that, Zoe decided to give them a try. Boy, was she glad she did. They were sweet, yet a bit tangy, and almost melted in her mouth. She couldn't place her finger on the exact taste, but if she had to guess, it was almost a mixture between raspberries and tangerines. It would be the death of her if she didn't have more.

"Where did you get these?"

"They grow wild near the far end of the mountain, just over the cliffs overlooking the ocean."

"They're delicious," Zoe said, her mouth full of juicy goodness. They were gone in minutes. "I'm sorry."

"Don't worry. I can get more." Brittany massaged her ankle as Zoe cleaned her teeth with her tongue, savoring the flavor of her new favorite snack.

"You know, I'd better be getting back home," Zoe said. "My caretakers might be getting worried."

"Of course. I should take care of this anyway. You'll come back tomorrow, right?"

It took a second for Zoe to realize why she asked, then smiled. "Yeah, of course. If there's a way to save everyone from the eclipse, I want to help find out what it is."

"Good."

"Good." Zoe smiled. Brittany smiled. Awkwardness followed. And then Zoe finally felt the time was right to leave.

Accusations

Z oe quickly made her way back to her house, where she called out for Maisy. She had to let her know she was all right (Maisy must have been scared out of her mind not knowing where Zoe was all night), but more importantly, she had to tell her about Brittany. It was all too incredible not too. But after searching the house (quite thoroughly, twice), neither Maisy nor Frances could be found. She then noticed a few ears of corn on the kitchen table and realized that they must have gone into Industry Quarters to make deliveries. At least Frances had. Maisy might have gone with him in Zoe's absence, but she could also very well be out looking for her, which was the more obvious possibility. Given that Maisy wouldn't know the first place to look (though checking in on Gertrude and Winter would have been the most likely of choices), she could be anywhere right now. Basically, there was really no point for Zoe to track her down, so she changed out of her damp clothes into something much warmer, and then darted out to Industry Quarters. There was someone there she hadn't seen in a few days that needed to know about this very same matter. If she happened to run into Maisy while doing so, points for her.

She was in such a hurry, as a matter of fact, that Zoe didn't even realize the dense quiet that hovered over the nearly empty streets of Industry Quarters. Odd to be sure, but nothing felt the same anymore to begin with, and Zoe's mind was on a million other things (including whether or not she should be out looking for JD, who must also be frantically searching for her by now; she really had caused a predicament, hadn't she?). She only finally took notice as she knocked on Kayla's door.

"Well, look who it is," Kayla said. It sounded a bit too snarky for Zoe's taste, but Kayla had a right to be a bit resentful. "Fancy seeing you here."

Zoe had no time to quibble over ditching her like she had. "You're not going to believe what I found out," she said, walking into the house uninvited.

"I'm a little busy," Kayla said. Zoe's rudeness didn't seem to bother her.

"You're going to want to hear this."

Henry came out of the kitchen, which stopped Zoe cold. "Oh," she said. She looked to Kayla. "Oh," she said again, this time with a bright smile.

Kayla burned a hole in Zoe's insinuation with her stare. "It's not like that."

"When did you...?"

"The same day you and JD became a single person. I was ambushed by Daniel and Catherine."

"Well... it's nice to know you finally found out... and are apparently okay with it."

"I know. Believe me, I know."

Zoe wasn't sure what to make of it, but smiled nonetheless. "I hate to be rude, but I need to talk to Kayla in private."

"Whatever you have to say, just say it," Kayla said.

"All right. I think I might have a way—"

A knock at the door interrupted her. Two nobles (Reynold and Gavin, as it turned out, with Henry announcing them) stood in front of Kayla, tall and firm.

"Kayla, ward of Daniel and Catherine?" said Reynold, the taller of the two.

"Yes."

"Come with us." Reynold grabbed Kayla's arm. She was quick, though, and yanked it away.

"Hey. Don't touch me."

"We need you to come with us," Gavin said, slightly more polite.

"Why? What's going on?"

"Susanna will explain. Please come with us."

Kayla looked to Zoe for support, to which she wouldn't get any. From Henry either. Her only option was to give in and follow them to wherever it was they wanted to take her. She again pulled her arm away from Reynold as she walked past them. When the door closed, Zoe ran to the window. Kayla remained a step ahead of the nobles as they walked south.

"I think they're heading to Factory Square," Zoe said.

"I know," Henry replied.

Zoe was a bit dumbfounded. "What?"

Henry looked ashamed.

"What did you do?"

"Zoe, I had to."

"What did you do?" Zoe's voice was raised. She walked to him with a heavy step.

"I'm sorry. It's just how things are done here. I don't expect you to understand."

"You rat piece of Heather's ass." Zoe hit him several times, and not with an open palm either.

Henry grabbed her wrists to stop her. "It's for the best, Zoe."

Zoe grunted and pushed Henry away, so angry she couldn't find any words (at least, not any words she felt were very honorable) to attack him with. It was best she let it lie. She stormed toward the rear of the house instead and called out for Lenny. No way was she going to leave her here alone with *him*.

"Lenny's not here," Henry said.

Zoe came back. "What do you mean? Where is she?"

"With Daniel and Catherine."

"This whole time? Then what were you and Kayla doing?"

"I was giving her a chance to change her mind."

"About what?"

"Taking Lenny away from me."

"Taking…" It suddenly dawned on her. "She told you that?"

"It may have slipped out."

"What did she say?"

"She said she was going to take Lenny with her when she left Heather. I couldn't let her do that."

"So you had her arrested?"

"Not for that, exactly. But it was part of it, yeah. Lenny's my ward, now, Zoe. I have to protect her the way I see fit."

"You make me sick." Zoe went to the door.

Henry grabbed her arm. "You don't know what she did."

"It doesn't matter."

Zoe ripped her arm away and stormed from the house, ignoring all of Henry's calls to stop, which she wasn't about to do until she found out once and for all what Henry (and by all accounts, all of Industry Quarters) thought Kayla had done. When she was in sight of Factory Square, she saw what had to be all of the residents of the Quarters huddled together near the lumber shop. Kayla was in front of them all. Her hands were bound together in front of her. Reynold forced her to her knees. It was then that Zoe realized this could only be Industry Quarter's version of a trial, made even more evident when Susanna stepped up to Kayla. Zoe had only read about trials in books of generations gone past, but she had no better explanation. If she was right, it was probably best she stay out of sight, not just because anything she had to say might hurt Kayla even more, but because this was an Industry Quarters matter. Any outside influence, especially that of a resident of Pasture Ranch, wouldn't even be taken into account. So she hid inside an alley between a couple of factory buildings (which for now had been shut down and deserted) to wait and see what the trial would yield.

"What did I do?" Kayla said, strong and tough. She wasn't about to let them get the best of her.

"Kayla, ward of Daniel and Catherine," Susanna said with soft authority, "you are being accused of inappropriate conduct and blasphemy. How do you plead?"

"Blasphemy? What are you talking about?"

"How do you plead?"

"I swear to you," Kayla said loud enough for everyone to hear, "whatever it is, I didn't do it."

"Okay," Susanna said. She turned to the group and nodded. They shifted apart, opening a pathway in the center of them all. At the end of the road, painted on the wall of the lumber mill, was art that stole Kayla's breath (and to a lesser extent, Zoe's as well).

HEATHER'S LOTTERY IS A SIN AND WE SHOULD ALL BE ASHAMED.
TO BE CLEANSED, THERE IS ONLY ONE WAY OUT.
WE MUST DESTROY THE ONE WHO TAKES OUR LIVES WITH THE HAND OF EVIL.
WE MUST DESTROY THE GODDESS OF CONDEMNATION.

WE MUST DESTROY HEATHER.

Below the text was a depiction of what could only have been Heather hanging from a noose above a pit of fire, a knife extending from her heart.

"Feather my tail," Zoe whispered. Kayla would have said the same thing, but her throat had closed.

"What do you have to say for yourself, Kayla?"

"You're crazy if you think I had anything to do with that," Kayla choked out, even though part of her thought maybe she somehow had. It's certainly something she thought about—not so vividly, mind you, but it wasn't a secret she didn't like what Heather stood for. But at no point had she ever fathomed going *that* far.

"We have testimony that claims otherwise," Susanna said.

"Testimony? From who?"

"That's irrelevant."

"Heather's feathers it's irrelevant."

"How many times have you been to church to praise Heather and all of her majesty over the last five years?" Susanna said clearly.

Kayla knew the answer, but wasn't about to convict herself. "I don't know."

"Would zero be accurate?"

It would, and Kayla lowered her head to answer.

"Did you attend the lottery this past week?" Susanna continued.

"No," Kayla answered honestly. She now knew where this was all going and had no defense for her actions.

"Can you tell us all why?"

"Because I don't believe it's right." Kayla's voice was clear and concise. If she was going to burn for this, she was going to do it with flair. "I don't believe it's fair. The eclipse is an asinine act of cowardice. Heather takes all of our lives before our time, and for what reason? What justification does she have to do such a cruel thing to us? To our families? She doesn't. Heather can burn in her own bile for all I care. But just because that's what I believe, doesn't mean I would hurt all of you to prove it."

Zoe half thought the Heather Biters would stand up in support of her, but they were all conspicuously absent. They knew better than to fight this, lest they, too, be condemned for the work of art that bled with contempt.

"If that's true, why not just leave Heather altogether?" Susanna inquired. "Take your chances on the outside?"

"I can't."

"Why?"

Kayla lowered her head again. She wanted to say, but didn't want to pull Lenny into this mess.

Susanna did it for her.

She waved Catherine forward. Lenny was draped across her arms. Catherine set her down and held her steady in front of Kayla. Lenny's chin rested against her chest as it usually did and she tapped her fingers, playing the music in her head with the fluidity of a river.

Kayla's tears were unlocked.

"Is this the reason you can't leave?" Susanna said.

Kayla held firm and quiet.

"Have you ever thought about, or spoken to anyone about, taking Lenoire, blood ward of Daniel and Catherine, and soon to be ward of Henry, away from Heather without permission?"

There were only two people who knew about that. One would never have said anything to anyone—she was too good a friend. The other she hardly knew, and now hated herself for believing he cared. How could she have let her guard down so easily?

"Yes," she admitted. "The reason I haven't left Heather is because of Lenny, and I have thought about taking her with me. I want to give her a better life, a longer life. If that means stealing her away from here, then so be it. She doesn't deserve any of this. None of us do. But it doesn't matter now, does it? Go ahead and do what you want to me. I don't care anymore."

Catherine stepped back into the crowd with Lenny. Susanna took a stand in front of Kayla. Never before had Kayla seen such impassioned conviction in the eyes of Heather.

"Kayla, ward of Daniel and Catherine," Susanna said with a tongue that lashed her like a whip, "it is with my greatest displeasure and a heavy heart that I must find you guilty of blasphemy and inappropriate conduct among the people of Heather. It is my duty, therefore, to punish you to the depths of Death Rock until your final execution of the eclipse."

Kayla may have said she didn't care, but Death Rock was the last place anyone wanted to be. Not only would she be banished nearly twenty feet deep into the earth, but the hole itself was infested with rats, maggots and who knows what other kinds of bugs and creepy-crawlers that would slowly ingest her living tissue until she finally succumbed to death. All kids are schooled on the starvation, dehydration and attack of nature that someone would endure within the hole—that is if their neck didn't break during the fall. Some accounts claimed death could take over a week (unless they bled out from cuts or breaks in the bone), which meant, if true, Kayla would still be alive when the eclipse rose to finally end her anguish. Her "normal" death was bad enough; did they really need to torture her like this?

"You can't do that," Kayla said. "Catherine, please. Say something."

"I'm sorry, Kayla," Catherine said. "You brought this on yourself."

Reynold and Gavin lifted Kayla to her feet. She immediately shook them off and ran to Lenny. Catherine, a bit shocked, took a step back, giving Kayla a clear opening to wrap her arms around Lenny. She hugged her and kissed her and whispered that everything would be all right. With the help of Catherine (and a few other residents), the nobles finally pulled Kayla off of Lenny and away from the group.

"I love you, Lenny," Kayla cried out. "Don't ever forget me."

Kayla's face was flushed red and her eyes burned when they finally reached Death Rock, which sat just to the south of the back woods trail connecting Industry Quarters to Pasture Ranch. It was named for a large rock that partially covered it. Most say that an earthquake rocked this region of the mountains long before time and brought the range sliding downward, flattening the land and bringing with it the seeds of growth. As the trees flourished, they sucked the water from the well, eventually exhausting its resources. It was now used to harbor those who would defy the rule of law, both of man and their god.

Reynold pushed Kayla to her knees at the edge of the hole (also known by many as "the pit"). She could smell the rot. "Reynold, you have to believe me," she pleaded. "I didn't do anything, I swear."

"It's too late," Reynold said.

"No, it's not. You can let me go. I'll leave. You can tell Susanna you dropped me in here and that will be that. Please."

"Do it and find yourselves down there with her," Susanna said from behind them.

"Susanna? Susanna, please. You can't do this."

"It's nothing personal. If I'm going to lead the people of Heather, they need to believe that when someone acts out of line, that my word holds strong. If I let the first person who defied our rules under my watch go free, what would that do for my reputation?"

"They won't ever know. I promise, if you let me go, you won't ever see me again."

"I believe you." Susanna walked up behind Kayla. She rested her hand on Kayla's shoulder, an ominous touch of affection and condemnation. "Gavin, Reynold. You may go," she said.

Reynold and Gavin hesitated, but left without objection. When they were gone, Susanna knelt next to Kayla. She, too, could smell the rot and it turned her stomach. "I do very much believe you, but look at it from my side. It's a fine line between order and chaos, you know."

Kayla lowered her head. She was done pleading.

"Terry raised me to lead and I intend to follow his teachings to the letter. But in all honesty, the only thing he's ever taught me that's truly meant something to me was that a firm hand may be strong, but compassion, under the eyes of Heather, can be so much stronger." Susanna grabbed the rope around Kayla's hands and sliced a knife through it. "I have to make them believe that I can follow through on my law, but that doesn't mean that I can't still find compassion in extraordinary circumstances."

Kayla couldn't resist; she hugged Susanna with the strength of a hundred bears. "Thank you."

Susanna took Kayla's hand to stand. "You must promise me that you will leave Heather by the time the sun sets."

"I promise. With the blaze of Heather's fingernails, I swear it."

Susanna smiled. "Zoe."

Kayla was confused, until Zoe came out from hiding behind one of the larger oaks. She had followed them there—to do what was unclear, but she couldn't stand by and watch her best friend perish alone. How Susanna knew she was there was also a mystery that would never be solved.

"Help Kayla collect whatever she needs and find her way out of Heather," Susanna said. "Just remember that no one can know that she's still alive, or else I'll have no choice but to send you both down the pit. And believe me, I do not want to have to do that."

"Yes, of course," Zoe said.

"Take care of yourself, Kayla."

Kayla had to hug Susanna one last time. Zoe then took her hand and headed for the one place she knew would protect Kayla while they figured a way out of this whole mess.

9

Into Hiding

Killing two birds with one stone had to be one of Zoe's most least liked sayings, right up there with being more than one way to skin a cat, or even looking like the cat who ate the canary. Condoning the death of any animal, even if it was just a metaphor, felt wrong and insensitive. However, she couldn't help but think that was exactly what she was doing with Kayla now. By leading her along the edge of the Horizon Desert, Zoe was able to get Kayla to triangle point without the fear of anyone seeing her, and at the same time was able to keep Kayla from having to step foot onto the "sacred soil" of Pasture Ranch (even if, for all she knew, Kayla couldn't have cared less about that anymore). It was a win-win for them both, though it did take them almost three times as long as it would have had they cut through the farms.

"Where are we going?" Kayla asked as the sun beat down hard on them. Thirst was growing and hunger rocked her stomach.

"Triangle point. At least that's what Brittany calls it."

"Brittany?"

"Yeah… oh, right. Do you remember that girl I told you about?"

"Snow White?"

"Yeah. Turns out her name's Brittany and she showed me this killer spot. No one will look for you there."

"Snow White?"

"Yeah." Zoe was confused.

"We're talking about the same person here, right? That chick that's been stalking you?"

"Well, I wouldn't say *stalking*."

Kayla laughed quite heartily. "Yeah, well. I would. When she came up to me and Lenny the day you set your claws into JD, the vibe I got was not a good one."

"She's not so bad. In fact, she's a child of the eclipse."

"Again, I have to ask. Snow White?"

"Yes." Zoe's annoyance grew faster than the heat.

"And when was it that you all got so chummy?"

"Last night. JD and I had to take cover in a cave… Heather's feathers. I completely forgot to tell you."

Zoe put the brakes on. She grabbed Kayla's shoulders, which if you were to ask Kayla, hurt quite a bit. But she was far too focused on the bright spark in Zoe's eyes to care, and not just because they were nearly touching her own. There was a heightened amount of passion in them that was totally affecting.

"You didn't," Kayla said, thinking a little further down the road than Zoe.

"We did. And it was just as we thought it would be."

Kayla's jaw dropped to her knees. Picking it up would take a forklift.

Zoe let go of Kayla and twirled away from her like a love-struck cartoon princess with her hands pulled tight to her chest colliding in a bouquet of fingers. "Just thinking about it again, Kayla…"

It turned out to be a lot easier to pick Kayla's jaw off the ground than originally thought. "How did it happen?"

"Well, we were hiking up to The Peak yesterday when it started raining."

Kayla was a bit confused. She didn't remember any rain; it had been sunny as far as she could remember, though she was inside all day with Lenny (and that rat, Henry), so it might have been possible. No need to interrupt Zoe's scintillating tale over such a minor discrepancy.

"We weren't going to be able to make it back down before nightfall, so we found this cave. We were soaked, I mean, *drenched*, by the time we got inside, and we started to horse around a bit. Before we knew it, we were in each other's arms and…"

The long exhale of breath said it all. "Kayla…"

"I get it," Kayla said, giving Zoe permission to put a period on it (though Kayla still felt oddly disappointed).

Zoe's smile stayed bright. "I wish you could have felt it."

Kayla wasn't sure whether she meant she wished she could have felt JD's kiss or felt a similar magic, but she figured, all things considered, it was the latter. "I'm sure I will," she tried to say. It was a lie. Zoe didn't care.

"I guess we ended up falling asleep soon after because the next thing I remember, Brittany woke me up."

"See, I told you that psycho's a stalker."

"Probably, but she had a good reason."

"And what, pray tell, was her reason?"

Zoe had her hands back on Kayla's shoulders. Importance and determination now filled her eyes. "She believes there's a way to stop the eclipse."

Kayla was now filled with the same tickle of anticipation and wonderment that swarmed Zoe. "Stop the eclipse? Seriously?"

"With the blaze of Heather's fingernails, I swear it."

Kayla was conflicted. If it was true, this was a chance to save Lenny without having to steal her away from Heather, not to mention living the life she had always hoped for. But there was still a chance (and a pretty big one at that) that this "Brittany" was deliberately lying to get something from Zoe. What that was, she couldn't say, but she was going to stay cautious and make sure to keep her hopes encased in steel until she was positively sure one way or the other.

"I thought you'd be more excited," Zoe said, absorbing the conflict.

"I will be, when it's verified."

"I know it sounds to good to be true. Believe me, I'm the first to say the whole thing reeks of desperation. But it's definitely worth the risks if it's even remotely true, don't you think? I know I'm willing to take that risk."

Kayla nodded. It was all she could think of to do. Zoe chose to hug her. It felt right. "I've had a lot of time to think, and I've decided I won't let you die. Not if I can help it."

There was no trace of a lie on her lips. Kayla returned the hug.

It took until the sun had once again set on Heather for Zoe and Kayla to reach their destination. Zoe smiled as Kayla's face lit up (which, if she could have seen it, was probably identical to hers upon her own first look).

"Wait here a second."

"Yeah," Kayla said, even if she didn't quite comprehend what Zoe had said.

"Brittany," Zoe called as she inched through the crevice. "Brittany. It's Zoe."

Brittany shocked the socks off of Zoe as she appeared from around a hidden corner. The swelling on her ankle seemed to have subsided, as she no longer walked with a limp. "Zoe? Oh, I'm happy to see you. Did you think about my proposal?"

"Yeah, but I have a huge favor to ask of you first."

"Anything," Brittany said. She was all bright stars and sunshine, which made Zoe somewhat indifferent.

"You know my friend Kayla?"

Brittany nodded. "Sweet girl."

"Yeah, well, something terrible happened this morning and I was hoping she could stay here for a few days, just until the eclipse."

"Of course. She's more than welcome to stay here."

"But you can't tell anyone she's here."

"Who am I going to tell?"

"Right." Zoe couldn't decide if she should get Kayla or confirm the situation. Eventually, she figured Brittany understood what she needed and called Kayla into the cave.

"Hello again, Kayla."

"Snow White."

Brittany smiled graciously, her cheeks powdered rosy.

"Brittany," she said with a child's squeak.

"Right, sorry."

"Don't worry about it."

If it was measurable, what came next was probably the most awkward silence of all awkward silences. Finally, Brittany said, "So, I hear you need a place to hide."

"I hear you know how to stop the eclipse."

"Not exactly, but I think I know how to find out. With Zoe's help."

Zoe nodded. "I'll do what I can."

"Thank you," Kayla said to them both.

"Great. We'll get started tomorrow." Zoe headed out but was stopped short of the crevice.

"Wait," Kayla said. "Where are you going?"

"If I don't get home, Maisy is going to have a fit, especially after I didn't come home last night. Don't worry, once I know I'm in the clear, I'll be back."

Now Kayla felt it was right for a hug. "Thank you," she whispered.

Zoe left, and if the last healthy silence was the most awkward, this one would have come in a close second.

10

An Alleged Accomplice

"Zoe!"

It was the frantic call of an extremely worried caretaker, which was inevitably followed by an angry, "Where have you been?" and a thankful hug. "I've been looking everywhere for you."

"I'm sorry," Zoe said, feeling her eyes moisten. "I got stuck in the mountains during the storm and then everything with Kayla happened. I should have come here first, I know."

Surprisingly, she wasn't scolded. Instead, Maisy said, "What happened to Kayla?"

"You don't know?"

It was odd, to be sure, especially if Maisy had been looking everywhere for her. Then again, even if Maisy had checked the Quarters, she may have done so before everything went quiet, making it possible that news of Kayla's trial hadn't spread yet. "Kayla was sentenced to Death Rock this morning for blasphemy."

"Blasphemy? What did she do?"

"They *claim* she wrote some death threat against Heather on the lumber mill. But she'd never do that. I know she wouldn't."

"I'm so sorry," Maisy said with another hug, this one more sad and warming. "I know how much she meant to you."

Zoe almost let it slip that nothing happened to Kayla, that Susanna let her go. But if she was going to keep her promise, she had to keep Maisy in the dark about her indiscretion, so she drummed up a few fake tears and said, "I'm going to miss her."

"I know. But it was going to happen no matter what. Still, I wish there was something I could have done to help her."

"Me too." It was odd to lie so freely, but once again, it was what Kayla would have done under similar circumstances. If they were going to get away with this, Zoe would have to remain in Kayla's mindset for the foreseeable future.

"Would you like me to make you some soup?" Maisy said. She had forgotten all about her having gone missing.

Playing along, Zoe said, "I think I just need some sleep."

"Okay. But tomorrow morning, we're going to talk about your punishment."

Heather's feathers. She hadn't forgotten after all. But it didn't matter; whatever the punishment might be, it wouldn't keep her from helping Brittany stop the eclipse. At least so she hoped.

Just before Zoe stepped from the room to complete her ruse, JD pounded at the door, his voice high and frantic. He didn't wait to be invited in as Maisy opened the door; instead he went straight to Zoe. "Thank Heather you're okay. I thought something awful might have happened to you."

Zoe kissed him for his concern. She just couldn't help it.

"Join the club," Maisy said with a laugh. She absolutely loved seeing their affection.

Zoe pulled his confusion back to her attention. "I'm sorry. I tried to wake you but you were out cold."

"No matter. Where's Kayla?"

"What do you mean?" Zoe said. She wanted to know exactly what he already knew before saying much else.

"She's not with you?"

"No." Again, the shorter the answer the better.

"Thank Heather." JD hugged Zoe.

"Why? What happened? What's going on?"

"The nobles are on their way here. They have it in their heads that you helped Kayla escape."

"They what?" The sound of Zoe and Maisy's high-pitched voices were right in tune with one another.

"How do you know that?" Zoe continued.

"When I went looking for you this morning, I thought you may have gone to Jack and Winter's, but when I got there, Nestor was there."

"Nestor? What happened? Is Winter okay?"

"She's fine. She thought she was going into labor last night, but it turns out they were false contractions. Nothing serious."

Zoe was relieved. She could only imagine how scary that must have been, to think that the child would be born prematurely. It was inconceivable to think what might happen to Heather if a child wasn't born with the eclipse. "That's good to hear."

"I stayed with her for quite a while after, just to make sure everything was okay, and then headed down through the hub for a bite to eat before coming to see if you made it back here. That's when I heard what happened. Rumor has it that before the nobles were able to take Kayla to Death Rock, you and the Heather Biters ambushed them and stole Kayla into the forest."

There are no words to explain how stunned Zoe was over this incredibly absurd allegation. "You don't believe them, do you?"

"I believe you may have helped Kayla escape, but not like that."

"That's ridiculous. I didn't do anything of the sort."

"But you were at the pit."

"Why would you think I was at the pit?"

"Susanna."

Zoe couldn't deny any of it any longer. "Loose lips," she mumbled. "She told you I helped Kayla escape?"

"She told Terry, but it was only to save her own skin."

"What? Why?"

"Apparently, someone claimed they saw Susanna cut Kayla free and ask you to take her out of Heather."

"Who said that?"

"I don't know. The nobles were already gathering to come up here and question you about the whole thing. I had to let you know they were coming."

"Is all of that true, Zoe?"

Zoe could already see the disappointment in Maisy's eyes even before her full confession. By the end, she was crying. "I couldn't just let her die down there, Maisy. I couldn't."

Maisy hugged Zoe tightly. She wasn't sure what she should do.

"It's a witch-hunt," Zoe said. "For whatever reason, we're being attacked. I swear to you, Kayla did not paint that defamatory stuff on that wall."

That was when the nobles knocked at the door. Zoe quickly grabbed JD's hand and held him close. She was afraid; he was afraid.

"Frances and Maisy, this is your quorum headmaster. We have reason to believe that your ward, Zoe, is harboring a fugitive. Open the door."

Maisy obliged. Her hands shook.

Terry entered along with all of the nobles, and, oddly enough, Henry. What he was doing with them (not to mention being in Pasture Ranch, though it did make some sense, now that his elected home was here) was beyond Zoe. He walked directly up to her and stared with a really unnerving grin. It gave her chills; she had to look away. The rest of the posse combed the property, both inside and out. When Kayla was nowhere to be found, Henry began his interrogation.

"Where is Kayla, ward of Daniel and Catherine?"

"My guess," Zoe said, confronting that grin with poise, "is down in Death Rock where she belongs."

Henry nodded. Zoe held back a shiver.

"Strong words from someone who hasn't hardly left her side since birth."

"What can I say? Heather is our grace, and no one shall ever speak of her with vitriol."

"Where were you this morning?"

"When? Before I yelled at you for being a rat, or after?"

"Watch yourself, Zoe," Terry said. He was trying to be strict (or as strict as Henry anyway), but Zoe didn't feel, with that attempt, that he believed any of this. Something told her that Terry felt

Henry had gone too far, but like Susanna, had to continue to present a mask of leadership.

"It's okay, Terry. She's a fighter. I respect that."

"I'll bet," Zoe whispered.

Henry chuckled, then said, "After you left Kayla's. Where did you go?"

"I went to see what you claim she did."

"And you saw what it was?"

"I did. I thought it was a sickening act of betrayal. To me and to Heather."

"Did you follow Reynold and Gavin to Death Rock?"

"No. When I saw what Kayla had done, I left. I lost all respect for her." Zoe felt sick, and wasn't sure anyone would believe her, not that they should.

"Where did you go, when you left?"

"I came back here."

"Can anyone verify that?"

"I can," JD said quickly. Zoe tightened her grip on his hand.

"You were here when she returned?"

"Yes. I was looking for her this morning. She got here shortly after I arrived."

"And what would you say her manner was?"

"She was upset, clearly," JD said.

"Right. Because she just saw her friend convicted of an incredibly heinous crime."

"Yes. She was in tears for most of the day. She only just now got over it."

Henry paced backward. He whispered something to Terry,

then turned back to JD. "Why were you looking for Zoe this morning?"

"We were up in the mountains last night and we got separated. I wanted to make sure she was okay."

"So, you didn't know anything about the incident with Kayla?"

"Not until Zoe told me, no."

"And you had no other contact with anyone today?"

"I was with Winter for a little bit. Other than that, no."

Henry turned to Maisy. Zoe tightened her grip on JD (if that were even possible). This is where the whole story could come unglued. Would Maisy back them up (and do it convincingly), or would she turn them in under the clear unwritten ethical law of Heather?

"Can you verify any of this, Maisy?"

Maisy paused. It was all over. Zoe almost broke down in tears.

"I can't," Maisy said, peering at Zoe and JD. "I was out of the house all day."

"What were you doing?"

"I was looking for Zoe. She didn't come home last night and I was worried."

Zoe felt like smiling but kept it hidden. Maisy had taken herself out of the equation and didn't even have to lie to do it.

"When did you get back?"

"Not much longer before you," she said.

"And Zoe was here?"

Maisy nodded.

"With JD."

Maisy nodded again. They were small white lies, and saying them with silence was a whole lot better than having to speak them out loud.

Henry nodded with her. "Where is Frances?"

"He was shucking corn all morning and went to Industry Quarters when he was finished."

"He's there now?"

"I assume so."

Henry pursed his lips and stared at Maisy. She didn't back down. Zoe loved her for that. He finally turned back to Terry and again whispered something.

"I'm very sorry for the intrusion," Terry said thereafter. "We'll be on our way."

The nobles left the house quietly, all except Henry, who stayed back for one last threat. He got right up close to Zoe and whispered in her ear. "I know you helped Kayla, Zoe, and when I can prove it, not even Heather or the eclipse will be able to save you from the torture I will inflict on you."

JD pushed Henry away, taking a stand between him and Zoe. "You can leave now," he said.

Henry nodded, courteously and with grace. "You have a good night."

When he left, Zoe had to sit. Her nerves were so tight. JD sat with her.

"What was that?" she said.

"I don't know, but Terry was definitely not in control of any of it."

"This isn't good."

Maisy stayed at the door, probably to make sure that Henry had actually left the grounds. When he was past the first field of corn (just a tiny toy soldier in the distance), Maisy took a seat across from Zoe. She set her hand on her knee.

"I need you to be honest," she said. "Did Kayla leave Heather?"

Zoe set her hand on Maisy's. This was going to be hard but she had to be honest, and had to be so with a clear direct line of sight. "No. She's still here."

"Where is she?"

"I can't tell you that."

"Why not?"

"I can't take the risk. She's safe now because no one knows where she is. I need to keep it that way, at least until the eclipse. You won't say anything, will you?"

"As long as you stay away from her until the eclipse, I promise I won't say anything."

"Thank you." And though Zoe knew that was an impossible promise to keep (and in some ways, she felt Maisy knew that as well), she hugged her, hoping it would appease her enough to turn a blind eye.

"Frances should be back soon," Maisy said to JD. "You'd best be getting back home."

"Yeah, I guess I should," JD said. He kissed Zoe's cheek and left.

Zoe and Maisy spent the next hour making dinner. They didn't say much until Frances got home with his own story. Meeting up with Henry just outside the Grand Hub, he, too, was thoroughly interrogated. For the most part, his story matched up with Maisy's, so the subject was dropped. Maisy and Zoe replayed their face-to-face with Henry shortly after over a hot bowl of corn soup and roast beef. It was a good night, all things considered.

Zoe woke extremely early the next morning. Her first instinct was to run out to the triangle. But thinking back on the night before, she couldn't leave without first telling Maisy that she was going, thus forcing the punishment issue (which Maisy and Frances had discussed over half the night). As Zoe predicted, the punishment (being home no later than sunset and cooking both breakfast and dinner every day until the eclipse) wouldn't at all hinder her from helping Brittany save Kayla.

After Zoe happily finished breakfast (including washing the dishes), she said she was going to visit Winter, which didn't raise any red flags considering what JD had said happened the day before. Maisy and Frances kissed her goodbye and she was off, free until sundown. And as long as she could control it, she wasn't going to waste one minute of it.

11

A Plan of Action

When Kayla woke up, the smell of the spring that flowed just above the cavern was scintillating, as were the berries that sat next to her. Starving, she wolfed them down as she had the night before. Why she had never had anything so delicious before was beyond her. She hadn't said more than two words to Brittany since Zoe left, but with so much generosity and kindness (she let her sleep on the ledge with the hand-made pillow of leaves and vines that was surprisingly soft), Brittany couldn't be as bad as Kayla first thought her to be, especially when she thought back to how comfortable Lenny had been with her. She had never before seen anything like that, and if Lenny was okay with her, perhaps she saw something in Brittany that Kayla wasn't able to see—yet.

Kayla stepped into the crevice to get a breath of fresh air when Brittany returned.

"I wouldn't do that," she said. Her speech was a little impaired, possibly because of the weeds she had lodged in the back of her mouth. "You never know who might be watching."

Brittany was right, though Kayla didn't want to admit it. "I need a drink."

"There's a small waterfall in the back. Here, I'll show you."

Kayla wasn't sure, but she thought Brittany might have deliberately brushed her arm against her as she passed (though she didn't complain; Brittany's skin was extremely smooth).

Brittany set her basket full of weeds and grains down at the base of the ledge. "Come on," she said. Her fingers delicately bounced ever so lightly as she held out her hand.

She led Kayla through a very small, secluded tunnel that led into a dark room lit only by a shimmer of sunlight breaking through a needle-size gap in the rocks. How it filled the room with so much light was an amazing phenomenon. At the back wall, a slow dribble of water leaked down from the ceiling (*some waterfall*) and pooled into a natural bowl. The water level stayed just an inch below the lip, leaving Kayla to wonder if the bowl ever overflowed, or if it was one of those supernatural entities that could never be explained, even with the most advanced science and theoretical deductions. The water was cold to the touch, but ever so refreshing on the lips. She wanted to drink the whole thing.

"How in the world did you ever find this place?" Kayla said.

"I'm a natural explorer, I guess. It's probably why I was able to leave so easily."

"What's it like?"

"What? The outside?"

"Yeah."

"I wouldn't say it was all that much different than it is here, really."

"Except for a longer, better life," Kayla was clear to interject.

"Well, yes. People live longer lives, but that doesn't necessarily make them better."

"What do you mean?"

"I mean, just because they live longer doesn't mean their life is any more fulfilling. Not when the majority of people waste half their lives, and that's with not even knowing when their life is going to end. At least Heather gives us the chance to live full, substantial lives before she takes us."

Kayla's thoughts were alive with questions, ideas, theories and contradictions, but none of them were clear enough to articulate.

Brittany could see her struggle. "I'm not saying it's a bad thing to have the chance to live as long as possible, I'm just saying that a lot of people take it for granted. No one does that here."

"Then why end it?"

"Excuse me?"

"If you think Heather's cleansing is such a good thing, why do you want to stop the eclipse?"

"There are a lot of reasons," Brittany said, "but the main one, I guess, would be because it's not fair, especially to someone like you. Yeah, you know it's coming, and have made every day count because of that, but what gives Heather the right to take your life just because you were born a year too early?"

"Two weeks, actually, but who's counting."

"My point exactly. There's no reason for it. It's wrong and it needs to be stopped."

"I agree, but then why would you even attempt to defend it?"

"Because it works. Everyone here makes every day count.

What's not fair is giving them the time they deserve to live, travel, explore. It should work on both levels."

"I don't get it."

"For all we know, the eclipse has plagued this land for as long as man could walk. It's something that everyone fears, but respects. I want to stop it because I believe that everyone deserves to live the longest life they deem worthy, but by doing so, the possibility that the next eclipse could end everyone's life would keep them from becoming complacent, as they have on the outside."

"Oddly, that makes a lot of sense."

"It's truly the best of both worlds, in my opinion."

"What if it doesn't work?"

"At least I tried, and I'll die with honor."

"In case it doesn't, how long would it take for me to get far enough away?"

"I'm not sure it even matters."

"Is that why you came back now and not in another thirty-four years? You think you're going to die anyway?"

Brittany remained silent but nodded ever so lightly.

Kayla bit her upper lip. If that were true, there was no chance to escape with Lenny if this didn't work. "It better work."

Brittany and Kayla didn't say another word to each other until Zoe finally arrived and let them in on everything that happened the night before.

"That piece of Heather's ass," Kayla hissed in regards to Henry. "Whether we stop the eclipse or not, I am not going to let Lenny live under that man's rule. I don't care if we both die at sea."

Brittany stayed silent on the issue.

"So what's the plan then?" Kayla continued. "You two do have a plan, right?"

"Of course," Zoe said and then looked to Brittany. Kayla followed. Their eyes were like daggers.

"I guess that's my cue," Brittany said with a fierce smirk. "Okay, here's what I know. Heather's curse can supposedly be broken with the sacrifice of the child of the eclipse."

"Supposedly?" Kayla said.

"Unfortunately, I don't know all of the specifics," Brittany confessed.

"If you don't know the specifics, what are we doing here?"

"You said you were chased out," Zoe said. "Someone was trying to kill you?"

"Sacrifice me, yes. David. He had just turned eighteen about a month before the eclipse."

"I know how that feels," Kayla mumbled.

"He came to me with the idea that because I was the child of the eclipse, that I had to be sacrificed in order to end the curse."

"Why did he think that?" Zoe said.

"That's what I asked him."

"The child of the eclipse has to be good for something," Kayla mused. "Why else would one be born every time?"

"You're not too far off," Brittany said. "But it was more than that. As you know, anyone that would make that type of accusation might well end up inside Death Rock if they weren't careful."

"All too well," Kayla said.

"There had to be hard evidence to the fact."

"So, what proof did he have?"

"He told me that he had found a book."

"A book?" Kayla said. Her belief was waning.

"A journal, of sorts, I guess. Super old, super secret."

"Right, of course. Is there any other kind?"

Zoe slapped Kayla, mostly to shut her up.

"He claimed that this journal laid out exactly what to do to stop the eclipse. He said that when the child of the eclipse was sacrificed in the light of the eclipse, Heather would gift the land with long life."

"Did you ever see the book?" Zoe said.

"What book?" JD said.

Everyone turned to him, their eyes larger than saucer plates. Kayla backed away, but her eyes remained locked on him as if she would melt him if he even thought about turning her in (which, if it was even possible, would actually have been really cool).

Zoe was the first to speak. "Did you follow me?"

"I didn't have to," he said.

"Then how did you find us?"

"It was actually pretty easy. I thought you would want to keep Kayla as close to you as possible while keeping her far enough away. Taking into consideration the accounts of Susanna and Henry, and the events that took place, I figured you to be around this area. When I got close enough, I heard you guys cackling away."

"Did anyone follow you?" Kayla said.

"No. I made sure of that. But if it was this easy for me, it's only a matter of time before Henry figures it out."

"You're not going to say anything, are you?" Zoe said. The concern for her friend's safety was wholly apparent.

"I wouldn't do that," JD said calmly. "You can trust me."

Zoe believed him, mostly because of what he did for her the night before. She whispered, "Thank you," and then turned back to Brittany and Kayla. "It's okay. He'll help us."

"Nice choice," Brittany whispered to Zoe, trailed by a wink and a smirk, which curled Zoe's lips with a blush.

"I'm JD." Had he heard?

Brittany thought so, what with the guilty shrug of her shoulders. She shied away a second but then shook his hand. She was redder than a rose. "Brittany. It's nice to meet you."

"Likewise," he said. "You're not from Heather."

"We'll explain later," Zoe said, interrupting. She had to bring them back to the matter at hand. JD was right; Henry was smart enough—he would figure out where they were before long. If they were going to do this, they needed to do it fast. "Did you ever get to read David's book?"

It took Brittany another minute to catch back up to speed (she was still a little disoriented by JD's sudden presence), but once she had, she jumped right back in as if nothing had happened.

"No, that's why I couldn't believe him. But he just wouldn't let it go. By the time the lottery came around, he had somehow convinced everyone that it was true. They decided to forgo the lottery in favor of locking me away until the eclipse so that they might stop the eclipse once and for all. They stormed my house and dragged me to the square like a rabid dog."

"How did you escape?"

"Terry came to my defense. He was the next in line for quorum headmaster and he wanted to see the evidence of David's claim before they went any further. But when David went to get the book, it was gone. He eventually went mad looking for it, but in the meantime, Terry convinced the headmaster to release me. I couldn't take the chance that David would find the book, so I left."

"What happened to it?"

"I have a theory," Brittany said, quieter than was comfortable.

"Go on," Kayla said.

"I believe it's somewhere in the headmaster's vault."

"The headmaster's vault?" JD said, speaking aloud what everyone was thinking. "I'm sorry to burst your bubble, but the headmaster doesn't have a vault."

"He does have a vault," Brittany said. Her confidence was unmatched.

"Where?" Zoe asked.

"It's in the catacombs below Quorum Circle."

"Quorum Circle has catacombs?" Kayla said.

"All of Heather has catacombs."

"What else don't we know about this place?"

"My guess?" Brittany said. "A lot."

"And what makes you an expert about all of this anyway?"

"My caretakers were nobles."

"You lived in Quorum Circle?"

Brittany nodded. Zoe might have said, "No, we lived just outside in the squalors," but that was her. It now made sense why Brittany was a little more proper than most.

"Did you know about these catacombs?" Kayla asked JD, who remained unbelievably quiet. Kayla threw up her arms, exasperated.

"Tell us about them," Zoe said, hoping to bring calm to the atmosphere—and ignoring the fact that JD hadn't trusted her enough to tell her about them. She just figured it was because it never came up in one of their multitude of conversations.

"They're a maze of darkly-lit passages that connect the center of Quorum Circle with all of the different communities of Heather. It's believed that they were built during the wars, in a way to avert the armies if they ever found us. They also came in useful to some of us kids when we needed to take a shortcut home, which didn't always work because we got lost most of the time. But it was always fun trying."

So that's how she got in and out of places so quickly, Zoe thought. "So what you're saying is we can get to this vault from anywhere in Heather."

Brittany nodded.

"If that's true, why haven't you already gone to the vault to get the book?" Kayla's skepticism could sometimes be downright infuriating, even when she was right.

"Because the vault has a coded lock that I wasn't about to try and break."

"Why not? You were a noble. Shouldn't you already know the code?"

"I was a noble, yes, but only the headmaster knows the code."

"Well, that's just wonderful." Kayla turned her back to the rest. Her chances of surviving were slowly diminishing.

"How do we go about getting the code?" Zoe said, unwilling to give up.

"I'll get it," JD said. His confidence warmed Zoe to no end.

"Are you sure you can do that?" Brittany asked.

"I'm the best bet. I live in Quorum Circle after all. It won't look suspicious."

"How are you going to do it?"

"You leave that to me," JD said. Zoe gave him a squeeze.

"Wait. Before we go running off on some fool's errand, I've got another question," Kayla said, whipping back around. "What makes you think this book is even in the vault? You said yourself it disappeared."

"I think Terry might have something to do with that. He and I were friends back then like you guys are now. We ran around those catacombs like wildcats on a prairie. It was our playground. I still believe that if I hadn't have been forced out, we would have been coupled."

Zoe tightened her grip around JD's hand. "He loved you."

"He wasn't about to let me get killed over some theory. I think that Terry, upon hearing about the book, found a way to steal it from David and hid it in the vault before asking him to reveal it."

"Genius plan," Zoe said.

"If it's true," Kayla said.

"Kayla."

"I'm serious. If they were such good friends, or in love, or whatever, then why doesn't she just go to him and get the book?"

"I can't do that," Brittany said.

"Why not?" Thinking about it, Zoe agreed completely with Kayla.

"It's complicated. Let's just say if anyone knows I'm here, it might not turn out the way we want."

"Enough with the cryptic—"

"Kayla," Zoe said. Kayla huffed her disapproval but trusted Zoe enough to let it go.

"I understand your trepidation, but everything will become clear when we get that book. I promise."

"Then it's settled," Zoe finished.

"I'm afraid I'll need to go with you," Brittany said, as if she knew Zoe had a plan all figured out.

"Why? You don't trust me?" Zoe knew how stupid that sounded the second it left her lips.

"The vault is hidden extremely well," Brittany said without a hint of offence. "Only someone that has actually been there will be able to find it. I could go on all day long about which path to take and when, and you'd still probably get yourself lost. At least on the way back."

"Fine. Whatever we need to do."

"But we need to hurry. The longer we wait, the less chance we'll have to find it."

"I agree." Zoe turned to JD. "Let's get going."

"JD should go on ahead," Brittany interjected.

"We're not going with him?"

"It's best if we take the catacombs. We'll meet you behind the physician's office."

"There's an entrance there?"

Brittany winked. JD couldn't help but smile. Neither could Zoe.

"Good luck," she said and kissed him. Kayla turned away; she had to admit it—she was a little jealous.

12

Into the Catacombs

Before she slipped into the crevice, Brittany pulled the hood of her cloak up over her head, helping her mix with the rock and the darkness like a chameleon. Zoe turned to Kayla, who was sitting on the ledge. One leg dangled off the edge, while the other sat up with her arm wrapped around it. Kayla still had quite a few reservations about following Brittany so easily, but she knew Zoe wouldn't do anything if she didn't feel in her gut that it was safe (though if she could have been able to go with them, she would have been a lot more comfortable). Zoe had thought about staying, to keep her company (and in some small part, to keep her from leaving), but retrieving the book had to remain her priority. If Kayla was right about Brittany (no matter how minor it was), she wanted to be there when they found the book—to be on the safe side.

She raised her hand as a feeble attempt to say a second goodbye, but Kayla wasn't paying attention. Her head was pressed back against the wall as she stared up at the ceiling. What she was looking at, only Kayla was aware (if she was even looking at anything; there was always a chance—no matter how slim—that Kayla was actually thinking, about Lenny for sure), but for all Zoe knew, Kayla figured they had already gone and she didn't want to interrupt her any further. If she did, Kayla might just well have stopped her, or worse yet, talked her way into going with them. That's when Zoe saw a small teardrop pass over Kayla's slightly pink cheek, almost causing her own to form. The conflict was too much for Zoe. She pretended that it was all in her imagination, choosing her original decision over second-guessing herself, which her gut told her was exactly what she should do.

Zoe slipped through the crevice and met Brittany a few feet from the cave. Pasture Ranch looked beautiful in the rich sunlight.

"She'll be okay," Brittany said. "Time alone will be good for her."

"I know." But did she really? "We better go. I need to be back home by sunset."

"We can't have you getting into any more trouble," Brittany said. She turned her head ever so slightly, to give Zoe the slightest visual at the curvature of her profile. "Can't stop the eclipse with you shackled to your bed, now, can we?" Brittany's lips curled slightly. Zoe wanted to be playfully upset, but the retort really wasn't smart enough for that. Kayla, she knew, would have had a much better zing.

It didn't bother Brittany any. For all she cared it was the best comment ever, and her assertive steps into Pasture Ranch proved that. The two trekked silently through Timber and Gail's cotton fields until they reached the oak in front of the main house.

What are we doing here? Zoe asked, but apparently only to herself. Or else Brittany ignored her as she traced her way around the tree, concealing herself from view of anyone who might be watching from the house. With her hand against the thick trunk, Brittany knelt down. She waved her hand above the grass line at the base of the tree like some kind of magician, and then pressed down at a spot about a foot in front of her. When she raised her hand up, the ground came with it, revealing a slit of an opening just underneath. Zoe's eyes went wide. It was amazing to think that she had walked and played over this very spot dozens of times and never knew what secrets were hidden just below her very own feet.

Brittany raised the wooden hatch (which could have been completely organic, for all Zoe knew) until it stopped at about a forty-five degree angle from the ground. She slid her feet inside and looked up to Zoe. "Are you coming?" Brittany pushed herself into the darkness below.

Zoe examined the gateway carefully. If Zoe was one thing, it was cautious to a fault. Focusing harder into the dark, Zoe saw Brittany glowing slightly. She didn't know how that was possible, but it excited her enough to give her what motivation she needed to slide her legs in as Brittany had done. She immediately felt a brush of immense heat against them and hesitated. That was until Brittany offered her a hand. Zoe took it gently and used the soft reassurance to jump down, allowing Brittany to ease her fall. Sweat washed over her instantly.

"Not so hard, was it?" Brittany said, not an ounce of moisture present. Zoe felt a bit jealous (and confused) but ignored it, feeling that if she put to much energy into wondering why Brittany wasn't perspiring, she would pass out. She wiped a pound of sweat from her forehead as Brittany grabbed a small rope latched to the back of the hatch. She pulled on it quite hard and made the ground a complete, seamless cover.

That's when her attention on the skin-melting heat (and the urge to both vomit and faint at the same time) gave way to a focus on the brilliance of the catacombs. The rocks glowed in a beautiful array of rainbows and sparkles as they lit up like a winter's festival. She had been wondering how they were going to be able to see within the catacombs (and partially if the darkness was why someone could get lost so easily within them), but now she knew—the rocks were the guide. The best part was, as Zoe followed Brittany along the first of many paths they would eventually have to navigate, the color of light would change upon each rock, making it feel as if her mere presence woke the rocks up and put them to sleep depending on the frequency of their color. Quite magical indeed.

"How does it work?" she finally asked, though her throat was dryer than sand.

"How does what work?"

"The glow-in-the-dark rocks. I've never in my life seen anything so beautiful."

Brittany smiled. "Thermoluminescence."

"Right, of course."

A laugh escaped Brittany's lips. "It's rare, I'll give you that," she said. "From what I remember from my old quorum history lessons, a few generations ago, some miners found a new mineral that glowed when it was under intense heat. To learn more about it, they continued to dig until they reached a point where the air was so naturally hot that it allowed the mineral to glow on its own. It was such a find that they spent two generations digging it out, ultimately using it as a foreign currency. That was when the first of the catacombs was built, as a matter of fact, running from Palisade Mines to Quorum Circle. Eventually they learned that the supply of rock was extremely limited. If they kept using it for trade, it was only a matter of time before it would be depleted. Hearing news of the wars occurring among the outside, the headmaster at the time, Killem I believe his name was, stopped the sale of the mineral, believing it was too rare and useful to be given to foreign hands. Instead, he tasked the diggers to build several tunnels under the communities of Heather, using the minerals to light their way. Because the earth underneath us was so hot, it was easy to create long, winding tunnels that stretched forever, keeping the rock where it was when it was naturally there, and transporting it to areas where the mineral wasn't, until the catacombs were completed."

"Fascinating," Zoe said, breathless (and not just because of the continuing heat).

"It's been a noble secret for a long time, to be sure."

"I still can't believe how the headmaster can keep such a secret from everyone."

"It's one of many secrets the nobles have, Zoe." In a light whisper, she added, "One of many."

"So what's happened since?"

"A few generations ago, the headmaster, once again seeing a great financial potential in the rock, and because there was no longer any danger, started stripping the catacombs and selling the rock to foreign entities. Mostly for profit, I believe. None of Heather sees any of that."

"That's appalling," Zoe said.

"That's Heather."

Zoe thought for a moment about asking what other secrets the nobles had, but she was actually interested in something else entirely.

"Do you think Terry sells it?"

"I'm sure he does. His caretaker made profit off of it, as did mine."

"And you didn't think that was even the slightest bit immoral?"

"It's the way it was. I had no reason to."

"That's a fat load of feathers. You should have known better. You're the child of the eclipse, for Heather's sake."

"That doesn't make us any different than anyone else, Zoe. I mean, I never showed any more prowess in anything than anyone else. I failed all of my mining exams and didn't do all that much better in Industry Quarters. You probably have your own stories of failure. We're not perfect; we're human. It wasn't until I left Heather that I learned how corrupt and dishonest it all was."

Zoe couldn't argue with her. A part of her felt as if Brittany was reading her mind because she was right about everything, which made Zoe feel a bit guilty for the accusation. Zoe and Brittany grew up in entirely different environments, but with the exact same reverence thrust upon them. It made Zoe wonder more about Brittany's past and who she had been as a young girl, but she didn't know what to say, or how to ask, so she remained silent for a mile or so before treading the waters once again (when she felt the tension had died down enough, that is). "How adventurous were you?"

"When?" Brittany's tone was light, without a hint of disdain.

"Back when you were a child."

"Extremely. I never stayed put, not even when I was punished for it. I just liked the freedom of it all. I could do anything, be anything. It was such a joy to be so carefree and independent."

"Was Terry as adventurous as you?"

"Heather's feathers, no. If anything, Terry tamed me. Don't get me wrong, I still did some crazy stuff when we were together, but just knowing that I might lose him kept me from doing anything too crazy."

A soft smile caressed Zoe's lips. "That and he wasn't willing to do most of it, right?"

"In a way, yeah. But under the right circumstances, Terry could be quite the wild man. I'm sure he hid that part of himself after getting his ward and becoming headmaster, but running around the catacombs with me was just the tip of the iceberg for us, if you know what I mean."

"I can imagine," Zoe said.

Brittany stopped. "Try not to imagine too much."

Zoe matched Brittany's smile.

"What I can't imagine," Zoe said as they started walking again, "is Terry doing what you're saying. He just doesn't seem to be that kind of a person."

"Like I said, the responsibility of caretaking changes people. Sometimes for the better, sometimes for the worse."

"He raised her well," Zoe said.

"I never doubted he would. Terry was always the most caring man I ever knew. He believed in compassion over anger, forgiveness over retribution."

"Susanna's the same. They deserve better."

"And we're going to give it to them."

13

An Unsettling Announcement

It felt like days before Zoe and Brittany finally weaved and turned and spun their way to a hatch hidden at the edge of the rose bushes that lined the fence separating Quorum Circle from Common Fields. Even from behind Brittany, Zoe could see the edge of the physician's building. It still amazed her that she had no idea about the catacombs.

Brittany slowly rose up out of the tunnel and cautiously slid across the grass until she came to a stop at the edge of the office. She pressed her back against it and waited for Zoe to join her (stopping her once to go back and lower the hatch—*but stay down!*). When Zoe finally laid her back against the office (and closer to Brittany than she realized), Zoe asked, "What's wrong?"

"I don't know," Brittany said. "Do you hear that?"

Zoe took a second to adjust, but finally did hear a soft commotion. It didn't sound close but it did sound important. Because the back quarter of the physician's office cut through the Quorum Circle fence (allowing special access to the Circle that only the physician could use), neither of them could see anything from where they sat. Brittany urged Zoe to move to the front of the building as slowly and as quietly as her little feet could manage, which was a lot tougher than expected, what with the pebbles and stones that lined the edge of the office along with a various number of plants, some that pricked at Zoe's sensitive skin. Each sting felt like a bite from a rabid dog, leaving behind a soft hiss and a thin bubble of blood. A step ahead of her, Brittany moved along like a ghost.

When they reached the front of the office, Brittany peered around the corner. The stillness of her body made Zoe want to see what was happening more than ever. Trying her best to remain concealed (believing Brittany might rip her head off if she didn't), Zoe got to her knees and wrapped her head around Brittany's legs. It was a bit awkward feeling Brittany's thigh brush against her ear, and even more so in her attempts to find a place to rest her hands for support. The best she could come up with was around Brittany's opposite thigh just above her knee. But any discomfort became moot when she saw several body-shaped pinpricks hovering about near what she figured was the entry gate to Quorum Circle. With the fact that those she could see weren't moving any farther, she knew someone (most likely Henry, as Terry wouldn't have risked bringing everyone so close to the Circle) had called all of Heather to an announcement.

"Why are they gathering for an announcement here?" Brittany said.

"I don't know," Zoe said, ignoring Brittany's psychic ability once again. "Maybe it's a protest. There's only one way to find out." Zoe slid around Brittany and stood back up, but kept her body slouched forward ever so slightly. She didn't get but a step before Brittany sunk her claws into her shoulder and pulled her back.

"What are you doing?"

"We need to find out what's happening," Zoe said.

"We need to wait for JD," Brittany countered.

"Stay here if you want. I need to know."

Brittany resigned to Zoe. "Be careful. Don't let anyone follow you back here."

"Yeah," Zoe said, more to appease her than to acknowledge what she said. Brittany slid back behind the office and readjusted her hood as Zoe jogged innocently enough (and as stealthily as she knew how) to as close to the back of the crowd as she could. She remained latched to the wall (as if it would help hide her) as she scanned the crowd. It became apparent rather quickly that they weren't there for any type of protest, or to seek answers to questions. The group was calm and laid-back, no doubt gathered for an announcement. And from the scuttlebutt that Zoe could weed out among the sea of conversation, it seemed the crowd believed that they were finally going to gain access inside the wall—which made absolutely perfect sense. Quorum Circle, because of its importance and sanctity, could only be accessed by those with the pass codes to the gates, which of course meant only those who actually lived in Quorum Circle (in other words, the nobles) would ever see what was actually behind the wall. Rampant speculation of what actually lied within, which ran from the mundane (gardens of rare flowers and plants and tech-nologies too advanced for the "ordinary mind") to the extraor-dinary (harboring alien spaceships and utilizing a time machine device) was a common topic of conversation. So turning off the security measures that kept everyone from breaching the gate in mutiny (people, as the past and the world would suggest, being extremely unpredictable beasts, after all) and opening the Circle to them with less than a week left to live would be a major gift for sure. Zoe would be lying if she wasn't a little bit excited for the prospect as well, as new and bizarre speculation had crept into her thoughts now that she knew a few of the secrets the nobles actually held.

It turns out Zoe was just on time. Before she had a chance to ask someone to confirm what was happening (a good thing, too, since doing so would have upset Brittany beyond comprehension), the hum of the gates overwhelmed the caw of the crowd. Zoe set her back against the fence and held still with her eyes closed—quiet as a whisper, as the crowd would soon become. She had no doubt that once Henry started to speak, she would have no problem catching every word. To her surprise, it was Terry's booming voice that swam over the crowd with the command of a general, thanking everyone for coming. If Zoe didn't know any better, she'd have bet that even Brittany would have been able to hear him.

"I have asked you all here," Terry said, "to clear up the rumors that you may have heard over the past day. It is true that my ward, Susanna, was instrumental in allowing the blasphemous Kayla, ward of Daniel and Catherine, to walk free. For her insubordination, she has been locked up in the holding cell until we are ready to pass judgment, which will take place here in two days time. Now, because of this heinous crime, Susanna will no longer become headmaster after the eclipse. My heart is heavy over these circumstances, but it is a necessary step to keep harmony in Heather. Therefore, I would like to announce that Henry, blood ward of David and Laura, has been selected, based on his tremendous leadership scores and prowess, to become Heather's new headmaster."

Zoe was beyond surprised, though it was kind of strange that she was at all. She should have seen this coming. Beyond that, though, was a simple question: what would happen to Lenny? There was no way to protect her the way she had hoped if she was stuck behind the walls of the Circle. Suffice it to say, Zoe didn't clap or cheer in any way along with the rest of the crowd, who all seemed far too compliant with the announcement.

"Beginning today, all decisions, including Susanna's sentencing, will be conducted by Henry," Terry continued once the cheers died off, "and I hope that you can show him the same kindness and respect that you have all given me over the last seventeen years. It has been a true honor. Thank you all for coming."

That wasn't about to happen. As the crowd cheered its approval once again, all Zoe could do to keep from exploding in rage was to slink away as calmly and quietly as she came and return to the physician's office. She made it rather quickly, constantly checking to make absolutely sure no one was following her. When she arrived, JD was waiting with Brittany behind the office.

"Did you hear that nonsense?" Zoe screamed.

"Keep your voice down," Brittany said.

"I heard," JD said softly, helping Brittany calm Zoe.

"Did you at least get the codes?"

"Not exactly," he said. "I was hoping to talk to Terry and let him know what was happening. With Susanna locked up, I figured he'd understand and want to help, especially if it meant protecting his ward."

"And?"

"His new little lapdog was following him around as if he were on a leash. There was no way I was going to get them far enough apart to say anything without Henry overhearing."

"Yeah. And there's no way to know if Henry would've talked him into telling him anyway."

"Exactly, so I did the next best thing."

"Susanna."

JD nodded. "I wasn't sure if that was going to work either, since Reynold had been ordered to guard her."

"Guard her?" Zoe didn't much care about any of this, but some small piece of her wanted to indulge JD's story. He seemed to be having fun telling it. And Brittany didn't seem to be in much of a hurry. "What for?"

"What else? To make sure someone"—*Kayla, no doubt*—"didn't try to break her free the same as she did."

"So what did you do?"

"I talked Reynold into giving us some privacy." It was a little arrogant, but Zoe still found it to be heavenly adorable—and surprising.

"How did you manage that?"

"Doctor-patient confidentiality." JD smiled bright with a quick wink. Zoe did too, if only because she couldn't resist his. "It took longer than I thought to convince her that giving up the codes was the right thing to do, for her and Terry. In fact, I didn't think she would, especially when Reynold returned before she had the chance to say. He wasn't about to give me more time alone. I thought it was over. Then she said it."

Zoe hated when people added extra drama to a story. *Just tell me already!*

"Follow the murderer of the mockingbird down the Mississippi," JD said as if he were reciting the greatest line Shakespeare had ever written.

"Cryptic much? What in Heather's name is that supposed to mean?"

"I don't know."

Zoe looked to Brittany for help but she looked to be just as befuddled. "Okay, well, let's think about it a second," she said, thinking hard about the meaning of those particular words. "Obviously, Susanna didn't want Reynold to know what you were talking about, or else he might have gone back to Terry. So, the code has to be embedded in the words themselves somehow. What's another name for a mockingbird?"

"A songbird?" JD said.

"A mimic," Brittany countered.

"Right, it absorbs the songs of other birds, mimics their calls. What, or who, do we know that does something like that? And why, or where, would we need to follow them?"

"I think you're looking at it the wrong way," Brittany said. "It has to be simpler than that."

"What, so you think we need to think abstractly? As in what? Who killed the mockingbird?"

"Atticus killed a mockingbird," JD said. "Figuratively speaking, anyway."

"Atticus Finch?" Brittany said. "From the book?"

"I *would* agree with you," Zoe said, "but Atticus Finch has nothing to do with the Mississippi." Her eyes suddenly lit up. "But Huck Finn does."

Brittany smiled as if she had been waiting years for them to come to that conclusion.

"What is it?" Zoe said. "What do you know?"

"*To Kill a Mockingbird* and *Adventures of Huckleberry Finn* were Terry's favorite books when we were kids. He always talked about taking a raft out of Heather to explore like Huck and Jim; to ride the wave of adventure."

"Great, but they don't have anything else in common," Zoe said.

"Injustice," JD said. "Both books deal with it in one form or another."

"The main reason Terry revered them so much. It only makes sense he would hide the book behind a code with those references."

"That still doesn't tell us what the actual code is. Based on that, it could be anything."

"At least we have a starting point," Brittany said. "It's something. We'll figure out the rest on the way."

Zoe wasn't convinced. But she was going to go along with it nonetheless. If anything, they should be able to figure something out once they got to the vault and understood more about what input was actually needed (whether it be words, numbers or a combination of such). Zoe nodded her approval and looked at JD. "Head back and check on Kayla."

"She doesn't need a babysitter," JD said, a little annoyed that

Zoe would even suggest such a thing. He put his neck out there to get the codes (well, the closest thing to the codes he could get). He deserved to go with them.

"I know that," Zoe said. Her eyes turned overtly compassionate as she reached out to touch JD's arm. "You said yourself it's only a matter of time before Henry finds the triangle. And now that he's headmaster, his resources just tripled. I'd feel so much better if there was someone else there with her, to make sure she's safe. Do it for me."

JD wasn't sure if her eyelids fluttered or not, but they sure seemed to. It was all so incredibly tender, how could he possibly resist it? *Girls and their sweet manipulation; it boggles the mind, and would so forever without end.* He nodded, words unable to escape him.

Zoe kissed him. "Thank you." She turned to Brittany. "We might as well get moving."

Brittany rubbed her hand across JD's arm, showing him a bit of sympathy as she walked past to join Zoe at the hatch. It was sweet, kind. And just subtle enough to convince him that Zoe was right.

14

The Vault

Several of the tunnels leading from the physician's office to the vault had been all but stripped of their luminous rocks (as Brittany had said), so navigating them was extremely difficult. How Brittany knew where she was going (if she even did; Zoe felt she was walking as blind as her) was beyond Zoe, but she made sure to keep her hand cupped to Brittany's so that she didn't lose her in this mess. At times, they did come upon a pathway that hadn't yet been stripped, but it only led to another (if it was at all possible) darker tunnel. When they came upon a path that had been stripped of the majority—but not the entirety—of its rock, Zoe was all but ready to throw her hands in the air in defeat. That's when Brittany stopped. To Zoe's amazement (and much needed relief), they had finally arrived.

In front of them was a large metal door that had to be at least twice the size of Zoe if she was lying down (probably as long if Zoe and Brittany lay head to head) and touched the ceiling, however high that might have been (which Zoe guessed to be around eight or nine feet in this area, though she didn't remember ever feeling as if they were going any deeper underground). Brittany quickly found a small block cut into the center of it, which lit up the moment it felt their presence. It gave Zoe a few goose bumps up her arms; never before had she actually seen such technology. As Zoe peered over Brittany's shoulder to get a good look, she saw an empty screen on the opposite side of the outline of a hand, with a keypad just below, all lit up in a fluorescent blue hue. Above the pads, in the center of the block, was a tiny ball, which Zoe assumed was a retinal scan device that, from what little she had seen and had been taught, was a similar type of lock that the gates of Quorum Circle displayed. Made sense, as whoever built the vault would have wanted to have it secured with the same guarded access.

"Are you sure about this?" Zoe said. It was the first time she was truly afraid they wouldn't get through. Even if Brittany was somehow able to bypass the retinal scan, and they were able to figure out the codes, if the rumors were true about access to Quorum Circle—that anyone who was not part of the Circle (or better yet, anyone whose DNA signature wasn't a part of the system) would receive a severe shock that wouldn't let up until they were unconscious or dead—entering the vault could be far more dangerous than either of them realized.

"Don't worry. If I know Terry…" Brittany placed her hand on the outline and lowered her head so that her eye sat directly across from the ball. As a swift blue flash of light scanned Brittany's hand from top to bottom and back again, the ball shot a laser beam directly into Brittany's pupil. When the scanner had finished with her hand, the laser disappeared and Brittany stood back. A series of lights flashed on and off, traveling in a circle around the eye scanner while a copy of Brittany's fingerprints highlighted in a successive ring around the hand. It took several seconds (too many for Zoe's sake) for the scanners to flash one last time as a whole and remain lit. No alarms went off and neither of them was severely shocked, so that was a good first sign.

No better than, "He wouldn't have taken me out of the system." Brittany's smile flashed brighter than the scanners.

"How did you know?" Zoe asked, taking her first breath since the system started.

"We were companions, Zoe. He must have kept me in the system in case I ever found the courage to come back."

"And knowing you, it was more than likely you would."

"If nothing else than to ride the eclipse away with him," Brittany said in a voice that was so soft and airy, Zoe could have floated away on it.

Zoe's heart melted. "That is so romantic."

Brittany blushed. For some reason, Zoe had thought that was impossible.

"What now?"

"We answer the riddle."

On the screen, in the empty box, was now:

ENTER CODE

Just below was a series of ten boxes separated in two groups of three and seven.

"So, what is it?" Zoe said.

"Well, we know it has to do with both *Huckleberry Finn* and *To Kill a Mockingbird*, right? So what are some key words or names from them that would fit this sequence?"

"Atticus is the lawyer in *Mockingbird*," Zoe said quickly, "and Jim is the slave in *Finn*."

"That's the most obvious," Brittany said. "Let's give it a try." She typed in

JIM ATTICUS

The boxes immediately flashed red upon the placement of the 'S' and the letters disappeared.

"I guess that means we were wrong," Zoe said.

"Obviously."

"Maybe it's more the themes of the books?" Zoe suggested brightly.

"Justice and what?" Brittany said.

Zoe was as perplexed as Brittany. "Adventure…? Fun maybe."

Brittany typed the words in and the red lights flashed them away (Zoe could swear it was quicker than before). But this time, a clock appeared just below the boxes and started counting backwards. They had less than a minute to figure out the right answer.

"What else you got?" Brittany said. She was calm, collected— the complete opposite of Zoe. She hated Brittany for that.

"Abbreviations of the books, maybe? Secondary characters? Other books in the series? I don't know."

Brittany shook her head to all of them. Time was running out.

"How about he authors' names."

Finally, a spark clicked in Brittany's eyes. Zoe was onto

something. "That's not right, though," Zoe said, dispelling her own answer. "Twain isn't long enough."

"But Clemens is," Brittany said and quickly typed in:

LEE CLEMENS

At just under ten seconds left on the clock, the boxes lit up green and the screen pronounced the words:

ACCESS GRANTED

The sounds of the locks clicking and the door hissing open were simply the most amazing sounds Zoe had ever heard (if she didn't count the sound of a baby laughing, that is).

"How did you know that?"

"From my time on the outside," Brittany said. "I learned that Mark Twain was only a pseudonym. The author's real name was Samuel Clemens. I don't know how Terry found that out, but it made the most sense."

"Brilliant," Zoe said.

They didn't linger long. Brittany pulled the door open (which was quite easier than she would have expected) and the two girls (cautiously) strolled into the vault with their mouths agape. It didn't look like a vault at all. In fact, it looked more like the warmest bedroom Zoe could ever have imagined. Brittany was nearly in tears over it.

"What's wrong?" Zoe said, feeling bad for her in some odd way.

"Nothing," Brittany said, faking a smile. "I just can't believe it."

"Believe what?"

"It's my room," she said with a quick laugh. Now it was clear: the tears weren't sad, they were overwhelmed.

"What do you mean it's your room?"

"I mean, it's not my room, but it's everything that used to be in my room, set up exactly as it was before I left. Terry must have taken my stuff and put it here."

If Zoe's heart could have melted any more, it would have. *Now that's love.*

Brittany took her time to gather her bearings and take it all in, to reminisce about the past and what may (or may not) have happened in that very room. "I can't believe it," she whispered as she sat on the bed. She picked up one of the stuffed bears—black as night—sitting in the gap between the pillows. "He gave me this," she said, "when I got ill after inhaling a bunch of soot. He said it was my little coal bear and would pull the soot from my body. I didn't believe him, but the next day my lungs were clear and I felt healthy and ready for anything."

Zoe was only half-listening, as a lot of her attention was on something a little more pressing. She didn't want to interrupt her, or make her think she was insensitive in any way, but there was a time to reminisce and a time for business. And now was the latter.

"I'm happy for you," Zoe said, "but we're running out of time."

Brittany caught fragments of what she said, bringing her back to the here and now. "Yeah, of course. The book. Right." She set the bear down and wiped the tears from her eyes. "Where do you think he might have put it?"

"I was hoping you'd know? He set this up for you. Did you have a secret spot or something that he knew about?"

"I did," Brittany said, lighting up. She ran to the bureau and crawled underneath it. She fiddled around with the lock on the latch attached to the false bottom; remembering the code was a little more difficult than she thought. "When I was little, I accidentally super glued the bottom drawer shut. My caretakers had to cut a hole out of it to get all of my stuff out. After that, I created a secret panel and hid my most treasured secrets inside." The lock finally slipped open. Brittany pushed the fake bottom away and reached inside the drawer.

"Well?" Zoe said.

Brittany sat back up. In her hands was a leather-bound book so thick, it had to be held by two hands. A strap was wrapped around the edge, keeping the book tightly closed. It smelled rich and musty.

"Is that it?"

"I've never seen it before," Brittany said, jumping to the bed, "but I assume so." She sprawled the book out and flipped through the pages.

"What is that?" Zoe said quickly upon seeing the unintelligible marks within.

"I'm not sure," Brittany admitted. The disappointment was evident in her voice. "Some ancient writing or something?"

"How are we supposed to translate this?"

"I don't know." Brittany was clearly as frustrated as Zoe.

"Come on," Zoe said. "Let's get out of here. We'll figure it out later. Maybe JD or Kayla will know something about it." Zoe grabbed the book.

"Yeah, okay," Brittany said.

Before they left, Brittany had to take one final look at the vault and the magnificence of Terry's undying devotion. She knew it was strong when they were together; she had no idea how strong it had remained.

"Come on," Zoe said, having to force her out of the vault so she could close and lock the door. The blue hue flashed off as they ran away. Brittany, holding Zoe's hand tightly, led them back to the hatch in Pasture Ranch—and a lot faster than Zoe had thought possible.

The sky beyond the desert had lit up orange, so Zoe handed the book to Brittany. "I need to get home. Take this back to Kayla."

"When will you be back?"

"I'll try to sneak out, but if I'm not able, bright and early tomorrow morning."

"Can't wait." Brittany pulled Zoe in for a long, tender hug. "We're one step closer," she whispered. "Thank you for your help."

"Decipher the text," Zoe said and then parted ways with Brittany.

Zoe made it home a couple of minutes late, but Maisy was understanding and didn't punish her any further. She cooked dinner and went to bed early, claiming that the day's activities had worn her out. It was a ploy to entice her caretakers to also turn in early, and though they did go to their bedroom earlier than usual, it was still later than Zoe had hoped it would be.

15

A Budding Friendship

It was only after doing a quick sweep of the mountains (and double checking that no one had followed him) that JD finally found his way back inside the cave. Kayla was apparently sleeping on the ledge and JD, for any number of reasons, couldn't take his eyes off of her. Not because he was enamored by her, not in the least. It was that her presence, even asleep, demanded attention.

"You can stop staring," Kayla said after a few minutes.

JD blushed and shied away. He hadn't even seen her open her eyes. "I'm sorry. I didn't mean to."

"You're a guy. I get it."

"Get what?"

"You're taken away by my awesomeness. Don't worry. I won't tell Zoe."

"That's not why I was staring."

"Oh really?" Kayla sat up. She was quite interested now. "Why then?"

It took JD a moment to come up with silence.

"You were picturing me naked," Kayla answered for him. "I know."

"I was not." JD was fire red, which cracked Kayla up.

"Sure. I totally believe that. Fess up. Our brilliant physician is infatuated with me. You can say it."

"Okay," JD had to confess, if only to get rid of the burn in his cheeks. "I'll admit. I did once have a crush on you."

"I knew it."

"But it was only a crush."

"Come on, admit it. You loved me." Kayla batted her eyelashes, just to see if she could turn JD into a firecracker.

"Not love," JD fought back. "To be honest, I don't think I've ever *loved* anyone."

"Not even Zoe?"

"Zoe's great, and believe me, I have deep respect for her. But do I love her? I don't know."

"Have you told her that?" Kayla said.

"No."

"You should."

"I think it's better if I wait to make absolutely sure before I do."

"Well, you better hurry your ass up. She's falling for you, you know—fast and hard. If you don't love her, you need to tell her now so she doesn't sink when you finally figure out what it is you need to figure out."

"How do you know she's falling for me like that?"

"She told me about your kiss the other night. She was glowing like an angel. I've never seen her so enamored with anything before. She made it sound like you two were destined for each other. Did you not feel the same?"

"I did," JD said (though it came off as a bit of a lie). "I mean, she's very attractive, she has a beautiful soul, and her kiss was…" The pause was abrupt.

Kayla smiled, knowing full well JD was uncomfortable talking about this. She decided to save him by acknowledging his thoughts with a light nod. "But," she said to move the conversation forward again.

"But, a lot of girls in Heather are like that, minus the heartfelt kindness."

"What are you saying? Everyone but Zoe is superficial?"

"I guess. A little."

"Then why are you wavering? She sounds like your perfect catch."

"I don't *want* to. I mean, Zoe deserves perfection, you know, a love that defies all gravity. There's just something missing that I can't quite put my finger on."

"Then you need to tell her that. Seriously, if she deserves a true love, then she deserves to know if that might not be a possibility."

"I know… and I will," JD said, knowing that it wasn't in the cards. "After the dance."

"Why after the dance?"

"If it turns out I can't truly love her by then, at least she'll have that moment. She'll have that memory. Something she'll never forget."

"I don't think that's a memory she's going to want to keep if it turns out you'd rather not couple with her." Kayla was right, but JD had no argument to counter it. "She's my best friend," Kayla continued. "My sister. I don't want to see her get hurt, even if it is from Heather's breast. The least you can do is give me the chance to be there to protect her from the fall."

"That's what it is," JD said as if his brain suddenly started functioning after a long winters nap. "That's what's missing."

"What?"

"That bond that you and Zoe have together. The need to protect each other, no matter the consequences. That's the love I don't know if I can give her."

"Did she ask you to come back here to keep an eye on me?"

JD chuffed a soft laugh, then seemed a bit confused. "Yeah."

"Did you want to come? Be honest."

"I'd much rather be down there with her right now, if that's what you're asking."

"So, basically, you gave up what you wanted for what she needed."

"I guess you could put it that way."

"Isn't that the kind of love you're talking about?"

"Maybe, but you have to understand. I'm scared as hell every minute I'm with her. But when I see the way she protects you... she has no fear."

Kayla wasn't sure if she completely understood, but she nodded anyway. JD felt as if he had to clarify. "She loves you unconditionally, no matter what."

"And I love her for that."

"Me too. I just don't know if I have that desire in me."

Kayla reached for JD. He accepted her hand (though felt a slight bit of guilt in doing so) and sat down next to her in silence for nearly five minutes. In that time, a small layer of sweat formed between their palms. Neither of them seemed to mind.

"Can I ask you something?" Kayla finally said. JD rolled his head to get a glimpse of her soft, quizzical eyes. "What does it feel like to kiss someone?"

JD was taken aback. "You've never kissed anyone before?"

"No, I have, but only my caretakers and a couple of guys on a bet or two. I've never kissed anyone I felt I could couple with, you know, like you and Zoe. Someone I could imagine living the rest of my life with, if I had a rest of a life to live."

"You kissed a couple of guys on a bet?"

Kayla laughed sheepishly. "I know, it was dumb, but hey. I take risks."

"Who were they?"

Kayla looked at JD with the most killer of smirks. JD sat upright, whispering "tell me" over and over. Sometimes, he'd throw in a "come on" just to change it up a bit.

"You're really going to make me tell you, aren't you?"

"That or I can get Zoe to tell me."

"Why would you think she knows?"

"We just established why. Best friends like you never keep secrets."

"Okay, fine," Kayla said, giving into the pressure like a tin can at the bottom of the ocean. "The first time was a few years back. It was more an exchange than a bet, I guess. I was in my studies at Pasture Ranch and a group of us were tasked to pick cotton for the day. Every couple of hours, we switched turns in leading the group. The one who got the group to pick the most cotton during their time as leader would get the highest mark, and so on down the line. You know how it works."

"I was last in my group. No one listened to me."

Kayla laughed. "It's brutal, huh? Anyway, so here I was, my time to be leader, and I was having a horrible time. I was, like, fifth in line, it was the afternoon, it was hot, everyone had been working the whole day. Torture. I'm so aggravated, I'm yelling at everyone for being so slow. Basically, doing everything wrong. So I ask Jason what I had to do to get them all to work harder. Instantly, like he'd been waiting to get me to do it his whole life, says, 'Go and give Bobby a big wet kiss.' I about lost it."

JD was laughing. Kayla knew why and couldn't help herself. Bobby, at least back then, was a plump (for lack of a better word) acne-plastered mess of a kid. Thinking back, it was really wrong to think of him that way and Kayla felt bad, but kids would be kids. He'd of course get the last laugh by winning a home in Quorum Circle.

"Just let me say that it took a lot of negotiation before I agreed to do it. In the end, Jason and a couple of others would work twice as hard for the rest of my time, but in exchange, the kiss needed to be on the lips for at least five seconds. And I'm not sure why they added it, but I couldn't throw up afterward. Long story short, I walked up to him, grabbed his face and plastered it into mine. I can't say if it was longer than five seconds or not, but the whole time I was wishing for it to end. I mean, just the smell of his breath was retching. But I did it."

"Did you get the top scores?"

"If I didn't, those guys were going to be bruised the next day, and not in any favorable places, if you know what I mean."

Kayla and JD enjoyed another hearty laugh at her expense.

"The other times weren't as memorable, though I'm sure the only reason they did it was because word got out of what I did. One guy bet me a dinner to walk up to Henry in the middle of everyone and kiss him—"

"That's why he has such a crush on you!"

Kayla raised her eyebrows, acknowledging her mistake. And since she didn't want to discuss it any further, she added, "Another said he would take a naked dip at midday if I kissed Courtney."

"You kissed Courtney?"

Kayla winked.

"Did he go through with it?"

"Oh, you better believe it. He was banned from the lake for two years because of that."

"Kenny, yeah. I remember that. I never knew why, though."

"Now you do."

"If I didn't know you any better, I'd think you were insane."

"You must not know me then, because I am definitely a bit insane. I mean, how many broken bones have you and Nestor patched up for me over the years?"

"Too many."

"Exactly. It wasn't just kisses I used to wager."

"Man, I wish I could be as daring as that."

"It's not hard. You just have to ignore what others might think and just go for it."

"That's harder than you might think."

"I'm actually a bit surprised you'd say that." Kayla had her legs up to her chest and rested her chin on her knees.

"Well, yeah, I mean, I've done a little bit of rock climbing and stuff, but nothing so wild or carefree that would get me in trouble."

"At least you have no problem courting anybody you want."

"That's different. I've taken care of most everybody in Heather at some point or another. I've even seen some of them in the nude. For medical reasons, of course."

Kayla thought having to add that last part was cute. So was the bright red blush filling his cheeks because of it.

"What I'm saying is that I already know everyone, which makes it easier for me to ask someone to court. That and I've never been turned down before, you know. I'm not sure why that is, but it really does boost your confidence."

"Are you kidding me? You are gorgeous." Kayla was shocked that she would dare say something like that to his face. Her stomach was shot with butterflies.

JD blushed slightly and said through a closed throat, "I appreciate that."

"Everyone thinks so," Kayla said, trying to turn the conversation away from her. "I don't know a single person who wouldn't want to be your companion."

"Does that include you?"

Failed. "I'd be lying if I said no," she said, giving in. "I've thought about us, about being with you… as a companion."

JD held back a chuckle, finding her adding the last part endearing. "Why didn't you ever act on it?"

"For one, I always knew it was impossible. I'm ten months older than you, plus I'm not going to last past the eclipse. Of course, none of that mattered anyway because Zoe and I made a pact with each other."

"A pact?"

A smile. "We promised that neither of us would pursue you as a companion so that neither of us would be jealous of the other."

"You did that so she couldn't have what you wanted," JD said, exposing the truth Kayla could only hide under her embarrassment. JD took it in stride. "Why is it okay now, then?"

"Because you sought Zoe out, not the other way around. And since I won't be here much longer anyway, if anyone was going to couple with you, I'd much rather it be her."

"And if the eclipse didn't matter?"

Kayla didn't answer, mostly because she couldn't, for the very reasons she already discussed. JD, though, took her silence as an affirmative, that if she had had the chance, she would, in fact, want to seek him as a companion. Suffice it to say, he was flattered.

"Do you think they found their way into the vault?" he said, clearly changing the subject.

Kayla was glad he did.

16

Looking for Clues

Z oe was quite eager to get back to triangle point, but she still contained her excitement for a full hour after the last remnants of conversation between Maisy and Frances were heard before she left. She would have to be back before dawn (to make sure they didn't wake early for some reason—that would be just her luck), so every minute counted. Running was more alluring than walking; cutting through the fields was more appealing than using the roads.

JD sat at the ledge with Kayla when Zoe finally stepped through the crevice. They scanned the book together, thick as thieves. Brittany was in the corner at the opposite end near a small fire, cooking what looked to be a rodent (and what she found out later was actually a squirrel). Not the most appetizing of midnight snacks, but to each his own. Where the smoke went wasn't even on Zoe's radar. She was too excited to get to work.

"Have you gotten anywhere?" She sat next to JD and took his hand. It felt cold.

"It's impossible," Kayla said. "It's nothing but chicken scratch and scribbles."

"So neither of you know what language it might be?"

"I don't think it is a language," JD said.

"What then?"

"Gibberish," Kayla reiterated. "A bunch of lines, symbols and codes."

"It can't be just gibberish," Zoe said. She grabbed the book and flipped through some of the pages.

"Careful," Brittany said. "Those pages are brittle. We don't want them to break."

Too late. Half of a page came off in Zoe's hand. "Sorry." She went through the rest much slower, being extremely cautious and only using the very edges of the corners to turn each page. "If it's not a language, then what do you think it is?"

"Gibberish," Kayla said again, knowing it might get her a slap from Zoe (though JD was between them, so maybe she'd luck out).

"Hit her for me," Zoe said to JD, who promptly did as he was asked.

"Ow." Kayla rubbed her arm where JD had planted his knuckles, then reached over and pinched his nipple. "See how you like it," she said.

JD quickly grabbed her wrist to try and push it away. When that didn't work, he twisted his hands around, burning a bright red mark across her skin. Kayla yelped and threw her arm around JD's neck, pushing his head to his waist. He laughed and pushed his body upward, causing them both to tumble to the floor. JD pulled his head up and around, and twisted his body so that he could get leverage under her leg. He promptly pulled it up to her chest, curled his other arm around hers and pulled together until she was in a tight little ball. And boy did she smell.

"Ow, get off," Kayla said. Her attempts at maneuvering out didn't work.

"Do you give?" JD said.

"No," Kayla barked back. Her lungs started to constrict.

JD squeezed tighter. "Do you give?"

All the while, Zoe stared at the book. She completely ignored the premature game the two of them played. Something had caught her interest in the way the symbols were represented, but Zoe didn't know what.

"Okay, all right. I give," Kayla said. JD laughed and let her loose. Just as he sat back to turn and give Zoe a smug smile (that she would never see), Kayla spun around on her back, twisting her legs up and around JD's neck and arm. She tightened her legs together at the ankle and arched her back against the floor. JD could hardly breathe.

"This is how you do it," Kayla said.

JD tapped her leg to try and find a way out, unwilling to give in. Not to a girl.

Zoe, meanwhile, started to see the gibberish in a different light. The longer she stared, the more the symbols morphed into something recognizable, but still utterly foreign. That is until she cocked her head to the side to get a different perspective. Doing so gave her a slanted vantage, which convinced her to turn the book slightly in the opposite direction. She eventually turned the entire book on its side, so that instead of reading the pages across, horizontally, she was reading them from top to bottom, vertically. And there, in that position, she recognized the sequence; she recognized the order; she recognized the *moves*.

"Feather Heather with honey and dip her in lye," Zoe said scornfully before tossing the book across the cave. Brittany had to duck away, it struck the wall so close to her. She collected it quickly and looked it over, hoping she might see what Zoe had seen. But for her it was still, as Kayla might say, all nothing but gibberish.

At the same time, Kayla's concentration broke with a slight chirp, allowing JD to slip his head from under her knee and take a breath. He quickly slid up to the ledge. Zoe wasn't interested in his touch or his comfort.

"What is it? What happened? Was it a spider?"

If looks could kill, Zoe would have dropped the entire population. "It wasn't a stupid spider."

"Then what?"

"They're chess moves," Zoe stated. She got up. There was no way she wanted to stay next to JD. She was too frustrated (and part of her just didn't want him to see this side of her; at least not yet).

"Chess moves?"

Brittany could see it now. "Heather's feathers. She's right."

"What do you mean?"

Brittany walked the book to JD. Kayla joined them on the ledge. "Take a look." She walked them through the configuration. The writing of each move of each game was so compact that to the layman's eye, it was simply a symbol, but for those really looking, the letters and numbers of each move could be seen—quite clearly, in fact.

"What does that mean?" Kayla said.

"It means we hit another dead end," Zoe said. "It's not the book we need."

"It has to be," Brittany said. "Why else would it have been hidden where it was?"

"Are you sure there weren't any other books in the vault?" Kayla said.

"I'm sure," Zoe said. Her disheartenment was overwhelming. "It's all bogus, the whole thing."

"There has to be something more," Brittany said, hoping to calm Zoe down.

"There isn't." Zoe couldn't stay any longer.

"Where are you going?" Kayla said.

"I can't think straight right now. I just need to be alone."

"Will you be back tomorrow?" Brittany said.

"I don't know. I think I need to spend some time with my wards. You know, keep up appearances." She looked to JD. "You'd be wise to do the same. Maybe a day away from all of this will help clear our heads. We'll jump back in the day after, with both feet, whether it be finding the real book or figuring out a way to get Lenny and Kayla out of Heather. Deal?"

Everyone agreed, and to be honest, Zoe was a bit surprised that she didn't get any push-back. Happy with the decision, she went back home. She didn't get much sleep; what sleep she did get was utterly dreamless, but incredibly pleasant.

17

Keeping Up Appearances

After making her caretakers a big waffle stack and freshly squeezed orange juice for breakfast (somehow feeling she needed to make up for being a little late the night before), Zoe left her house in a better mood than she had expected. She took the back trails through the forest into Industry Quarters, taking a detour past Death Rock as a reminder of what was at stake. It was only four days until the eclipse, and though she would lose this day to her wards, she was more than happy to see them knowing that they might be able to remain with their current caretakers after all—though that idea was still only a glimmer of hope among the horizon.

The hustle and bustle in the streets of Industry Quarters was riveting. Everyone had begun their preparations for the Parting of the Eclipse dance, which was always (according to those old enough to remember) a massive party that filled the Grand Hub with food, activities, and plenty of music and dancing—a celebration of the lives that would be lost to those who were just beginning. The party usually lasted until the rise of the sun, marking the last few hours before the eclipse. It took the residents three days to set up completely, and most would participate to take advantage of the communal spirit of the festivities, what with this being the last time they would get to spend with friends, companions and loved ones alike. Winter (and maybe Jack) would be spending their last few days until the dance at home, so Zoe figured she would spend most of the day with Janette and help Gertrude set up her storefront for the dance. Before she could do that, though, Zoe had a brain worm she had to extract.

Having been studying the page she ripped out of the book, Zoe needed to figure out what it meant. The game, as written, didn't make much sense. How could the queen possibly move from a8 to f3 when there was clearly a pawn sitting at d5? Either someone cheated or this was, in fact, complete gibberish as Kayla believed. It was times like these Zoe wished she hadn't been so quick to gift Lenny that chessboard, though she wouldn't have had much use for it otherwise (except maybe to enjoy its decorative company). At least it was in a place she had access to—for the time being. Besides, swinging by to take a look at it to help understand the game would more than likely give her a chance to speak to Henry alone—a necessary evil to keep him, and the community as a whole, from believing she had anything to do with Kayla's "disappearance."

She was right, as even before she was able to knock at the door, Henry had it open. She didn't have time to slip the page into her pocket.

"Zoe," he said. "It's nice to see you."

"Thank you," Zoe said graciously (or as graciously as she could muster).

"I didn't see you at the announcement yesterday," he said. His eyes were cold.

"Yes, I'm sorry I had to miss that. I had to shuck some corn for the dance. But I did want to come and give you my congratulations. You are a very deserving replacement and I am very much looking forward to your leadership." Zoe wasn't sure if he could read her lies (especially with the way she spewed them past her lips like bile), but he seemed to accept them either way.

"Thank you," he said. "Would you like to come in for some tea?"

Odd. "Yes, please. Thank you."

Lenny was sitting in front of her chessboard, scribbling in her notebook.

"So what brings you by?"

Feeling the texture of the parchment caress her hands, Zoe was quicker than a fox with an answer. "I was playing around with some stuff the other day and I wanted to show it to Lenny." She handed the page to Lenny, who snatched it up quickly and examined it. Her eyes were like darts against the page.

"How is she?" Zoe asked, brushing her hand against Lenny's cheek, which Lenny rubbed into Zoe's hand like a little kitten, an indication of affection if there ever was one.

"She's doing fine," Henry said. "She doesn't appear to miss Kayla at all."

Zoe had a hard time believing that. It might be true, as Zoe wasn't sure if Lenny was truly aware of anyone, except maybe that they come and go. Did it really matter to her? She sat down across from Lenny, who pushed her queen's pawn to d4 and wrote the move down in the book.

"Looks like she wants to play," Henry said as he brought the tea. "I can never beat her. But I was never all that good anyway."

"She's a force to be reckoned with, that's for sure." Zoe took a sip of the tea. Apple and cinnamon—delicious.

"Good luck."

Zoe smiled and set the tea down on the table. She moved her queen pawn up to d5 and the game was on. But this wasn't any normal game. Lenny moved as fast as she ever did, but every move seemed a bit weaker than the next, allowing Zoe, for the first time ever, to stay on the offensive. Forty moves later, when Zoe landed her knight for checkmate, she had no doubt in her mind that Lenny let her win.

"I guess your title is well deserved," Henry said.

"I guess it is," Zoe said, but remained silent otherwise.

Lenny stood up and handed Zoe her notebook. She kissed her on the cheek, tapped it five times and left the room.

"She doesn't like to lose, huh?" Henry said.

Zoe stared at the notebook. What a wonder it was. Even though her heart fluttered, she masked her disbelief from Henry. She couldn't allow him to know that anything was out of the ordinary. "I better be heading out anyway." She didn't take another sip of tea (even though she was tempted, simply by its radiant aroma). Henry set his down and escorted her to the door.

"She seems happy," Zoe said. "Comfortable."

"You can imagine how comfortable she'll be when we move into the mansion," Henry said.

"Yes, I can," Zoe said and left, but not before Henry snaked the notebook away from her. She didn't argue (not even an attempt to take it back), she simply pretended she didn't even realize what happened.

All the way to the Grand Hub, Zoe tried to make sense of what Lenny was trying to tell her. It wasn't enough to purposefully lose the game, she had to go and freely hand over her notebook (with a kiss, no less). Now what she believed to be unthinkable just a few days ago had become a sign of something much bigger. Zoe tried to make herself believe that Henry's presence was helping her, changing her for the better, but that didn't seem at all likely. If only she could have run to Kayla to find out what it might have meant, her anxiety over it all would have been quenched. But if she strayed from her plan in any way, suspicions might rise. It wasn't a risk she was willing to take.

Janette hugged Zoe to bits and wouldn't let go after Zoe arrived. She held her hand, urged her to play a few games of make believe with her toys and all but fell asleep in her arms. Afterward, Zoe tasted several new cupcake recipes, even going so far as choosing the one Gertrude and Christian would use for the dance. They didn't talk much about anything that didn't involve how much frosting was too much frosting (answer: there is no such thing) or how much flour and sugar should go into what cake, but Zoe did find out what the community was saying about her and Kayla, which seemed to be pretty evenly divided—at least where Zoe was concerned. Gertrude and Christian's thoughts came from a middle of the road perspective—they believed Kayla's sentencing was right and fair, but they admired Zoe for doing what she did (which, in their circles was that Zoe, with Susanna's help, beat Reynold and Gavin to a pulp, going so far as to threaten to push them into Death Rock if they ever came near them again). It may have been on the extreme side, but that's what true friends and families do; it's exactly what a caretaker would do for their ward. Zoe decided it best to keep up the ruse (though it wasn't entirely a lie) that she had nothing to do with any of it, and both Gertrude and Christian were more than willing to believe her. They trusted her.

Janette woke an hour before Zoe had to leave and automatically started filling her mouth with the test cupcakes. The little garbage disposal even ate the ones that had either too much sugar or too much flour. It was so much in such a short amount of time that Zoe had to apologize for leaving Gertrude with an overly hyper, sugar rush-fueled little disaster waiting to happen.

"I've been through it before," Gertrude mused.

Janette grabbed onto Zoe's leg and wouldn't let go. It took Christian coaxing her away with the last of the cupcakes to get her off. She would be a sick little one tonight; forget about dinner. But they loved her regardless. Oh how badly Zoe wanted to tell them they might not have to lose Janette. It took everything she had to keep her mouth shut. If it was possible, they would all know in due time.

There were still a couple of hours before Zoe had to be back home, so she had plenty of time to make a quick visit to see Winter. Maybe it was the lighting or maybe the way she wore her blouse (hitched up and above the stomach so that it could breathe), but Winter's baby bump looked bigger than it had just a few days earlier.

"Feel," Winter said, wishing to share the baby's karate moves.

"She is a fighter," Zoe said.

"Wait 'til she gets going." Winter laughed. Even though they wouldn't know what gender the baby would be until it was born, they still referred to the baby as a *she*—and for very good reason. For as long as it had been documented, every child of the eclipse had been a girl, most believing the child to be, in some way, a representation of Heather. Zoe never really believed that before, but now that she had gotten to know Brittany, she could definitely see traits of Heather inside of her. And if you had asked Winter, she would have said the same thing about Zoe.

"I heard what happened the other day," Zoe said.

"Did JD tell you?"

"Yeah. He said you almost gave birth."

"A false alarm, thankfully."

"That certainly would have been weird, not having a child born on the eclipse."

"It might have been the end of Heather as we know it."

"That already may be happening," Zoe mumbled. When Winter asked her to repeat, Zoe just said, "Nothing. It's not important."

"Your companion was the perfect gentleman, by the way," Winter said to help Zoe out of whatever funk she had slid into.

"He's not my companion," Zoe corrected (though wasn't entirely sure why she thought she had to). "Not yet, anyway."

Winter smiled bright. "I've seen that before."

"What?"

"That look. You are smitten with him."

"I am not." There comes that fire red again.

"You don't have to pretend around me, Zoe. I was in the same place as you when Jack first courted me."

"How did you meet?"

Winter paused. Was she trying to hide something or was she just trying to find a more comfortable position to tell her tale? "Have you ever heard of a lottery romance?"

"I don't think so," Zoe said. She couldn't get enough of the little one's kicks. "What is that?"

"It's when a caretaker falls in love with their ward."

"Jack was your ward?" Zoe felt slightly ill.

"I was his," Winter cleared up.

That didn't seem to help Zoe. "Still."

"It's not as bad as it sounds. It happens, especially when a caretaker chooses a fourteen-year-old as their ward."

"You were fourteen at the last lottery?"

"And Jack pulled my name out of the cup. It wasn't like he tried anything; in fact, he couldn't have been more of a gentleman as caretaker. But being that close in age, and living together for three years, by the time I had come of age, we had grown quite attached. It was the most logical next step. A year later we were coupled."

"I want to say that's beautiful, but…" Zoe's skin crawled like ants on a molehill.

"Most say the same thing," Winter said. "People just don't get it. But I don't care. You never know when or where you're going to find love, so when you do, you can't let it get away." Winter shifted up. Whatever she had to say next was extra important. "Don't ever let the good ones slip through your fingers."

Zoe smiled. Winter wasn't happy.

"Listen to me, Zoe. When JD came here the other day, he was nothing but kind and gentle to me, going as far as making sure

I was comfortable with every step, even when he had his hands where not even Jack has been."

"I don't need to hear that," Zoe said, squeamish to all get out.

Winter laughed. "Skipping forward, after it was deemed a false alarm and Nestor left, I was still feeling some tenderness and pain in my abdomen. JD sat with me, made me some tea and helped massage the pain. He held my hand, he washed my hair… he did everything he could to relax me. I swear, if I hadn't have fallen asleep, I'm sure he would have stayed until Jack got back, which that night, wasn't until really late, since they're pretty deep in the mines bombing out that new passage.

"The point is, Zoe," Winter concluded, gripping Zoe's hand tightly, "when I was a little too deliriously close to sleep, I asked him why he was being so nice. You know what he said?"

Zoe shook her head, but knew what was coming.

"He said it was because of you."

A tickle ran through Zoe's body. She shook and Winter kissed her hand.

"Don't let the good ones slip through your fingers."

Zoe got up to leave.

"Before you go," Winter said, "I have something for you. It's hanging on the clip in the bedroom."

An elegant white gown that sparkled in radiant glitter hung against the mirror in the corner. The upper torso and chest area were covered in three layers of satin, while the actual dress was a tapestry of silk, leveled as if it were the outer wrapping of a bouquet of flowers. Blue streamers highlighted the ensemble. It took Zoe's breath away.

"Bring it here," Winter called from the other room.

Zoe was a bit afraid to touch it, but brought it to Winter nonetheless. The texture was so smooth it was almost wet. Winter smiled brightly, just at the expression on Zoe's face.

"This was the dress I wore at the last Parting of the Eclipse dance," Winter said. "And now I want you to have it."

"I can't," Zoe said quickly. "It wouldn't be right."

"Please. I don't have any wards to pass it along to and I would never fit in it even if I were able to go to the dance. Please. Consider it my day of breath gift to you."

Zoe was utterly speechless. All she could do was hug Winter. How long to keep the hug for a gift like this was unknown, but if Zoe held it for too long, she didn't care. It was worth it, knowing that Winter appreciated it.

When she left, her legs were numb; she was hardly able to walk. What was most evident was the smile that just wouldn't go away. She had to relieve this feeling of adoration—no, affectionate devotion—she had swimming through her veins. And there was only one way she could do that.

Just a mile down the path, deeper in the mountains, was Caleb and Barbara. If she were at all lucky, JD would be there with them.

"I love you," she said as JD opened the door with Connor around his waist. Zoe wrapped her arms around him as if they were alone and kissed him more passionately than with their first kiss; longer than she could remember ever holding her breath, and with a tenderness that became the definition of tender. She squeezed Connor so hard against JD he started to cry. Zoe laughed, ending the kiss with sweet joy. She wiped her mouth and bit her lips affectionately.

"I love you," she whispered again and left.

JD was stunned solid until Connor's wriggling got so bad he almost dropped him. He caught him before that happened, but watching Zoe fade into the sun gave him something he had never before felt. And at the same time, confusion remained his dominant emotion.

Conflict had become his ultimate foe.

18

Deciphering the Moves

That night, Lenny's kiss kept Zoe from finding any rest whatsoever. Her behavior played on Zoe's mind like a pinball, bouncing from one obstacle to the next—Kayla and the lumber art she had been accused of creating led to Death Rock and Susanna being locked away for doing the right thing, which made her angry at Terry for handing over the reigns of headmaster to Henry so that he had the authorization to pretty much take control over all of Heather. Whether that was a good thing or a bad thing for everyone wasn't the point; Terry had gone against his better judgment and allowed himself to play right into Henry's hands, which begged the question: who else was Henry manipulating? Was he playing Lenny, so much so that her walls had been broken? Was he playing Zoe in an attempt to show what type of power he could eventually command? Or was he playing them both in some ultimate game of three-person chess, where there could only be one victor. It was in that victor, she was convinced, that would determine Heather's future, for better or worse. But how could she play an effective game when her moves were being dictated for her?

Dictated for her?

Not by Henry—certainly not by Henry. He wasn't at all cunning enough (or smart enough, for that matter) to create a children's game all by himself, much less a three-person ruse. No, Lenny had to be running this game; it was the only thing that made sense. Once Zoe understood that, she also understood what move Lenny had just made. She was giving her the answer; she was giving her the code.

Zoe was far too excited to sleep the rest of the night. As the rooster signaled the rising of the sun, Zoe cooked a small breakfast of bagels, homemade cream cheese and milk, and left it in the icebox with a note letting her caretakers know where she had gone—

HELPING DECORATE FOR THE DANCE AND MAY GO ON A HIKE WITH JD LATER.
BE BACK AT DUSK.

The lying was certainly starting to get to her, but she didn't want her caretakers to be accused of being accomplices, or worry about her getting caught if any of this suddenly went south. Leaving them in the dark was the best way she could think of to protect them.

When she reached triangle point, Kayla was sleeping on the ledge. No one else was there (not even Brittany, which seemed extremely odd) and the absence of JD disappointed her. She knew he probably wouldn't be there, but she still hoped he would be, if nothing else than to hold his hand or feel his warm breath; just thinking about him gave her chills. Paranoia also factored in—his absence made her think that what she did had scared him off, made him feel trapped or smothered; if he had been at the cave, it would have given her validation that he felt the same. That was just crazy; she was being crazy.

"Kayla," Zoe said. She slapped her shoulder and said, "Kayla, wake up."

It didn't take much more to get Kayla up. Wondering what all of the ruckus was about, she rubbed her eyes, brushed the crust at the corners of her eyes away and stretched her shoulders. Sleeping on that rock every night, though comfortable enough at first, wasn't doing her body any favors.

"She gave me the code," Zoe said.

"Code? What...? Who gave you what code?"

"Lenny," Zoe said, excited.

That woke Kayla up. "When did you see Lenny? Is she all right?"

"Yesterday. Yeah, she's fine."

"Henry's not doing anything to her, is he?"

"No. Look, that doesn't matter. The point is she gave me the code. I know she did."

"The code to what?"

"To the book," Zoe said. She picked the book up and flipped through the pages.

"You think Lenny gave you a way to decipher that nonsense?" Kayla said. It was clear she was beyond doubt.

"I know she did. It's the only explanation."

"To what? Zoe, you're not making any sense."

Zoe paused to catch her breath. She hadn't realized the run she made to get to the triangle had taken so much out of her—and jazzed her up so much. "Okay, look. When I was at your house yesterday, Lenny and I played a game of chess. You know what happened?"

Kayla shrugged. "She won?"

"No. I did."

"Good for you. Why is that so earth-shattering?"

"Because I've never beaten her before. Not once, you know that. Even when I play my best game, she's always eighty moves ahead of me."

"That doesn't answer my question."

"Yes it does," Zoe said, showing her the book. "As long as I've known her, Lenny has written down every move of every game in her notebooks."

"Yeah, I know. But Zoe, she's got dozens of those books with lots of different things in them."

"But has she ever given you one before?"

"Ha! Are you kidding me? I touched one of them once and she nearly had a conniption." Zoe's smile radiated the point she was trying to make. "Wait. Are you trying to tell me that Lenny *gave* you one of her notebooks? Without force?"

Zoe bit her lower lip and nodded.

"That's impossible," Kayla whispered.

"Apparently it isn't. After the game she just gave it to me. Like it was a gift. She even kissed me."

"She kissed you?" Now Kayla knew she was lying. If she wasn't, Kayla was downright jealous. What had Zoe done— Brittany also, to a lesser extent—that Kayla couldn't crack in over eight years?

"Exactly," Zoe said, agreeing the whole thing felt like a dream. "She had to be telling me something. I think she deliberately lost that game because it was the only way she could get me a message."

"And you think this message is a way to decipher the book?"

"I know it sounds insane, but it would be super easy to make a cipher out of squares on a chess board."

"It's more than insane, Zoe." Kayla paced in front of her. "How would Lenny even know what was in the book?"

"I showed her that page we tore out."

"That *you* tore out."

"Yeah, whatever. The point is it was right after she saw the page that she wanted to play. It has to be connected."

"Where is it, then?"

"Back at your house, I assume."

"You don't have it?"

"Henry took it back before I could leave."

"Why would he do that?"

"I'm not sure. For all I know, he may be thinking the same thing I am."

"How would he know about the book?"

"Brittany said the nobles know more about Heather than anyone. Maybe Terry told him about it. I don't know."

"So how do you expect to get it back?"

"You let me worry about that. You just keep this book safe. It could still prove to be useful after all."

Kayla saw a clear determination in Zoe. It was inherit with her, that zeal; it was one of the reasons Kayla loved her so much. No matter how insane an idea could get, or how dubious something was, if Zoe believed it, she could make anyone believe it. And that would never change, not for anything—and not today.

Kayla took the book from Zoe. "With the blaze of Heather's fingernails, I swear it."

Zoe hugged Kayla. It didn't matter if she didn't believe her. "Tell Brittany and JD where I went. If I'm not back an hour before the sun sets, assume the worst."

"Don't you worry."

Zoe left with one small look back to flash Kayla another smile. Her excitement drove her to run as fast as the wind until she reached Industry Quarters. It was still quite early and most of the residents would either be asleep or nearing the end of their shifts, so the streets themselves were quiet enough (in terms of the amount of people, anyway) for Zoe to easily slip through undetected—seen only by a few lumber artists who were finishing up a good nights work before heading back home for some much needed rest. She thought about going to them to ask about the art Kayla was accused of doing, but even if they knew anything, they wouldn't squeal on one of their own. It would certainly be a dead-end, thus a complete waste of time.

When Zoe reached Kayla's house, she climbed in through her bedroom window. Lucky for her, Catherine and Daniel hadn't locked it after Kayla was sentenced. Most of Kayla's stuff (including a lot of her clothes and most of her furniture) had all been moved out. All that remained was a stripped down mattress on a cold bedspring, her dresser (absent of any drawers) and a few items of clothes still hanging on the rack in the closet, most likely choices Catherine had made to keep as hand-me downs when Lenny got older and could wear them. If that was true, there might be a clue there. She spent several minutes searching the clothes for anything (thinking the page with the code might be in a pocket, or pinned inside a blouse) that might scream **WARNING**. Nothing came of it, obviously, and without Kayla here for her memory, it was really impossible to know if there was any meaning to these particular garments, so it was of no use to continue down that path. Catherine would be up soon enough; Zoe had to hurry.

The obvious choice for the notebook's whereabouts was Lenny's room. That's where she kept all of the others. Then again, the notebook in question was only half full (not even half-full when she thought about it), so it might still be in the living area next to the chessboard. That was a good place to start. It would at least keep her from worrying about waking Lenny if the door was even the slightest bit squeaky. After searching the living area from top to bottom, from side to side and inside out, Zoe found she was going to have to enter her room anyway. At least the hinges were oiled.

Zoe slid into Lenny's bedroom with the quiet steps of a spider. It was an odd feeling; as many times as she had been in this house, not once had she ever stepped foot in this room. It was as empty as Kayla's was now, with only the barest of essentials. Of course, that could simply be because all of Lenny's stuff had been moved into the manor, though Lenny dealing with that type of change without so much as a peep… Zoe didn't buy it. If Lenny was still sleeping in this room, nothing had changed, and if what she knew of her was correct, all of her notebooks would be kept under her bed and in some type of order.

Lenny looked so sweet and innocent—like most every child in Heather—as she slept. Here, in this world, she was not an outsider, she was not any different; she didn't have any rare disease or disorders. Lying here, sleeping, Lenny was exactly the same as the next person. Which, in a strange way, robbed Lenny of the one thing Zoe loved so much about her—her uniqueness. Zoe held her hand over Lenny's forehead, wavering between touching her (and waking her) and doing nothing, which turned out to be the better option. If Lenny woke, there was no telling what she might do. Zoe couldn't take that chance. She curled her fingers back. "Sleep tight," she whispered.

Before long, Zoe was down on her hands and knees looking under the bed skirt at the dozens of notebooks stacked so precisely and meticulously. Trying not to disturb them too much, Zoe reached for the top-most notebook on the shortest stack on the right side of the bed. It was completely full of chess games, scribbles, lines of numbers coming from all different directions, and complete texts from books she must have read and transcribed back down here. Flipping to the back, she saw something that caught her completely off-guard. At the top of one of the last pages, Lenny had written:

LITTLE SNOW-WHITE

Completing the last few pages of the book was the entire story, word-for-word, in a calligraphic scrawl that looked ancient. At the very end, at the bottom of the last page, the following was written in big block letters:

WE SHOULD ALL BE ASHAMED—
THERE IS ONLY ONE WAY OUT—
HEATHER MUST BE DESTROYED—
Z & K

Zoe closed the notebook and placed it back under the bed (unsure if it was because of the text or the sound of the pipes running water with fervor). She got to the door quickly and peered out through a small crack at the baseboard. Catherine, barely awake, walked past and into the kitchen. Zoe took that as her cue to slip back into Kayla's room and out of the house, making absolutely sure to close the window behind her (she couldn't have anyone suspecting anything, now could she?). She took two steps away from the house and had to stop. Her body shook. What had she just read? What was Lenny doing? And where was the unfinished notebook?

As her nerves calmed through a few uncontrollable teardrops, Zoe started to put some things together. The text that Lenny had written must have been her response to seeing the lumber art. But Zoe couldn't remember there being a Z or a K written anywhere on the wall. What that meant, Zoe was uncertain, unless, of course, that was just how she closed all of her notebooks—with the first letters of her two favorite people. Yes, that was a little arrogant, but Zoe had to believe it was true or else Lenny was in a lot deeper than she originally thought, and she certainly didn't want that to be the case. She convinced herself that she didn't know what it meant (and was even able to push it to the back of her mind and forget about it). What she did know for sure was that the unfinished book was not in the house, which meant there was only one other place it could be—

With Henry at the manor in the center of Quorum Circle.

19

Infiltrating the Manor

Zoe couldn't think straight. It was impossible to get through the Quorum Circle gates, much less get into the manor, but without Lenny's notebook, she saw no other way to decipher the code. As far as she could tell, if what she believed was even true, it was officially over. Other than going to Henry and asking him to give her the notebook (yeah, that was going to happen), what other choice did she have? All that was left was to get Kayla out of Heather.

Dragging her feet through the nearly deserted hub, Zoe caught a whiff of that delectable French toast she so enjoyed. She wasn't in the mood to eat, to say the least, but she was famished and couldn't pass it up. At the very least, grabbing a bite might help her think. She sat at her normal booth (and for a second, the image of Frances was sitting right there, smiling back at her), completely unaware of its emptiness.

"I'm sorry, Zoe," Greta said. "I'm afraid I've shut down for the morning." Never before had she kicked Zoe out. It must have been those ugly rumors.

"Why?" Zoe said, hiding her aggravation. "What happened?"

"Susanna's sentencing," Greta said. "You didn't hear?"

Zoe felt slightly relieved. "No one talks to me much anymore." Which was true, but not for the reasons Greta might think. Zoe would let her believe it anyway.

Greta sat down. She took Zoe's hand. "I've heard what people are saying about you, Zoe. I have to say, it doesn't make a whole lot of sense. I just want you to know I don't believe a word of it."

Zoe tightened her grip, gracious for her support.

"Susanna, on the other hand, deserves whatever's coming to her."

The change in Greta's demeanor was alarming. But once again, Zoe had to play along, even though it hurt her to do so. "No doubt she does. What was she even thinking letting Kayla go like that after what she did?"

"Unforgivable," Greta said.

Zoe was a bit disgusted. Was there any way she could change her mind? "I've heard some say Susanna showed great courage by giving Kayla compassion."

"Compassion for what? Susanna sentenced Kayla to Death Rock and then turned around and let her go. That isn't compassion, it's hypocrisy. It's cowardly. If Susanna truly believed Kayla deserved compassion, she would have let her go in front of all of us, not in the shadows of the woods."

Zoe hated to say it, but Greta actually had a point. "That may be true," she said, "but if it is, then shouldn't we show her how it's done and give her a second chance?" For a second, Zoe thought she might have gone too far.

"There's some truth in that, too, I guess," Greta said softly. "But I don't know how I could trust her again. She certainly won't ever be able to lead."

"Being headmaster is all she knows, it's all she's ever wanted. To take it all away from her—wouldn't that be enough of a punishment?"

"Someone has to pay for what Kayla did," Greta finally said after a bit of reflection. She tapped Zoe's hand and got up. "Come on. We'll walk over together."

Zoe didn't really want to go, but she couldn't look like she wasn't in favor of Susanna's sentencing either. She was playing a role—she had to keep playing.

Henry and Terry flanked Susanna just outside the inner gate of Quorum Circle. Her hands were tied together in front of her with rope. Henry had his hand tightly clutched to her arm.

It seemed at first glance that everyone was present to witness the sentencing. And why not? It's not every day something like this happens in Heather. In fact, other than Kayla's trial, as far as she knew, the last time anything like this had happened was the incident with Brittany. They say a full moon brings out the crazies and the werewolves. In Heather, Zoe was beginning to believe it was the eclipse.

Greta wasn't much taller than Zoe (only by inches) and she wanted to be able to get a better view, so she squirreled her way through the crowd to find it. Zoe, on the other hand, remained back, away from what she knew was wrong but had no real way to fight against it. Not yet, anyway.

A light bulb finally went off as she stood away from them all. If she was right, she only had one more pawn to place before beginning her offensive, and now was the right time to take advantage of Henry's arrogance and make her move. The trick was finding a way of breaching the walls without being electrocuted, and since it was impossible to get in by herself, she would have to use a noble.

Lucky for her, she had one of those at her disposal.

Zoe hoped that JD was back at the triangle with Kayla and Brittany, but she had to be certain he wasn't here (avoiding her at all costs) before she headed back. At the same time, Zoe thought it would be a good time to make sure that as many people as possible saw her there. That way, if anyone asked (more specifically, Henry) if she was at the sentencing, there would be plenty of witnesses to the fact. If enough people say they saw her there, he would have to believe them, making her innocent of any crime he might accuse her of later. When she was happy with the number of eyeballs that spied her (and some uncomfortably so), Zoe became eager to find the right time to step away. It was a very fine line she had to walk; no one could question her for leaving, and at the same time, no one could know she was even gone.

She made her way back through the crowd (in one final JD check) and found a spot to settle far enough away from the main gate, where only a few Heather Biters had made camp. By this time, Henry was up on his soapbox, proclaiming some nonsense about order and justice. Zoe rolled her eyes and tried to think about what she was going to do to get away without being fingered for it.

"...So I want to thank you all for your support of the unfortunate decisions I am forced to make today."

Zoe wanted to scream out that he didn't *have* to make them. But that would be like moving her queen to a pawn's capture square for no other reason than shock and awe. That wasn't what she needed.

"Susanna, ward of Terry, you have been accused of treason against your people and your very own law. How do you plead?"

"I did what I thought was right, and what all of you should know was right." Susanna's voice was louder and more forceful than Zoe had ever heard it. "The only thing I regret is doing it in secret."

"She pleads guilty," Henry translated. The crowd erupted.

Sick, pathetic sheep. The only ones smart enough to find this whole thing outrageous were the Heather Biters, who screamed in protest of the verdict. It was a shame Zoe hadn't seen before what they had seen all along. Then again, in some odd way, the Heather Biters might very well be her ticket in. Perhaps shock and awe was exactly what she needed after all.

Two birds with one stone.

"Shut your mouths," she screamed. Her eyes locked on Harper, but only because she was a girl and a lot less intimidating than the others.

"What did you say?" Harper asked, leading the rest to stop chanting their cries of protest to zero their focus in on Zoe.

"I said," Zoe reiterated, each word long and forceful, "shut your mouth." Zoe pushed Harper away. "Someone deserves to go down for what Kayla did. If it's not her, then Susanna's the next best thing."

"I can't believe you would say that," Harper bit back. "I thought Kayla was your friend."

"That was before she threatened our beloved god for her own selfish needs."

"Zoe, what is wrong with you?"

"What's wrong with you, Harper? What's wrong with all of you?" She had everyone's attention now, including Henry's. "Heather has given us all everything we ever wanted, and you fight it like it's a plague."

"It is," Harper screamed, "and if you weren't such a mindless sheepdog, you would see it too." Harper shoved Zoe. Unwilling to back down, Zoe pushed back (though deep down, she wanted to laugh).

"Don't touch me," she said. "You should be ashamed. All of you. Susanna deserves what's coming to her, and I think all of you Biters should be dealt the same sentence." Zoe stepped up close to Harper. "Bite the hand and find the thorns." Zoe punched her to the ground. The pain in her knuckles was excruciating, but she fought it enough to spit out, "The way it was, is and always should be." To add one last ingredient to the fire in hopes of an explosion, Zoe said, "Worthless squatter." It was derogatory, to be sure, and Zoe hated herself for saying it. But she figured Harper wouldn't take too kindly to it. She was right.

Harper tackled Zoe to the ground and pulled her hair. Zoe quickly hit Harper's cheekbone with her elbow, knocking her off of her. Luke and one of the Palisade Miners quickly went to help Harper up. Alan got in between her and Zoe and held out his hand. Zoe pretended to continue her attack, but she had done enough. Blood trickled past Harper's lips and her eye was swelling.

Henry stood next to Zoe as the Heather Biters helped Harper to her feet. "Take her to the physician," he said. They walked away, angry with Zoe for what she had done (but more so for what she had said). Henry, on the other hand, was proud.

"I never thought I would see that," Henry said to Zoe. He smiled and rested his hand on her shoulder. "If I didn't believe it before, I believe it now."

Zoe winced slightly from the sharp pain that bit at her knuckles. She grabbed her hand and held it to her chest. Blood dripped down her fingers.

"Let me see," Henry said. The wound looked worse than it really was, what with the dirt and blood that covered it. "You should see the physician, too."

Zoe hid her proud smile.

"But not with all of the Heather Biters there," he added.

"Why not?"

"They'll kill you."

"Yeah, you're probably right," Zoe admitted. "I'll get JD to help back at my place."

"Don't be silly," Henry said. "I can take care of this at the mansion. Come on."

Zoe pulled back. Her eyes glowed with fright. "What about...?"

Henry chuckled, knowing exactly what scared her. He leaned in to whisper in her ear. "None of it's true." He walked Zoe through the dispersing crowd to the main gate, which consisted of two barriers. The first, which was already open for the sentencing, was a simple access code that would usually need to be plugged in to allow entry to the second gate. They had to wait for it to close before they were able to access the second gate, a defense mechanism set in place under the idea that should anyone ever find out the code to the first (through the slip of a tongue or something of that nature), they would be caught between the gates and punished for their indiscretion, as they wouldn't have the biometrics necessary to access the second.

Once the first gate had locked, Henry opened the access port (which looked exactly like the one on the vault, to no surprise of Zoe) on the right-most pillar, and placed his full right hand on the scanning pad followed by placing his right eye in front of the retinal scan. Taken together, the scanner flashed blue. Henry put in the necessary code (*Lee Clemens*, Zoe thought, but knew there wasn't a chance it was the same) and the gate slid open.

"Take Susanna back to the cell," Henry said to Terry. "I'll announce her sentence later." Terry nodded, hiding the relief in his eyes (at least he would have at least one more day with her) and pulled Susanna away.

"Sorry for interrupting the sentencing," Zoe said, fighting the smile that wanted to break free.

"It's not your fault. It was in defense of my decision, so I'll let you off the hook with a warning."

Zoe nodded. Henry smiled; she had him in her back pocket now.

Henry didn't take Zoe through the gates right away. In case any stragglers were still watching, Henry pretended to encode Zoe's biometrics into the system so that Zoe wouldn't be "electrocuted." When he had finished, Henry waved for Zoe to step through. She did, but quite cautiously, still afraid the rumor might be true and this was just Henry's way to end her once and for all. To her relief, there were no electric shocks, no lightning and no death traps of any kind.

Walking to the manor wasn't as glorious or magical as she had once imagined either. Instead of exotic and rare plants lining the walkways with a beautiful scent, there was hardly any sign of any flowers, except for those that grew alongside the weeds at the base of the trees, which in and of themselves were smaller and less impressive than she had pictured. Some of them even looked like they were dying. Most of the grass was patchy brown at best, and near dirt at worst. In some areas, it was hard to distinguish between the weeds and the real plants. For the first time, she was amazed that anyone would want to live in Quorum Circle at all.

The manor wasn't all that much more impressive. It was large, to be sure, the largest house Zoe had ever laid her eyes on. But the rustic look, with faded and rotted wood linings, scratched paint and warped bearings, left a lot to be desired. For collecting so much hidden wealth from the glow rocks, it was a wonder the entire Circle wasn't covered in lavish extravagance. She couldn't see any of the houses the other nobles lived in since they were all on their own two acre plots and were spread across the circle, but she didn't believe they would be any better. The steps leading up to the front door (which looked as if it was once a gloriously sparkling sight, now just an unpolished rusted mess) creaked and bent as if they would snap in two if enough weight was applied. Zoe had to believe that this house (and its land) had once been one of admiration, but for whatever reason, had been slowly rotting away, much like, as Zoe was slowly discovering, the quorum leadership itself.

"What are you planning for Susanna?" Zoe asked as they walked into the manor—where all the money had clearly been spent. The foray glistened in a rich sheen that reflected almost everything in the room, which included dozens of exotic and rare furnishings.

"She will be sentenced to walk the Horizon Desert," Henry said. He closed the door. The click of the lock sent a small chill down Zoe's spine.

"Really? When?"

"The morning of the eclipse."

"You did the right thing," Zoe said. It was becoming easier for her to lie. She smiled and held Henry's hand. The gesture was all she needed.

"Come on," he said. "Let's get that cleaned up."

He walked her to the nearest bathroom (one of four on the ground floor) and cleaned her wound the best he knew how, adding a little iodine and bacterial cream for good measure before wrapping it up with a soft bandage.

"Will you stay for dinner?" he asked.

"I can't," Zoe said. "I have to be back home before sunset."

"Are you sure?"

"It's because of you I was punished, you know."

"What if I talk to your caretakers? Get them to forgo the punishment for tonight?"

"If you can do that," Zoe said, her smile bright with affection, "I would be happy to stay for dinner."

Henry nodded. His hand sat gently on the back of Zoe's neck, which made her a little uncomfortable. "You look tired," he said.

She was. He saying so forced her to yawn.

"How about you get some rest and I'll wake you for dinner."

"That would be great," Zoe said and stretched. She rubbed her eyes.

Henry walked her upstairs to one of the six guest bedrooms on the second level. It was smaller than she thought it would be, but was still twice the size of her own. It wasn't decorated all that much, either, though all of her amenities were there—soft bed, comfortable blankets and an utterly sleep-inducing pillow. She was out even before her head hit the cushions.

Kayla and JD

Kayla's face was buried in her hands. She was bored out of her mind, having been left alone for who knows how long. The walls around her were shrinking. She couldn't sleep (which, being trapped in the cave, was all she could do besides eat) and the urge to get out into the open to breathe the fresh air grew exponentially. She wasn't built for this type of confinement. She had to get out; she had to do something.

No one will see me. No one will see me. I swear it. No one will see me.

Was she trying to convince herself or her invisible body-guard—Brittany's ever-present aura perhaps? It would only be a short climb up the mountain, just past where she was allowed to go to use the facilities (a spot that was really starting to stink, by the way). She would be cautious, extremely so, remaining low, looking around every crack in every crevice. It was a good plan, a safe plan.

It was time to go—

That is until she ran hard into the wall of JD's rock-solid chest. Seriously, she could have broken her nose had she been moving any faster. She stumbled away, a little hurt, but more so because now she had no other choice but to stay put. Her anxiety overwhelmed her. She bent over and gripped her knees.

"What's wrong?" JD placed his hand to Kayla's back. She shoved it away. Her breaths came in small spurts—sucking air was like trying to suck up a good thick chocolate milkshake.

"Breathe," he said, returning his hand.

Stubborn jerk.

"Come on, sit down." He sat Kayla on the ledge, making sure to keep her upper body bent low. Her chin nearly touched the sides of her knees. She wanted to lie down but JD wouldn't allow it. "Take nice, short breaths," he kept saying. If he was trying to calm her down, he wasn't doing the best job of it.

After minutes with absolutely no progress, JD grabbed the top of Kayla's shirt and pulled it up over her mouth and nose, cupping and holding it just under her chin. "Short, easy breaths," he said. Though Kayla was unsure of what he was trying to do (*just another guy looking for a way to cop a feel*), his new method actually worked. Within a few minutes, Kayla had calmed. He let go of her shirt and let her sit up.

"Are you okay?" he asked. His hand still lingered in the middle of her back. It felt nice, reassuring—comfortable.

"Yeah, I think so," Kayla said, taking her time with it. "I'm sorry. I don't know what that was."

"It was a panic attack," JD was quick to answer.

Kayla was confused, but then realized why. "I guess I'm feeling a bit trapped lately," she said. She lied down. It felt good, but unbelievably static.

"I can understand that." JD's hand had somehow found its way to her knee (either an accidental after effect of her lying back or a deliberate way to keep touching her without seeming skeezy). Kayla wasn't sure she liked it, but at the same time, she didn't know if he'd take it the wrong way if she moved her leg to inadvertently brush it off. "Where is everyone?" he finally asked.

"I don't know about Brittany—she wasn't here when I woke—but Zoe's gone off to get Lenny's notebook."

"Why?"

Kayla sat back up (a good way to push his hand away, though when it had, she didn't feel quite as safe). "She thinks it holds a key to translating the chicken scratch."

"Translating? You mean it's a codebook?"

"I'm not sure I believe it, but hey, it's worth a shot, I guess. If she ever gets back, that is."

"When did she leave?"

"You think I can tell time in here? Please, I've lost all sense of the word being cooped up like I've been in the pit the whole time. If I had to say, I'd guess a few hours, but as far as I know, it could've been ten minutes ago."

"If it's been a few hours, she should have been back by now."

"I guess… if she didn't get caught."

"Who got caught?" Brittany slid into the cave as if out of the shadows. She lowered her hood. The sparkle she brought with her calmed Kayla's nerves to the point that they seemed to have melted away completely.

"We think Zoe may have been caught looking for Lenny's notebook," Kayla said. For some reason, that was all Kayla felt Brittany needed to know, as if she already knew the rest. As if confirming, Brittany didn't ask for any further information.

"Where have you been?" JD said.

"I was at Susanna's sentencing," Brittany said. Her voice was a quiet crystal.

"Susanna was sentenced?" Kayla said, shifting her legs to sit upright against the ledge. Her thigh rubbed up against JD's. She didn't notice it, but JD did.

"Fortunately, no. There was a disturbance before the sentencing took place."

"What kind of disturbance?"

"The Heather Biters got into a fight."

"What in Heather's name would they be fighting about?"

"The same thing as you would be," Brittany said.

"Good for them," Kayla said. "Who did they put in their place?"

"Zoe."

"Zoe?" JD stayed seated as Kayla stood, but they couldn't have been more in sync with each other.

"Why would they pick a fight with Zoe?"

"I don't know the details," Brittany said. "All I know for certain is that Henry took her into Quorum Circle."

"He did what? How?" Kayla said. JD simply rolled his head.

"How?" Brittany was genuinely confused. "He walked her through the gates."

Kayla wanted to punch something. "I knew it. I knew that whole vaporize stuff was a lie. You quorum fools make me sick." Kayla pushed JD.

"Hey," JD laughed. "Don't blame me for their stupid rules."

"I'll blame who I want to blame." Kayla turned her back but

had to take one flash look back at JD.

Brittany smiled.

"Why did Henry take her into the Circle?" JD said, calmly.

"She cut her hand during the skirmish. Since he sent all of the Heather Biters to the physician's office, I guess he thought it best they not be in the same room together."

"That's not like Zoe," Kayla said. "She'd never accept help from Henry, not unless…" If JD could have seen it, the light bulb that went off above Kayla's head would have blinded him.

"Unless what?" JD was on his feet now.

"Henry has the notebook."

"How can you be sure?" Brittany said.

"Why else would Zoe risk going into the Circle, and better yet, pick a fight with anyone, if she didn't think he had it?"

"Why would Henry have it?"

"I don't know. But if he does—"

"Then Zoe's in trouble." The fear that washed over JD was infectious. "I have to get her out of there."

Kayla let slip a light crack of a smile. Her adoration for JD grew, just by knowing how much he cared for her best friend, even if it turned out not to be true love.

Brittany stopped him before he could leave.

"Use the painting," she said.

"What painting?"

"There's a painting of Heather at the back of the foray. Behind it is a secret passage that leads down to the catacombs. Get her down there and I'll guide her out."

"Are you sure?"

Did she really have to answer that?

"Right. I got it."

"JD," Kayla said, again keeping him from leaving. His anxiousness was palpable.

Kayla looked at him, lost for words. JD smiled and nodded, hearing her loud and clear.

21

Searching the Manor

eautiful colors painted the sky when Zoe finally woke
up. Her hand throbbed lightly and was a bit itchy. She
scratched at the bandages (not doing much good) as she
lowered her legs over the edge of the bed. For a few minutes, Zoe
stared out at the stunning view of the lake. It was so far the best
part of being in Quorum Circle.

Zoe walked to the window to get a better look. If she had
nothing better to do, she probably would have stood there until
the lake was blanketed by the night. But she was only in the manor
for one reason, and she figured that once dinner was served, she
wouldn't have any more time to look for the notebook, that is
unless she decided to stay the night, the thought of which made
her skin crawl. Now she hated herself for falling asleep in the
first place. If she hadn't, she might have already found the book
and made some excuse for getting back home. As it was, she had
very little time left.

Shoulda, coulda, woulda. No point in crying over spilled milk, as Maisy
used to always say when Zoe broke a vase or accidentally burned
down an acre of crops after being spooked by a crow. *Circumstances
are circumstances, sometimes you just have to go with the flow; don't worry about*

the past, just keep moving forward; mistakes happen, and when they do, figure out how to correct them. Maisy's witticisms remained in Zoe's head as she crept through the halls, checking every room she came across (some larger and more dressed than others, but all relatively the same) and making sure she didn't cause any suspicion. When she came up empty after searching every corner of the second floor, it was apparent that it must be somewhere on the main floor in the drawer of a counter or a desk that Henry uses—to do what? It would be risky going down there; the smell of roast beef, potatoes, corn and steamed vegetables (very similar to what Maisy always used to make on a cold winter Sunday afternoon) filtered through the house. Dinner would be ready soon enough.

As she reached the stairwell to head down, she felt a gust of hot air hit her arm. It didn't last long—in fact it felt as if the house had spit the air at her—but it was enough for her to check to see where it came from. She couldn't see any cracks or holes in the wall, but as she pressed her ear up to it, the wall blew into it like a gentle lover (reminding her of the night spent in the cave with JD). Something was definitely hidden behind it. Examining the wall ever closer, Zoe noticed that the picture above her head of Terry and Susanna sitting posed for a portrait when Susanna was about eight or maybe nine years old was slanted a smidge off of straight. (Susanna was so cute back then, you just couldn't help but want to squeeze those pudgy little cheeks of hers.) When Zoe reached up to fix it, the frame wouldn't budge—not until she pushed up on it. With that, a lock clicked open and the wall slid forward. Zoe jumped back with a squeak. She covered her mouth and waited. Had anyone heard? If they had, it was better they not find her there. She quickly opened the wall and curled inside, pulling it shut behind her with the small lip on the metal at the back of the door locking it tight.

The room was nothing but a stuffy hole (which almost made her faint despite having dealt with the extreme temperatures before) with a glow rock-lined stairwell that curved up and around to a third story. From outside it wasn't apparent that there was any type of upper level (or attic), but Zoe had found the entrance, wherever it led. The steps were old and warped, and it took some time to get to the top (trying hard to keep each step she made from creaking). When she did, the space took Zoe's breath away.

It was highly decorated with all types of strange and unusual knick-knacks (most of which were jewelry, books and a slew of rocks of varying sizes and shapes), packed from corner to corner with furniture. Off to the side, opposite the luxuriously made up bed, was a large desk. Papers were sprawled about and stacked in sporadic, chaotic piles. Searching through them, Zoe found all kinds of things from recipes to scribbles of what looked like someone attempting to write their own stories, one of which was about a ghost haunting the lake. From the page Zoe actually read, it wasn't very good. The syntax was all over the place, it felt extremely labored and was so wordy, it came off extremely dull and dry. It had to be Henry's.

Well, at least he tried.

Zoe set the papers back down and rummaged through the drawers. The left side didn't reveal anything but more writing attempts, some bad drawings (she didn't want to go as far as terrible, but in all honesty, they were) and some folders labeled with each generation. Flipping through one, Zoe learned it was a catalog of all of the major events that took place in Heather over that particular seventeen year period between eclipses. This would be a gold mine of information had she had more time to actually go through it. Oh well. She shoved the folder back into the desk and reached deeper into the drawer, pulling out the farthest one. It was dated about eight generations earlier, which meant the rest had been stored someplace else. (Zoe's best guess: the vault.)

Zoe put the folder back, making sure not to show any signs of tampering, and closed the drawer. She started on the other side. The top held mostly writing tools and other normal household items like a can of glue, some butterfly clips and a screwdriver. The bottom drawer had more files, but these were far more personal, so much so that they frightened Zoe to the marrow of her bone. Each folder was labeled with the name of a resident of Heather. Some had one to two sheets of paper (a birth certificate and ward designation, to be exact) while others were quite thick. Kayla's was one of those. When she pulled that out, inside were reports of almost every step Kayla had ever made (though in actuality, it only followed her from about the age of eight, the day after she first met Zoe). Questions and concerns flowed through Zoe's head like a wild fire and she didn't know how to handle it. What was the head-master hoping to accomplish spying on the residents of Heather? How was he doing it? Why did he need so much information? What purpose could he possibly have? But most important of all, why did it seem that the only ones he followed were those that had made any significant attachment to Zoe? Kayla, Lenny, Frances,

Maisy—even Greta had a nice thick file—each one starting at the time they would have made first contact with her.

A file, which she would come to find out, didn't exist at all.

The thickest of all the files was Lenny's, and there was a reason for that. The notebook was inside. Zoe dropped it on the desk and flipped through the pages. Déjà vu as it looked identical to the other book she saw in Lenny's bedroom. But this one had what she was looking for. On the last written page was the chess game the two of them had played. At first glance (or at least to a laymen or a novice) it looked like any other ordinary list of moves. But to anyone who knew how it worked, it was obvious that it wasn't just an account of the game. All of Lenny's moves seemed to be correct, but a lot of Zoe's had been clearly altered (one move, QR1-QB3 was entirely impossible, as even if the rook wasn't blocked entirely at that point in the game, the piece couldn't legally move diagonally like that) or X'd out, as if the move had been taken back. Even the captures were written wrong. Now all she had to do was figure out what Lenny was trying to tell her. Yeah, that would be as easy as shaving a cat.

Before she had a chance to review even half of the message, the doorbell rang.

Zoe wasn't sure what that meant, but it confirmed that she had spent enough time here. Besides, dinner was almost certainly ready, which meant Henry would be looking for her soon enough, if he wasn't already. She couldn't possibly take the notebook with her without getting caught, so she ripped the page from the book (clean and without any indication of its absence), put it back in the folder and hoped to Heather that

Henry hadn't already examined the book thoroughly enough to know it was missing.

Zoe closed the drawer and inched her way back down the stairs. How to get out was a puzzle all its own. As she looked around, she caught sight of a candle on the wall at the bottom of the stairs, odd because the rest of the corridor was lit with the rocks, so why the candle? Zoe grabbed hold and twisted it to the left, opening the locks. *Eureka!*

Cautiously pushing the door open, Zoe heard JD at the door asking for her. She was happy and excited to see him, to say the least, though it wasn't clear how he even knew she was there. Several possibilities included witnessing the fight she started, or hearing about it secondhand through the Heather Biters at the physician's office. It didn't matter, really; he was there. But from the sound of it, he wouldn't be much longer. Henry was growing irritated and was just about ready to slam the door in his face.

Zoe slinked out from behind the wall and closed the door as quietly as she could muster, holding her eyes tight as it locked. When the conversation continued without pause, Zoe knew she was safe. She stood up straight, messed her hair and clothes up, and forced herself to yawn as big as she could.

"What's going on?" she said through the yawn as she stepped down the stairs. Both of the boys looked to her.

"I heard what happened," JD said, "and I came to check to see how you were doing."

Zoe cracked her neck as she took her final step off the stairwell. JD was chilled a bit when she wrapped her arm around Henry's.

"I'm fine," she said. She looked at her bandaged hand. "Seems to be doing fine, anyway."

A smile and a wink later, JD wanted to vomit. "As I said to Henry, I'm thankful for his taking the initiative, but he's not a medical professional. I would be much more at ease if I were to take a look at your hand and make sure it hasn't become infected."

"You think that's possible?" Zoe said. She tightened her grip on Henry's arm.

"I think it's very likely," JD said, "especially after seeing what you did to the others."

Zoe looked to Henry. "Maybe he should take a look," she said, her eyes dropping slightly. "Just to be safe. I mean, it does hurt a little." The wisp of her angelic smile was enough to convince Henry to let JD in. She still had it.

"Where's the bathroom. I'd like to examine it under some brighter light."

"Zoe will take you there," Henry said, and then to Zoe, "But hurry. I talked to your caretakers and they were both happy to have you stay for dinner, which is being served as we speak."

"Okay." Zoe tapped Henry's shoulder and gave him a squeeze before leading JD back to the bathroom farthest from the kitchen and dining areas of the house. Once the door was closed, Zoe had her arms around JD's neck with her lips planted on his.

"Thank Heather you're here."

"I hope all of this was worth it," JD said.

"It was." Zoe pulled the page out of her pocket. "It's here. I know it is."

All JD saw was a mix of letters and numbers jammed together into nonsense.

Zoe could see his confusion. "It'll make sense once we get it back to Brittany and Kayla."

"I hope you're right. Now, let me take a look at that hand."

JD lifted Zoe up onto the sink and unwrapped the bandage. For not being a physician, Henry had certainly done a good job, though JD wasn't ready to acknowledge it out loud.

"So, what's the plan? How are we getting out of here? You going to say it's infected? That I have to go to the office to get antibiotics or something?"

"Not a bad idea, but I don't think he'd buy it. I think it's best if we play out this dinner thing you've got going. It should keep him off guard enough to get you out."

"Get me out how? If we do dinner, Henry's going to insist I stay the night. JD, I can't do that."

"You won't have to. There's a painting in the foray of Heather."

"Garish thing, if you ask me. It's two stories tall and I don't think the artist even knew what he was doing."

"That's beside the point. Behind the painting is an entry to the catacombs. Brittany's going to meet you there to lead you back out." JD had cleaned the wound and re-wrapped it with a fresh bandage from his bag.

"What about you?"

"Once you're in the catacombs, I'll leave. Don't you worry. Henry will be happy to see me out of here."

"Won't he suspect you helped me, though, once he knows I'm missing?"

"Maybe, but he'll have no proof, so I'm sure nothing will come of it."

"I don't know."

JD clipped the bandage and cupped her hand in both of his. "Don't worry." His eyes said everything else. Zoe kissed him graciously. She could feel only a hint of love in return, but she ignored it.

Henry knocked at the door. "Dinner is served."

"Coming," Zoe said and then kissed JD again. She hopped off the sink and opened the door. "I invited JD to join us. I hope that's all right." She didn't wait for an answer as she pulled JD past Henry into the dining area, one of the more elegantly dressed rooms in the manor. A pair of crystal chandeliers sat above the slickly polished cedar-wood dining table, which was covered in a silk tablecloth. Silver candle holders lit the room in what Zoe was sure was meant to be a romantic atmosphere. Only two chairs were at the table, though Zoe could see the others stacked just past the corner of the entry to the kitchen. She immediately grabbed one and placed it at the table.

"Won't Terry be joining us?" Zoe said as Henry sulked into the room.

"Terry is with Susanna tonight," Henry said.

Zoe nodded. Made perfect sense. She sat down with JD next to her, leaving the chair at the end of the table for Henry. He sat as Paula, the headmaster's housemaid, brought the rest of the dinner to the table. It looked and smelled delicious, and Zoe was as hungry as ever. She dug right into all of the dressings, grabbing a pile of asparagus and two spoonfuls of garlic mashed potatoes. And, of course, what was a meal like this without one of her own freshly picked cobs of corn. She bit in and savored the juicy flavor of the freshly buttered cob. Henry and JD watched with delight, both wanting to ravage her the same as she was doing to the food, both wanting to tear the other apart for even thinking it.

"Aren't you two going to eat?" she said and cut a huge chunk of meat from the roast. It tasted like heaven, moist with clam oil and a hint of carrots and broccoli. When Paula returned, she brought with her an elegant Moranis red wine—named after Moran, one of the first known settlers of Heather who owned a small vineyard just west of Pasture Ranch where he grew and fermented his grapes with the delicacy of a lover. The vineyard went dry long ago, swallowed up by the encroaching desert that had been slowly eating up Pasture Ranch for the last century or more. The last of the bottles produced had been stored in a cellar under the manor in Quorum Circle to be used for only the most special of occasions. Zoe was flattered he thought she was one.

Zoe clutched Paula's arm. "This is all very delicious," she said, knowing Paula probably didn't get very many compliments. Paula smiled graciously, and though Zoe might never know if it meant anything to her, she had to believe that it had.

The boys finally served themselves and Henry poured each a glass of wine. Zoe had never before tried wine and the taste was a bit bitter for her liking. She opted to stick with the lemon water. JD and Henry, though, both drank as if they were competing to see who could down the most without ending up a pile of slush on the floor. Halfway through the meal, Zoe caught JD slyly watering his down with each new glass. She had to smile;

it was absolutely brilliant. If it were possible, she would have kissed him right there.

By the time Zoe finished her meal, which, incidentally, wasn't that long after she started (having wolfed it down like a duck on steroids), Henry was rattling off about some exploit he and his friends had done on Fallen Island a few years before—something about swimming naked together during the winter solstice at the crack of dawn (a phrase that just cracked him up, using it in reference to not only the sunrise, but as the split in his ass as well). JD and Zoe laughed right along with him, helping to fuel the fire the best they could. Zoe used it, in fact, to excuse herself from the table, claiming she had to piss like a faucet—a phrase that sparked Henry's laughter even more. Zoe squeezed JD's hand lightly and left the table. Once in the foray, Zoe was all business.

She traced the edges of the painting with her fingertips. About eight feet up, she felt a small metal latch that she was barely able to reach on her toes. Once unlatched (after a couple of failed attempts), Zoe slid the painting to the side. Behind it was a thick, concrete wall. For a second, Zoe thought it was over. Then she felt a soft nip of air whisping through the seam between the manor wall and the concrete. It was another trick; it had to be. Zoe couldn't see any latches or hinges, so she did the only thing she could think of doing—she pushed. It took all of her weight and then some, but the concrete slid backward on a couple of small (but extremely thick) hinges that revealed a thin opening below it. What was noticeable right away was that familiar staggering heat and musty smell—except intensified like nothing else. A ladder sat against the dirt wall at her feet. She wrapped around it, and when she was a few rungs deep, Zoe reached out to grab a hold of the painting. Standing down the hall, watching inertly, was Paula. Zoe froze, sweat beading along her forehead; she had been caught and there was no excuse she could think of that would get her out of this one. Then Paula did the unthinkable—she raised her finger to her lips.

Shhh.

Zoe smiled, her body tingling with relief. She winked at Paula in appreciation and pulled the painting back over the hole. It automatically locked back in place and Zoe was left in absolute darkness (except for the slight aura of light etching past the corners of the painting). She knew right away that there was no way she was going to get the concrete back in place (or how anyone could), so she ignored it completely, praying to Heather that Henry didn't grow a brain and check it (or hear or smell something funky and out of place if he ever walked by to admire—or otherwise check on—the painting). She inched her way down the rest of the ladder, making sure each rung could sustain her weight. She let out the breath that had been caught in her lungs when she finally felt the ground under her feet.

"Brittany," she yell-whispered (if that's even really a thing). She followed the wall to her right, repeating the call with every step.

"Zoe," Brittany finally said. Her voice was like a dream. The second Zoe felt Brittany's touch on her arm, she grabbed hold and pulled her into a hug. She couldn't help herself.

"No time," Brittany said, though she was thankful. "We need to get as far away from here as possible before Henry figures you out. Did you get it?"

"I got it." There was nothing else to say.

Brittany pulled Zoe along the catacombs with fluid speed, maneuvering through them as if she had some sixth sense homing beacon set in her brain. She knew she was good, but this felt a lot farther and a lot more twisted than the trail to the vault.

"The vault," Zoe said, stopping Brittany.

"What? What is it?"

Zoe thought twice about telling her about what she thought might be there. If she was right, Brittany already knew about what it was, and would probably argue that it wasn't a necessary concern right now. And she'd be right.

"Nothing, sorry. Let's get back to the triangle."

22

Cracking the Cipher

Hugging seemed to be the thing to do today. And Kayla held Zoe for quite a long while.

"I'm okay, I swear," Zoe assured.

"With the blaze of Heather's fingernails?"

"And the rapture that comes with it," Zoe said. Kayla hugged her again.

"Where's JD?"

"Still at the manor, maybe. I don't know. He may have left by now, but from the look of it when I left, JD may have switched tactics. I'm sure he's okay."

Kayla nodded. Her concern was sweet.

"This is what we need to focus on right now." Zoe handed Kayla the page.

Kayla could have stared at that page until the next eclipse and still wouldn't have been able to figure it out. "I still don't get it."

"What's not to get? It's a cipher. A puzzle. If you need to, think of it as a game. Each of the moves represents a letter in the alphabet."

"How do we know which letters go with which moves?"

"Lenny's trying to tell us through that game. If I'm right, it'll be a quote or something of that nature that will help us translate the book."

"All right. So… where do we begin?"

That was a good question, and Zoe was on top of it. "A chess board is eight squares by eight squares," she started, drawing a picture of the board on the bottom of the page. "Each one has a specific designation. Now, if we were using the algebraic chess notation, it would be a lot easier, but Lenny, she has to make it hard by using descriptive notation. But that's what the book is written in, so I'm sure that's why she did it that way."

"If you say so," Kayla said, lost already.

"In descriptive notation, there are two distinct codes, if you will, for each specific square based on the king and queen of each side, each one numbered one through eight. What we need to figure out is which letter represents what square based on the notations listed here."

"And how are we supposed to do that?"

"I have no idea," Zoe said.

"That's good, because I have another pothole to fill. There are only twenty-six letters in the alphabet."

"Yeah, and…?"

"If there's sixty-four squares on the board, what are the other thirty-eight squares for?"

Zoe was stumped. And she remained stumped for half the night. She tried hundreds of different things (well, maybe not hundreds, but it sure did feel like it) while Brittany tried a few others. Kayla mostly slept. When Zoe was about to give up and take her own much-needed nap, Brittany chimed in with, "What if it's subtraction."

It took Zoe a couple of seconds to comprehend what she was saying, but when she did, it all clicked into place. "You mean take the beginning square and subtract it from their ending square?"

"Right, using the dash between each one as a minus."

"That's a good idea, but how do we get what numbers to subtract?"

"You said that each square on the board is represented by a number and a letter."

"Yeah, okay, I think I see where you're going with this. So, if Q2 to Q4 in algebraic terms is B4 to D4, then that would be zero, which wouldn't represent any letter."

"Maybe if we use the number representation of the letter along with the number."

"Like a multiple? So, in this case it would be two times four minus four times four, which is eight. So the first move is an H."

Using that logic (and using the moves that Lenny crossed out as spaces between words) Zoe and Brittany cracked the code quite easily, deciphering the sentence to read:

HE WHO SACRIFICES A QUEEN LETS KNIGHTS
PROTECT THE KING AND REIGN OVER THE LANDS

"What does it mean?" Brittany said.

"I'm not sure," Zoe said. But after reading it over for the bazillionth time (and attempting to use the same formula to crack the text of the book to no effect), four words suddenly popped out like they had been bolded in bright hot pink highlights. "Wait," she said and slid over to Brittany, who had gone to the corner of the cave to think upon the message while eating several fresh blackberries she had picked earlier that day.

"You get it?"

"I think so, thanks to Kayla."

"Go on," Brittany said, matching Zoe's excitement.

"Okay, so, I was thinking about what Kayla said about there being too many squares to match the letters of the alphabet, which got me wondering how I could possibly reduce the amount to make it work. Lenny's message tells us exactly which ones to take out."

"I'm intrigued. Which ones?"

"The king, the queen and the knights," Zoe said through a squeak. She just couldn't contain herself.

"Why those?"

"Because those are the pieces she lists in her message. Those are the most important pieces on a board as well. So, if we set up the alphabet on both sides of the board, while leaving the opening squares of those pieces blank, we can fill out the board correctly."

"It's a good theory, but that only removes eight squares. That still leaves four squares we need to leave empty."

"Right. The center four squares."

"Why those?"

"Controlling the center of the board is a strong strategic move. I figure those would be the squares that would help 'reign over the lands.'"

"All right. I'll buy that. Let's give it a shot."

"You bet." Zoe went right to work, placing the alphabet one letter per square, where A was in the left most bottom square and

Z was in the far right square four rows up on one side, and then mirrored the pattern on the opposite half. When she was through, she wrote down the notation of each square in a line and matched it to its alphabetical counterpart. Now all that was left was to see if it actually worked on the text.

"Use this," Brittany said, handing Zoe a clean, fresh notebook. "I bought it the other day in case it all worked out." Zoe took the notebook (the smell of the pages was refreshing) and sat on the ledge at Kayla's feet.

"Here goes nothing," she said and translated the first line of text, finding out quickly that the empty spaces on her alphabet board were designated spaces between words of the text. Her heart raced as she saw it working brilliantly before her eyes. Before she knew it, she had the first several pages translated—something about several gods she had never heard of and their adventures across the high seas, or some such rubbish. The point was she had cracked the code. Several more pages in, Zoe started dozing and couldn't see straight. She woke Kayla, showed her how to work the translations, and went to sleep.

It was just past dawn when Brittany woke her (the smell coming from the small spit-fire being far from pleasing). Kayla relayed what she had been able to translate. Most of it was ramblings and rants about how the authors of the book felt about the tyranny of the gods. But toward the end, it got ever so closer to what they needed. A young, beautiful girl named Hærothestî (at least that seemed to be the translation) was introduced as a wandering spirit who made the lives of fallen men pure again. Zoe wasn't sure if it was meant to be a metaphor or taken as fact, but she knew that this Hærothestî had to be the goddess that would eventually rule over Heather.

Just as fast as she was introduced, though, Hærothestî disappeared from the text for some sidebar on the best ways to brew alcohol, which Zoe couldn't have been less interested in. Kayla hadn't gotten much further than that, but it was certainly a start. There were still several hundreds of pages to translate and only two days to figure it out. To speed things up, she suggested they tear out the pages so that all of them could translate at the same time. Brittany agreed and took several pages near the middle. Zoe tore out the rest of the pages and got to work.

Hærothestî, it turns out, was, in fact, a goddess who represented purity and second chances. Over the course of her young life (in relation to all other gods, that is), she grew saddened by the state of man as they became ever more corrupted and tarnished by the law of man. No matter how hard she worked, this plague multiplied, torturing her until her essence was nearly depleted and forgotten. To remedy her life, she went against the wishes of the gods and created a disease of war and famine, hoping it would eliminate the sins of man and allow her to find her place among them once again.

(There was a portion missing here because it had yet to be translated, but judging from the pages that Zoe had completed, which dealt with some sort of supreme trial, Hærothestî fought the gods in a massive war that cost many lives. Hærothestî was on trial for her insubordination, so whether she won or lost was unclear, but Zoe was eager to read about it.)

Hærothestî was eventually sentenced to lord over a land that she saw fit, the caveat being that every seventeen years, everyone over the age of seventeen would become her servant, and live eternity in a black hole. They would be unable to breathe, unable to move, and unable to speak, but remain completely capable of pain. Anguish was all Hærothestî felt. Exiled and alone, she cried and hasn't stopped since the first day her subjects were given breath.

"That's something else," Kayla said. "I never thought that Heather might not have any control over the eclipse."

"Makes you think, doesn't it?" Zoe said. Her pages were more about other gods, and some other wars involving mortals taking a stand, leading to a band of demigods known as the titans to rise up and all but defeat them. All in all, Zoe wasn't quite sure why any of it had to be hidden in code, as it seemed to be a history book more than anything. But then again, it was also somewhat of a rulebook for defeating a multitude of gods of various powers, so keeping that aspect a secret, especially from the god himself, definitely made sense.

"What does?" JD said under Connor's loud coos.

Zoe's aura lit up. As she hugged him (happy he was okay, like there was ever any doubt), Kayla collected Connor, bouncing him up and down gleefully. She then ran Connor around the room, holding him flat on his stomach as high as she could. JD kept his eyes on Kayla, enamored by her amusement.

"You got out okay," Zoe said. "What happened with Henry?"

"Not much," JD said after finally turning to Zoe. "After you slipped away, I kept him talking about himself and continued to get him drunk. By the time we finished desert, he had all but forgot about you. When I said I had to go, he walked me out and that was it. My guess is he passed out shortly after. I'm not sure if he even realized you had gone."

Zoe was relieved. She hugged JD. "Thank you for that."

"Anything for you," JD said. Zoe kissed him gently and held her smile close to his for a long while. She just couldn't let him go; his presence was far too powerful. If she could stay glued to him for the rest of her life, she would have, and by all accounts, so would he. Their connection blushed her cheeks with love.

JD kissed the top of her head and went to Kayla. She sat with Connor on the ledge, blowing zerberts onto his stomach. He laughed like crazy every time her lips rattled across his little outie of a belly button. "You're good with him," he said.

"I had a lot of practice," Kayla said. Another zerbert and a laugh so wild, it caught on around the group. "Lenny loved it when I did this, too."

"Let me try." JD bent over. Connor laughed just the same, but JD's zerbert was nowhere as good as Kayla's.

"You'll get it," she said. "It's all in the amount of spit and moisture on the lips." She showed him, this one huge and loud, cracking Kayla up more than Connor as drool dripped off her lip. She wiped it away, unable to stop her uncontrollable laughter.

"A little too much?" Zoe said, sliding her arms through JD's and around his waist. He grabbed her hands and curled their fingers together. "Okay," she continued as Kayla's laugh finally died away. "Let's get back to it, yeah?" She dropped back to the floor, pulling JD with her.

"What are we doing?" he said. He grabbed a few of the pages. "You cracked it?"

"Don't be so shocked," Zoe said. She playfully shoved him.

"Have we found anything yet?"

"Mostly the how-to on killing a god," Zoe said.

"And how Heather got to be where she is," Brittany added.

"Yeah, but not how to stop the eclipse."

"It's in here," Brittany said. "We just need to keep digging."

And they translated all day—with the exception of a few breaks when they all took turns playing with Connor (unless he needed a diaper change, then it was all JD) or when one of them needed a quick power nap to clear their eyes. With the sun setting and no further clues about the eclipse (just some tips on how to clear your mind of thoughts and a few warrior techniques, including fencing, fisticuffs and what sounded like kickboxing—which Kayla had a good laugh with—but was probably more about how to defend against a supernatural attack), Zoe curled the rest of her pages together and kissed JD farewell.

"I had better get going as well," JD said. He picked up Connor (who looked dead straddled between Kayla's legs) and caught up to Zoe just outside the cave. Zoe leaned up and kissed him softly, lingering again for nothing more than to feel his breath on her lips.

"I can't wait for tomorrow," Zoe said.

JD nodded. "Yeah." He kissed Zoe and said his goodbye. It was extremely hard for Zoe to let go of his hand, reaching as far as she could until the tips of their fingers fell away due to distance. Zoe held firm, cupping her hands in front of her chest and lifting herself on her toes (though it felt more as if she were floating) until he had disappeared behind the rocks. Even so, she couldn't help but continually look back in hopes that he would be running back for her.

He never did.

23

The Rules For Breaking the Curse

After finishing dinner—and talking in depth about the meal she had had with Henry and a few lies on the side to fill in the gaps, which included spending the night in the guest bedroom after falling asleep to Henry's rendition of *A Tale of Two Cities*—Zoe took to her room to continue translating the pages. But she could hardly stay focused. Her mind continually wandered to thoughts of JD, whose aura was sucking at her soul (in a good way, mind you). It was intoxicating and, some would say, dangerous if dealt with in the wrong way. As she had been taught, when a person falls this hard for someone, there was always the possibility of getting emotionally killed. But she didn't care—if she got hurt, so be it. The breathless rush of euphoria that had gripped her was nothing shy of otherworldly.

Halfway through the night (Maisy and Frances had gone to bed some time before and the house was as quiet as it would be), Zoe was growing drowsy, having almost slipped unconscious a couple of times. But when she translated that sentence—the one she had to read a couple of times before she actually comprehended the actual words—she was wide-awake. Her heart pumped wildly as if she had just run the entire circumference of Heather twice over.

HÆROTHESTÎ HAD A WAY OUT.
THROUGH THE UNSELFISH SACRIFICE OF THE FIRST-BORN,
THE CURSED WOULD BE FREE.

Brittany was right. There was a way to stop the eclipse and it involved a sacrifice. What it didn't say was how the sacrifice actually worked. It occurred to her that if David *had* known about this, he didn't know anything about the *how*. There were still several pages left to translate and having learned several ways to destroy a god in full, concise detail (and several ways to skin a cat, which answered the question of where that phrase came from), she knew the method had to be in these pages. Zoe wasn't about to go to sleep until she found out.

What she wasn't expecting was what she ultimately found.

WHEN THE CHILD, BORN OF THE RECKONING, STEPS INTO THE LIGHT OF THE ECLIPSE AND GIVES HER LIFE FREELY FOR HÆROTHESTÎ, WITHOUT DOUBT, WITHOUT FEAR, WITHOUT COERCION, THEN HÆROTHESTÎ SHALL BE FREE TO LIVE AND HER PEOPLE WILL BE GRANTED AMNESTY WITHIN THE LIGHT.

IF THE CHILD SHALL SACRIFICE AGAINST HER WILL, LET THE CROWS PICK THE EYES OF THE CHILD AND GROW BLACK AND WILTED AMONG THE LAND, EVEN AFTER A TRUE SACRIFICE IS PERFORMED.

Zoe had always believed that Brittany had returned to perform the sacrifice, willing to give her life to save Heather. But now she knew that was impossible. If the translation was right, there was no way Brittany would be able to perform the sacrifice, which meant it fell on Zoe's shoulders to do the right thing. A week ago, Zoe would have been perfectly ready to step in as sacrificial lamb for the good of the land and its people. She had been, for as long as she could remember, a true believer that Heather was a gift, and that she would return that gift in kind whenever the day might come. But now, after the events that had transpired, and what she had learned about Hærothestî, Zoe wasn't sure Heather deserved her help, or that she was ready to give up what she had gained. It scared her to think what might happen if it didn't work, if the texts were wrong, or if JD's love would keep her from completing the sacrifice as freely as she needed, which would in effect end a life—a love—in vain. With everything she had to lose, how could she not be afraid? How could she push away all doubt, especially after what she had learned? It was near impossible and it made her quite sick.

The rest of her night was sleepless. After breakfast, Zoe decided to take her normal jog around the lake and clear her head (a routine that hadn't been routine for some years) instead of going directly to the triangle, though doing so was a lot easier in theory than actual practice. Kayla was her best friend and doing this for her would be an unselfish act for sure, but she couldn't help thinking that there had to be other options. Perhaps Brittany would be able to do it after all, though that was highly unlikely. The abandonment of her destiny ended any such possibility. If that were the case, maybe Zoe could pass it along to Winter's child. She was going to be her ward, after all. She could simply raise her to be the sacrifice. At least she would have more time to prepare, more time to make it right for herself; more time to live and dream. It wouldn't come as a surprise; it would be her fate. But then again, it would also have to be her choice.

No coercion.

That and raising a child to be a sacrifice, especially after promising her birthrights to take care of her, was wrong on so many levels. That she would have even considered such a ludicrous thing made her feel utter contempt for herself, not to mention that the idea wouldn't do anything to save Kayla, which was the whole point of all of this, wasn't it?

Stopping to catch her breath (running for dozens of miles takes a lot out of a person), Zoe took stock of her whereabouts. She had never been in this particular area of the mountains before and wasn't quite sure where she had actually wandered off to. Then she caught sight of a large building slightly off in the distance. Stepping closer, she could make out the Quorum Circle fence extending off both sides of the building. Somehow, Zoe had absently meandered onto Prisoner Path, a natural cut between the mountains that could only be accessed by crossing Serenity Lake and then hiking around the edge of the right breast. It was the only way anyone could visit criminal offenders in the holding cell (unless you were a noble), so being here meant only one thing—the cell, which by all accounts still housed Susanna, was calling for her. Unwilling to tempt fate, Zoe jogged down to the holding cell (finally noticing her wet feet sloshing about inside her damp shoes).

The room was an empty space with nothing but a glass partition separating her from the prisoner cell, which itself was a large padded room with multiple sets of beds that didn't look at all comfortable lined up across the center. To the left sat a large bathroom facility with a shower and a pair of toilets and sinks, and to the right, a small eating area, including vending machines for healthy and non-healthy treats alike. It seemed more like a studio apartment than a cell, if it wasn't for the fact that the occupant was locked in with no access to the outside—not even a window.

As Zoe walked up to the glass, she wondered if anyone had ever attempted to break someone out, thus leading to the line of metal bars that sat about a foot away on both sides of the glass (spaced off-center with each other so that the gaps between were hardly gaps at all). It gave her a smile to think that Terry might have tried it had Brittany been locked up here the way Susanna was now, but in all odds, it never happened. When she was finally able to get a clear line of sight inside the cell (without the obstruction of the bars), it wasn't Susanna that sparked her interest. Terry, who as far as Zoe knew had been with Susanna since Henry sent them away at the gate, sat with Susanna on the bed near the vending machines and brushed her back with his fingertips. She looked as if she had been crying.

"Good day, Terry," Zoe said. "Susanna." They both looked to her, Terry standing forcefully. His height overpowered Zoe, even from a distance, and he didn't look pleased to see her.

"What do you want?" Terry said.

"I have some questions about the eclipse." Zoe wasn't one to beat around the bush. Not when it was something of this importance.

"What about it?"

"Well, I'm not sure if Susanna has told you about Brittany—"

"Yeah, she told me," Terry said, his voice gruff and droll. His eyes matched his tone. "And I don't find it funny at all."

Okay, Zoe was now confused. "I'm not trying to be funny."

"You're doing a mighty poor job of it then."

"I don't understand. What did I say?"

"Who told you about Brittany?"

Zoe paused. She couldn't find what words she needed to say. When she was able to string a few together, she said, "Nobody told me about her. I've met her. I've talked to her."

"That's impossible. Brittany's dead."

"No, she isn't, I swear. I'll bring you to her, if you let me."

"Stop that. Just stop it."

"What makes you think she's dead?"

"Because I buried her." Terry bellowed. "I watched her die. I felt her die. And then I took her body to the edge of the Circle by the lake and buried her." He was right up on the glass now. Zoe swallowed, focusing on remaining calm. There was a barrier between them after all; he couldn't harm her. "They killed her thinking it would stop the eclipse and save everyone who was set to die. It didn't work. I loved her and she was murdered. For what? She died for nothing." Terry's eyes were a deep red and his throat clenched, but he calmed enough to say, "I don't appreciate people playing games with her memory, especially you and your friends, who've done nothing but harm my family."

"I'm sorry," Zoe said with a slight lump in her own throat. Her eyes were glazed in confusion, doubt and betrayal. "I didn't mean you any harm or ridicule. And I certainly didn't want to see

Susanna put in the position she's in. I was simply there to help my friend. Susanna chose to free Kayla, not me."

"But you haven't come clean about the whole thing, have you? You haven't confessed or told Henry and all of the others that you know where Kayla is, that you were the one who rescued her."

"What would that accomplish?"

"It would save Susanna." As if it were obvious.

"And what about Kayla?"

"Kayla deserves what she has coming."

"But she didn't do anything and you know it. If you think about it, you're actually sentencing Kayla to the same fate as Brittany. She's got to die anyway. What's an earlier death going to prove? Nothing."

"It will prove a point."

"What point?"

"That crimes against Heather will be met with strict punishment. If we show weakness in that regard, then we might as well throw all law out the window."

"Like Heather herself?"

"What are you talking about?"

"Heather wasn't some saintly, righteous god. She was selfish and sought to end humanity for her own personal gain. It's only when she failed that she was sentenced to this world, to continually punish us for her own sins. I used to believe the same thing you did, Terry. I believed Heather was good and kind, and only did what she did out of love. But the truth is, she's a coward and a phony."

"And how do you know that?"

"Because I translated the book."

"What book?"

"The book from your vault." Now she had his undivided attention.

"How did you get into my vault?"

Zoe didn't want to open that wound again. "It doesn't matter. The bottom line is, I have it, I translated it, and I learned what needs to be done. The problem is, I don't think anyone deserves to die—for her, with her or against her. Whoever it was that put that message up on that wall was right. The only way we're going to be able to live free is to destroy Heather."

"By destroying her land?"

"If that's what it takes, yes. Maybe chaos is exactly what we need to destroy her soul."

"I don't believe that. And neither do you."

"All I'm saying," Zoe continued, calmer "is that Susanna doesn't deserve her sentence, and neither does Kayla. Neither do any of us. That's why I want to stop it. That's why I want to stop Heather. But to do that, we have to think differently about what this eclipse actually means and how we can go about stopping it without having to sacrifice anyone."

"And how do you suggest we do that?"

"I don't know. It may take time, much more time than we have before the next eclipse. But I'm willing to take that time to figure it out. I can't do that if I'm dead."

Terry knew what she meant. He had to accept it. He sat back down and held Susanna close. "I just want this to be over."

"So do I," Zoe said. "And if I might add, Terry, regardless of how I came by the information, I find the devotion and love you and Brittany had for each other incredibly inspiring. I can only hope for the same in a companion."

Terry blushed now, too, but his was in soft embarrassment.

"What happened at the last eclipse?" Zoe asked, eager to know. She aimed to find out why Terry was so adamant about Brittany's death.

Terry was lost for words. Every time he tried to speak, only air passed his lips. Susanna took his hand. "Don't be afraid," she whispered. Her smile was enough to open his heart to them both.

"It feels like just yesterday," he began, supposedly using the opener as a way to build his courage. "Brittany and I were the best of friends, companions. We had been for some years. We hardly ever left each other's side. It was always a surprise to me, too. I mean, what would the child of the eclipse want anything to do with me? The headmaster's ward at that. But she was sweet, compassionate and generous. I didn't care if she only hung out with me because she felt sorry for me, the shy kid down the street who could barely talk to anyone without stuttering, because we had something that others didn't—some special spark. Something unexplainable that once you have it, you don't ever want to let it go."

JD's essence swarmed her skin. She knew exactly what he was talking about.

"Anyway, like you, when the lottery came around, she was sixteen. I had only just turned fifteen a few months before. Being the child of the eclipse, she chose her ward first." He squeezed Susanna's hand and she snuggled her head against his chest. "Susanna."

"Wait a minute," Zoe interrupted, a bit confused. "Susanna was Brittany's ward?"

"Yeah. Because of my age and placement in line, I didn't even get to choose a ward. But in my mind, Susanna was always mine as well. She would always be ours."

"That's all well and good, but it's not what I'm getting at. Brittany told me that they postponed the lottery because of her."

"That's not true. David didn't even consider the sacrifice until the dance."

Zoe was befuddled. *Why would she lie about that?*

Terry thought about stopping, asking Zoe more about what "Brittany" had said, but instead chose to continue his own tale and let Zoe work out the truth for herself afterward.

"After the lottery, Brittany and I spent almost all of our waking time, and some of our other time, with Susanna. She was less than a year old, so I don't think she remembered much, but we were a family. A couple of days before the eclipse, David started spreading a rumor that he had found a book that explained how to keep the eclipse from taking everyone's lives. David was an excellent speaker, which made him a master manipulator. Within a day, the majority of Heather was on his side and believed that the way to save Heather was to sacrifice the child of the eclipse."

"What did he say, exactly?" Zoe said. She had to know.

"He said, 'The blood of the child of the eclipse had to run cold in the light of the eclipse. When her last breath lay upon the apex, Heather's curse would be seized in the eclipse and lasting life would reign among us.'"

"He was lying," Zoe said. "That's not what the book says."

"It doesn't matter. They believed him."

"Without any proof?"

"A fool is easily manipulated," Susanna said, "when they are promised a better life."

No better words could have been said.

"Just as Kayla was branded without proof, so was Brittany," Terry continued. "Brittany had to go into hiding in the catacombs, but David was a noble too, so he knew just as much about them as she did. When she didn't show up for the dance, he rounded up a team to head down and swarm the tunnels until she was found. I tried to get to her first, but the catacombs are long and twisted." (*That's putting it mildly.*) "It was impossible for me to know where she had gone. Suffice it to say, David caught her before I could and locked her up here, in this cell, bound and gagged like some serial killer.

"The next day, a few hours before the eclipse, they dragged her to the center of the Hub, to the same stage that we had had the lottery, and waited. I begged for them all to reconsider, but none of them would listen. There was nothing I could do short of killing the lot of them to get to Brittany. So I watched as the eclipse came, burning the light from the sky. As it fired its final rays of light, David took his knife to Brittany's throat…"

The last word, *throat*, was dry and got lost in his building tears. Zoe knew he wouldn't be able to say anymore about it, and she wasn't about to push for more. She could infer the rest herself. After the eclipse, Terry took Brittany's body and buried her as anyone would do for a loved one.

She also understood what was happening now. "Henry's trying to do that very same thing to me, isn't he?"

Terry cleared his eyes. He nodded.

"Why would he think it would work this time when it didn't work before?"

"He may have thought he would find the book, or force me to give it to him."

"How would he even know about it?"

"David was Henry's birthright."

"I thought he died with the eclipse."

"He did. But his companion, Laura, was already pregnant with Henry at the eclipse, and watching him die must have pushed her over the edge. She must have told Henry everything that happened."

"If you knew all of that," Zoe said, "then why would you give him so much power?"

Terry was stricken with tears. His answer was in his tight grip around Susanna.

"Then why have you been following us?" Zoe said cautiously.

"Following you?"

"I found several folders in the manor attic filled with incidents of everyone I've ever spoken to."

Terry looked as confused as ever.

"You don't know anything about it, do you?" Zoe asked. She now knew (and she suspected both Terry and Susanna did as well) to whom those files belonged. Henry had been watching them, looking for a way in. And for all she knew, Laura before him as well.

"I'm sorry," Terry said, his regret apparent in the tremble of his voice.

"It's not your fault."

"No, it is. I should have seen what he was doing earlier. Fool me once, shame on you; fool me twice…"

Susanna hugged him. "It's not your fault."

"If I had to guess," Terry said, much more composed, "it was Henry who painted that lumber art."

It made complete sense. "He framed Kayla hoping that I would stop her from being sentenced. That way, he would have something to use against me to convince everyone I should be sacrificed." *Nice play, Henry. Nice try.*

"Except I got in the way of that," Susanna said.

"Yeah, but that gave him the chance to slide into a position of power. He knew Terry would have to recuse himself and he took advantage of that. Now he's headmaster and he can say anything about me or Kayla and the sheep will believe it."

"I'm sorry," Terry said again.

"Don't be sorry," Zoe said. "Henry's using the same bogus translation that David was. But I have the evidence that proves it won't work. I can stop him."

"I don't think it'll matter. It's what he wants. To draw the book out."

He was probably right. "What should I do?"

"Leave."

Zoe lowered her head. It was all she could do. "Thank you," she said. "Both of you." She put her hand to the glass and curled the tips of her fingers. She smiled; there was nothing else left to say.

24

Planning to Leave Heather

"**Y**ou awake?"

JD stood at the mouth of the cave. Once again, he had been staring at Kayla for some time. For whatever the reason, he couldn't take his eyes off of her. Every part of her was genuine. Not that Zoe wasn't, far from it. Zoe was as pure as pure could be, what with being the child of the eclipse. It then occurred to him as if someone had slapped him upside the back of the head, knocking sense back into him—Zoe was *too* pure, *too* innocent, whereas Kayla, even in sleep, seemed more…

Natural.

"You finished watching?"

JD rubbed his mouth, hiding his embarrassment. Kayla opened her eyes and gave him a smile. "Don't worry. With this perfect body, I'd always be watching me, too."

JD had to laugh, a giddy chuckle that might have been considered a giggle had he been an eight-year old girl holding hands with a crush for the first time.

Kayla laughed with him. She sat up.

"How's Connor?"

JD finally sat down next to her. Not on the ledge, but on the floor where he could rest his head next to her knee, which if they hadn't been covered, would have revealed a knobby curvature that Kayla utterly despised. If there was anything she could change about herself, it would definitely have been her knees. (Her toes came in a close second, but even those were still cute in their own sordid way.) She rubbed her hands over them nonetheless and kept them there, as if it would help to hide them.

"Since yesterday?" JD mocked a little playfully. "I'd say fine, but that trip he decided to take through the mountains really messed him up."

"Crawling around rocks at a steady pace can do that to a kid," Kayla said, not missing a beat. "At least he's got street cred now." They both laughed. When it had faded, they sat in silence for a few minutes, thoughts and questions neither really wanted to ask running through each of their heads. Finally, Kayla said, "You ready for the dance tonight?"

"I'm not so sure I should go," JD said a lot quicker than Kayla would have expected.

"Why not? Zoe'll kill you if you don't. She's been looking forward to the dance since birth. I know. I was the same way. I'm pissed I can't go."

"Why is it so important?"

"Typical." Kayla rolled her eyes then slid off the ledge to sit next to JD. The sides of their bodies lay gently touching. "It may be a sordid attempt at closure, but deep down, this dance isn't some hokum… it's a blessed event. It's the last time, really, that everyone is ever going to see each other. It's the last time we can really have fun and forget about everything. It's where you go to find out what truly matters to you and who you are among a sea of others who don't have that choice."

"But you wouldn't have that choice," JD said, "even if you were able to go."

"I know, and thanks for bringing that up." She punched JD in the upper shoulder. It wasn't painful; it just made him laugh. Kayla followed suit. As it tapered off, she said, "I don't know. For me, it's like one last hooray. One last time to truly enjoy life, do something I wouldn't normally do—"

JD laughed again. This time, Kayla lightly punched him in the gut for interrupting.

"It was supposed to be the night I threw caution to the wind, tore my walls down and just gave in to whatever temptations came my way. It was going to be magic. And I was going to dance, not with the looming eclipse resting on my shoulders, but with the light, airy step of a woman who has the rest of her life to live."

JD was silent. Kayla turned her head and wiped away a tear.

"You believe in magic?" JD finally said. He thought about wrapping his arm around her and giving her a small comforting squeeze, but decided against it. It was better for him to keep his hands laced across his knees (though for the life of him, he wasn't exactly sure why).

Kayla looked back to him. Her lips curled slightly. "You have to, or else, why is life worth living?"

JD nodded. He then decided that on a day that is supposed to be full of life and joy, this conversation was really a downer. Something had to be done about that. "You know what…?" He flipped around so that he was facing Kayla and crossed his legs together. "Spin around," he said.

"What are you doing?"

"Just spin around." He almost had to force Kayla to face him and sit as he was. "Now hold out your hands, palm down."

"Why?"

JD yanked her hands out in front of her. Kayla fought it at first, but quickly gave in. "Hold them still, just like that," he said and rested his hands underneath, palm up. "Now, the object of this game is to move your hands before I'm able to slap them. Ready?" JD waited a few seconds before quickly (and without Kayla realizing it) curling his right hand around Kayla's left and slapping the top of it—hard.

"Ow," Kayla screamed. She pulled her hand in tight to her stomach, rubbing the top of it. "What was that?"

"It's a game I learned from Janette. Come on, let's go again."

"No," Kayla said. But JD was just too cute to refuse and so she cautiously put her hands out again.

"Don't forget to pull them away when you think I'm about to slap them."

Kayla nodded and did the dance with JD, repeatedly getting slapped as she got used to the speed of the game and the tricks JD would play, such as tapping her palm with his finger to make her think he was moving, slapping before her hand was barely in position, or going across the body to slap the opposite hand (the first time he did this, Kayla was almost ready to punch him, he hit her hand so hard). Eventually, Kayla got used to it (her hands soaking red) and finally pulled away quick enough to avoid the slap.

"Ha!" she said gleefully. It was JD's turn to take some abuse. The problem was, he was too fast on this side as well. On Kayla's first attempt, she completely whiffed. The battle raged on as Kayla got better and better, her drive to defeat him overwhelming her sense to end the game, even if her hands were almost numb and as bright as a lobster. She wondered for a second if she would ever have stopped the game if Zoe hadn't interrupted them.

"Where's Brittany?" Zoe screamed as she stormed into the cage, a jackal ready for a hunt.

With JD distracted, Kayla slapped her hands together over his with a sting that resonated up his arm. He fell back and stared at Kayla—stunned but extremely proud.

Kayla fell back herself, laughing and cheering her defeat (even though it wasn't really a defeat, as it appeared there was no actual end to the game, not until someone decided to throw in the white flag, which made it somewhat pointless, really).

"Well?" Zoe said as she came back in from the watering hole.

"I don't know," JD said. "She wasn't here when I got here. Why?"

"She lied to us." Zoe was burning red. She swiped the pages of the book off the ledge toward Kayla and JD. None made it to them, though, as they caught the friction in the air and floated to the floor as scattered as Zoe's thoughts.

"What do you mean?"

"I mean… she's not Brittany."

"What? Why do you say that?"

"Because Brittany's dead. Terry buried her. He said so himself."

"You talked to Terry?"

"He told me everything about the last eclipse."

"That doesn't mean she lied," Kayla said. Zoe was a little stunned she would be defending her.

"No, it doesn't. But I went out to where Terry said he buried her. I saw the grave, Kayla. I saw it. She's been playing us" (*playing me*) "this whole time with half-truths and outright lies. Even the urge to end the eclipse was only half honest."

"Why? What does it take to stop the eclipse?"

"She was right about the child of the eclipse sacrificing herself. What she didn't say was that she couldn't possibly do it because she's already dead."

"Zoe, you're not making any sense."

"I thought that when we found out exactly how to make the sacrifice happen, Brittany would do it. But even if she was the child of the eclipse, she wouldn't be able to because she was already sacrificed against her will. Once that happened, her destiny was severed, even if she wanted to do it this time."

"Which means what?"

"It means that I have to sacrifice myself, without any pretense, fear or regret. And right now, I'm really not feeling up to it."

"So what are we going to do?" Kayla said, much quieter than usual.

"Not that." Zoe stopped and took a moment to actually absorb Kayla's unspoken fear. She suddenly felt bad, regretting her complete lack of empathy. "I'm sorry, Kayla," she said softly. "I want to protect you, I do. But what's the good of saving Heather if I can't live the same life as everyone else. What's the good of saving Heather if it's just going to be corrupted?"

"Corrupted?" JD said. The word didn't sit well with him.

"Henry," Zoe said, and it was all she really had to say. "Listen, Kayla, if I thought Heather would remain the peaceful place it is forever, and I didn't have so much to live for right now"—she looked to JD with a cockeyed smile—"I would do this for you; for Lenny. But I can't abide Heather anymore, or what this place will become if I stop the eclipse."

"Zoe, I get it," Kayla said, though Zoe wasn't quite sure she meant it. "No one should be forced to do something they're not ready to do."

"That's why we go with plan B," Zoe said. "It may not work, but at least it's worth a shot. We just need to get both you and Lenny out of Heather by midnight tonight."

"You're playing with fire, Zoe," JD said.

"We have to take the chance."

"So what do you suggest we do?"

"We've talked about it already," Zoe said. Her stance and demeanor were like that of the most beloved of rulers. Her voice was stronger than Kayla had ever heard it and she felt ten years older, with clarity in her eyes and command on her lips. "Tonight at the dance, JD will cause a commotion. It doesn't matter what it is, or what you do, just make something happen near midnight to distract everyone. Whatever it is, though, make absolutely sure Henry, Daniel and Catherine are all there. That's when I'll scurry Lenny away. All you have to do, Kayla, is get to Frances' boat, which by all accounts will be mine tomorrow anyway, and wait for us there."

"Do you really think that will work? I mean, Catherine isn't just going to let Lenny out of her sight."

"You let me worry about that," JD said, absorbing Zoe's confidence. "I think it's a solid plan, so long as you can get far enough away before the eclipse."

Kayla looked worried. There was nothing more that she wanted than to escape Heather and her wrath, but at the same time, the idea of living anywhere but Heather chilled her marrow. The unknown was known to have that effect.

"Will you be coming with me?" Kayla asked.

Zoe answered by taking JD's hand and sliding the other up the course of his inner arm. She lowered her head to his shoulder and took a breath. Kayla happily nodded, ready to break into tears. "You'll be fine," Zoe said. "And you'll be alive."

"I'll come back for you," Kayla said and hugged Zoe as hard and as long as Zoe was willing to let her, which if she could, would have been for the rest of eternity.

But the sound of bells rang through the air. They were sweet and loving chimes announcing the beginning of the dance. At the same time, they were cold and heartless, for in just over half a day, the eclipse would be upon them, and the lives of so many would be extinguished.

Kayla wiped her eyes. "That's your cue," she said. Her voice cracked a little, but Kayla was good at hiding her sadness.

"Are you going to be okay?" Zoe said.

"Yeah. Now you two get going." Kayla pushed Zoe and JD away. Zoe stumbled into JD's arms and laughed a little at the inadvertent swipe of JD's hand along the underside of her breast. She went red and Kayla lit up with her own slight embarrassment. JD apologized, but really, why should he? There wasn't anything to apologize for. It was just one of those things that they would look back on and laugh at when they reached the next eclipse and reminisced about their love, just as almost every other couple would be doing over the next half a day—before, during and especially after the dance.

"Get, you two," Kayla said. Her spirits were high, but that was still only a very good and strong mask. "This is your night."

"I'll see you at the boat," Zoe reminded her.

"Yeah. I'll be there."

Zoe nodded and pulled JD from the cave like a sprite on a sugar high. When they got outside, Zoe kissed him (she just couldn't help herself any longer). She looked at him after for what felt like the life of a third eclipse.

"You better get ready," JD said.

"I'll see you there." She gave him one last passionate peck (which she hoped would have lasted longer, but knew if it had, she would never have left him) before she skipped away, turning back several times to wave and blow a kiss his way. By the time he was out of view, Zoe felt as if her heart had grown wings and was flying her back home.

25

The Parting of the Eclipse Dance

The reflection in the mirror was far more beautiful than Zoe was expecting. The dress flowed over her body like the waves of the ocean and though she couldn't see it full on, the back was tapered with lace that resembled the complexity of a pair of wings ready to take flight. Maisy could see them and it took her breath away. The curls of Zoe's soft hair (*softer than the cotton of the heavenly clouds*, she thought) bounced gently upon her shoulders. And though she didn't originally want it, Maisy insisted that she highlight her features with a touch of rouge and some eyeliner. Zoe was glad she had. Her eyes popped with a luscious blue under her darkened eyelashes, flowing into the curvature of her cheekbones and down to the tips of her radiant smile. It was a picture of perfection. It would no longer take the eclipse to kill JD.

"My angel," Maisy said. She wanted to hug her, or kiss her, or hold her in some way, but refrained from doing anything in fear that it might hurt the portrait that stood in front of her.

"Thanks Maisy," Zoe said, turning and twisting to look herself over as much as she could. "You're absolutely amazing."

The two of them left shortly after with an awe-struck Frances in tow. Zoe held an open umbrella across her shoulder, not only to hide herself from the setting sun, but to keep the wind from playing games with her (again, at the insistence of Maisy). She stayed behind Maisy and Frances, who walked hand-in-hand, shoulder-to-shoulder all the way from their home to the main square of the Hub, where the lights lit the street with a brilliance of color. Over half of Heather was already enjoying the pleasantries of food and drink and company when they arrived. The second Maisy and Frances split apart, the benign chatter abruptly stopped. All eyes were on Zoe.

If there was ever a need to crawl into the nearest hole and hide in utter embarrassment, this was when Zoe wished she could have done it. Zoe's cheeks flushed with the pain of her incessant smile (even after she tried to stop; boy did she ever). It wasn't quite clear how long it was before Zoe stepped through the crowd to find her way to the food, or when everyone finally stopped staring and returned to their own personal conversations (a lot of which had switched over to Zoe), but she finally found a comfortable medium where she was able to eat and fill her stomach without feeling the need to throw it all back up. Not that she would, as the food was delicious and hit the spot perfectly—and gave her a reason to hide as best she could from the festivities, at least for the time being. Several friends and acquaintances bid her their wishes and extolled upon her their praises. She accepted them all with a genuine heart, but after the umpteenth time of hearing, "You look so beautiful," it just became rather rote. When Gertrude and Christian brought Janette over to say hi and grace her with a hug, they didn't say anything. In fact, they played it off as if nothing had changed, or that she was just the average young girl that had won over Janette's heart, possibly because they could sense her admiration fatigue. It didn't matter; it was a nice change of pace.

"Have you seen Winter?" Zoe asked after a nice, quiet conversation about some of the more mundane quirks that Janette had displayed over the past couple of days, which included the bout of sickness she had shortly after gorging on cupcakes. If Zoe didn't know any better, just the sight of them now made Janette's stomach turn—an unintended consequence that fell in her favor.

"I haven't," Gertrude said. She looked around while answering, like it would somehow help.

"I don't think she's coming," Christian chimed in. "You know she had that scare about a week back. I talked to Nestor the other day and he mentioned he had her on a pretty strict bed rest."

"That's too bad," Zoe said. "I really wanted to show her the dress."

"That's where I've seen it before," Gertrude said brightly. "I knew it looked familiar."

"You remember it?"

"How could I not? Winter looked just as beautiful as you do." It slipped, but Zoe didn't mind one bit.

"I'll have to stop by later."

"You should."

From there, Zoe didn't have much more to say, and in some way, was hoping JD would arrive and pull her away from it all. But until then, the group had to sit in that awkward silence that says, *I have nothing left to say but I don't want to hurt your feelings by walking away.* Gertrude felt exactly the same way. If only someone had said something, they could have avoided the whole thing. It was Henry who broke the moment as he took the stage to address his people.

"My people," he said with that strong, booming voice. "I just want to welcome you to the Parting of the Eclipse. I know for everyone here this is a bittersweet moment, but I urge you all to look upon this time not as a departure, but as a blessing. This isn't a time to ask yourself what might have been, it's a time to reflect on the life you had and how many people you have affected along your journey—a journey that will not end tomorrow among the eclipse, but will continue on in the glory of our protector, our love, our god."

Everyone cheered. Zoe could only roll her eyes. *If only he knew.*

"Now I bid you take heart in hand and enjoy the blessings that Heather has provided us, and if nothing else, have fun." Henry jumped from the stage and was swallowed up by the crowd, all giving him their congratulations.

That was when Jonah, Kerry, Bradley, Paul and Ingrid (dubbing themselves the Eclipsers, which wasn't all that original, but at least made a little bit of sense) took to the stage to start playing what they liked to call music, but which was actually what a lot of others might just consider a lot of noise. It wasn't that any of them individually was any worse than any others, but as a group, it seemed that each one was trying to do their own thing, blending about as good as fried chocolate spinach. It didn't seem to matter to most; the second the music started, everyone moved their feet and joined in celebration, swiveling their hips, bobbing their heads and swinging their partners around with exuberance and reckless abandon. Zoe noticed Janette had wandered off somewhere as Gertrude and Christian took to the dance floor. She knew she should be concerned for her, but JD was front and center on her mind. He was all she cared about.

Where is he?

As she weaved through the crowd (taking up a quick step here and there when prompted by some overzealous hoofer), Zoe looked just about everywhere she could imagine for him. She finally gave up when she reached the final lighting post, where she caught sight of Janette horsing around with a few of the other kids on the grass up the hill. She sat on a bench there to watch over them like a good little caretaker (but mostly to get away from the crowd and the noise) and wait for JD. Her interest on the kids quickly waned as she looked past them up the road to Quorum Circle, hoping against hope that she would see JD rise above the horizon like a Greek god coming to claim his nymph. She could see his billowing hair blow across the wind (which was funny because JD didn't have much hair at all), his beauty dressed in his finest suit and tie, holding in his warm, moisturized hands a corsage that she would slip across her wrist, which over the coming months would be replaced by the ring that would couple them as one. He kissed her and rested his hand on her shoulder. The dream was haunting in its forgery, yet mesmerizing in how real it all seemed. It turned out the hand wasn't that of JD's at all—far from it. The hand that rested on Zoe's shoulder was that of the person who had hurt Zoe the most—the last person she wanted to see right now.

Brittany.

Zoe backed away. Her brow was shriveled forward across the top of her nose and her eyes sliced together. "What are you doing here?"

"We need to talk," Brittany said. Her voice was gentle and kind. Zoe hated it.

"I have nothing to say to you."

"But I do you. Just listen, and after you hear what I have to say, you can have me arrested and thrown in the pit for all I care."

The offer was tempting. Brittany held out her hand. "May I have this dance?"

Zoe wasn't sure if she should. She had hoped her first (and every other dance for that matter, especially the last) would be with JD. But Brittany looked sweet and remorseful (and in some ways, oddly fearful); to abandon her now, even after the lies she had told, would go against everything Zoe was brought up to believe in. Who would she be if she didn't at least give her the benefit of the doubt? After all, Brittany had done plenty to earn her trust (all the while doing just as much to harm it), so it was only right that she lend her an ear and consider what she had to say. Zoe took Brittany's hand and then walked back to the sea of dancers to blend within like a needle among the pines.

Surprisingly, Brittany wasn't a bad dancer. She led Zoe with such a delicate smoothness it felt almost as if the two were simply floating on ice. It was a shame Zoe had to muddy the moment with words.

"So what do you have to say for yourself?"

"I know sorry isn't a strong enough word for the lies I've told, Zoe. But I want to make things right. I do."

"I'm not sure you can."

"Believe me, if I could have done it any other way, I would have. I respect you far too much to seek to hurt you in any way."

"How can you respect me so much? You've known me for less than a week. Hardly a chance to truly get to know anyone."

"That is true, but you have to admit, the lies aside, you felt a connection to me beyond the norm."

Zoe wanted to argue the point, but couldn't. There was no way to deny it.

"There's a reason for that, Zoe. I just couldn't tell you what that reason was before now. I hope that you can believe me when I say that I wish this could have been different, that our meeting could have been under better circumstances. It simply wasn't possible, and no amount of words can express my sincerest apologies."

Zoe grew more irritated with every word that passed her lips. Was she simply here to grovel for forgiveness? If so, Zoe had no more room in her heart.

"I'm not here to grovel, or try to convince you that I'm a good person and should be given a second chance," Brittany continued, as if she knew exactly what Zoe was thinking (which kind of freaked Zoe out, if she was being perfectly honest). "I only want you to know the truth, and whatever it is you do with that is up to you. You can accept my word and embrace it, or you can reject it and leave me to be cursed with the rest. It's Heather's will and nothing more."

"What do you know of Heather's will?" Zoe snapped. "I don't even know who you are."

The next three words answered everything for Zoe and sent her mind, her life and her entire world into the tizziest of tizzies. As Brittany leaned in close and closed her eyes, nothing could have prepared Zoe for the whisper that transferred from Brittany's soft lips to Zoe's cold ear.

"I am Hærothestî."

26

The Dance of Nature

It's hard to truly appreciate the beauty of a setting sun until it becomes the last one you'll ever see. This sunset in particular held a bounty of rich depth in its color pallet that Kayla thought Heather might have painted it especially for her. She leaned quietly against the cooling rocks of the cave, visualizing herself on the very edge of the horizon, melting into the picturesque canvas as if a roaring sea of magma was covering her. She didn't fear anyone seeing her—not tonight. Everyone was going to be at the dance, which gave her one last chance to gaze out at the only land she had ever known; the land that she was going to be giving up one way or another.

She climbed up the side of the cave and took a perch on its lip. From here, she could see a shade of the river that she would soon be taking to meet up with Zoe after the moon settled into the sky. Tonight, that current would take her and Lenny to the unexplored. And that not only excited Kayla, knowing that she had a one in a million shot at outliving the eclipse (and being able to do so with Lenny by her side for always), but it scared the living soul out of her for hundreds of reasons she didn't want to sift through at all. It wasn't that she hadn't been down that very river many times;

in fact, she had probably been down that river more than anyone in Heather, except for maybe the fishers, who spent almost all of their waking hours on the docks, floating about in their rickety old ships. Thinking back, it always amazed her how stubborn the fishers were, especially with their boats. She once asked Tommy, a boy she met when diving near the drop point (a very dangerous thing to do, and not endorsed in the least) why his caretaker never fixed his boat. Tommy's response:

"Fishers are superstitious. No matter the boat, no matter the name, if it's catching the fish it will remain the same."

Kayla thought it was cute. At the same time, it was pretty ridiculous. It was hard for her to believe in any of that. Superstitions were, after all, a way to continue to believe that nothing would change. But Kayla knew better than to believe that she, or anyone else, could keep anything the same. Life is change, after all. Without it, no one would grow or evolve. What would the world be like if everything remained stagnant and constant? *Boring as hell, that's what.*

Then again, she might lose Lenny simply by forcing her out of Heather, a change she didn't know if Lenny would ever be ready for. Was she willing to break that small inkling of superstition for her own selfish need to keep Lenny safe, keep her protected, and in a way, keep things the way they had always been?

A cool brush of wind wrapped Kayla's arms around her. Although it chilled her bones, it was invigorating nonetheless. But nowhere near as invigorating as the sound that came with the next gentle gust.

"Are you cozy?"

It took a moment for it to register, and still yet another few moments to find where it had come from. Her heartbeat quickened as she thought she'd been caught and would be taken back to the pit; she was so close to escaping, to lose Lenny now would be the most painful of all. To her relief, she finally caught sight of JD, who awkwardly made his way up the mountain, all the while trying to hold onto a bouquet of freshly cut roses and a small bottle of what could only be a very rare Moranis wine. Kayla knew that only the most privileged ever had access to it, so where he got this one Kayla wasn't sure. Regardless, she thought he might have stolen it from a drunkard after passing out (or else he had been drinking it himself) because the bottle was half empty.

"Getting the party started a little early?" Kayla said smiling. She shifted over (as best she could without falling off the edge) to let JD sit next to her. In the space they occupied, it forced them to sit with their arms and legs pressed firmly against each other. The funny thing was, neither of them cared in the least. It felt comfortable; it felt right—like JD's smile.

"I was actually saving it for you," JD said softly.

"Well, thank you." She took the bottle up in her hands and examined it. The label was so elegantly designed she was amazed that anyone in Heather could have created such a masterpiece. "I've never had wine before."

"Not many have."

"I thought all of these were locked up tighter than a nun."

"They are. I snaked this one from Henry after I helped get Zoe out of the manor. Thought it would be nice to have for a special occasion."

"Why bring it to me?"

JD didn't answer, but it hung in the air between them loud and clear. A smile pulsed across Kayla's lips as JD turned slightly red. To avoid any further discomfort, Kayla quickly pressed the tip of the bottle to her lips and let the wine pour across them. The taste was sweet and a little bitter, with just the right amount of fruitiness and what seemed like a hint of walnut. It was as satisfying as the touch of JD's hand against hers. Kayla lowered the bottle and flipped her eyes to JD. With the light of the stars glistening across them, she suddenly realized something more important than her.

"Wait. Shouldn't you be at the dance with Zoe?"

"Yeah," he said. "I was on my way when I thought you might like a little bit of company."

"That's sweet," Kayla said, though the words tasted extraordinarily sour. "But she's probably expecting you. You should go."

"I will. After I do what I came here to do."

Kayla's eyes were wide, curious. But whatever she thought he was going to do, she was dead wrong. Instead, he stood (balancing himself carefully across the edge of the rock) and held out his hand.

"May I have this dance?" he said with the most charming pinch of a smile. Kayla had no reason to resist. She took his hand. He pulled her close, and they danced, gently, quietly, and with all things considered, breathlessly for a lifetime and then some.

Neither of them realized when, or even why it happened, but the kiss was warm and delicate. The pair of them were no longer dancing as their bodies had become non-existent. They were no longer animate, but instead had become everything, from the rock to the trees, to the sky and the clouds. Everything touched harmoniously at the tips of their lips, and it was nothing that could ever be written, now or forevermore.

The next hour was like a dream, as they carefully made their way back into the cave (unaware that they had even moved at all) where the passion of their kiss continued on without respite or remorse. If Kayla had had any sense, she would have known that what she was doing to Zoe was wrong, breaking the bond they had together as friends. But Zoe was the furthest thing from her mind, which was only focused on taking the kiss even further than either of them had ever gone before, or thought they would ever go with each other. By the time that they lay together, the cool air tickling the rush of warm blood flooding through their veins, no words would ever again cross their lips that meant more than one another's touch.

27

Revelations

Zoe had to sit or else she would faint. Despite her reluctance, she used Brittany for balance to help walk her behind the stage. If she hadn't, she might have ended up on the ground in the middle of everyone trying to dance. Boy would that have been a super party spoiler. Zoe pushed Brittany away as soon as she found solace against the stage and held her hand to her forehead to focus on controlling her errant breaths. Brittany stood away from her and waited.

"You," Zoe finally said. Brittany knelt down and rested her hand on Zoe's knee. She didn't try to brush it away.

"I know this may be hard to believe—"

"Hard to believe? Hearing that JD wanted to court me was hard to believe. This is beyond lunacy."

"But it is true."

"I don't know what's true anymore," Zoe said. She still wasn't willing to look directly at Brittany. "You've been manipulating me this whole time. I don't even feel like my life is my own anymore. How in Heather am I supposed to accept this?" Realizing what she had said, Zoe finally looked up. In that moment, when her eyes connected with Brittany's, Zoe knew. Brittany wasn't lying, at least not now; at least not about this. She wanted to come clean; she wanted to let Zoe in.

Should she let her, after what she'd done already?

"Hear my words, that's all I ask."

Zoe curled her eyes down. Slowing her breaths helped her calm her chaotic mind. After a small hesitation, Zoe covered Brittany's hand with her own. She nodded.

Brittany relayed her story. As it was, Hærothestî was the daughter of Ananke, Greek goddess of destiny and fate. Revered by the gods, Hærothestî spent most of her youth learning and becoming one with the Fates, giving her love to what was always meant to be, raised to one day inherit her mother's station. Until that time, Hærothestî blossomed into purity and second chances, granting a man her hand when she felt his absolute remorse for actions were out of his control. Over the generations, Hærothestî grew less observant, spreading second chances among those who didn't deserve them, or who otherwise begged for them rather than seeking redemption, to the point that so long as someone asked, Hærothestî would grant them their request.

Hærothestî was on the eve of her seventeenth generation when she overheard the Fates whisper the demise of a group of mortals seeking to rise up against the gods, which on its face was nothing out of the ordinary. An uprising was always inevitable every few generations, and with each one, the gods would prove their dominance with the hand of power and strength (and the deaths of those who would remain defiant). However, a hint of sorrow bled through Hærothestî's body in relation to this new premonition that urged her to seek answers. It turned out that the mortals involved in this new uprising were kids, none of which were older than seventeen. Never before had such a young group of mortals been so defiant, and at no time had it ever been considered by the gods to lay waste to so many young hearts.

To end it before it ever began, Hærothestî stole her way to the land, hoping to speak with the group and change their minds before their transgressions led to the mark of death. Her words fell hollow upon their ears, pushing them to seek out many of the gods, which led to the successful destruction of one and the near maiming of another. It pained Hærothestî to the point of deep anguish and constant rest. But not even then did she give up on her people. The night before the gods were to attack, Hærothestî pleaded with them to give her more time. She could barely stand on her own and her voice was all but gone, but she was determined to keep them from following through. To keep her from doing so, she was sent away with Hades and held prisoner among her thoughts, contemplating what it meant to act on her impulses and what it would mean not to. When Ananke heard of her insubordination, she went to her and explained why such an act was necessary—if these kids were not dealt with upon a strong hand, their uprising would signal a change between gods and mortals, which would lead to the death of all that they know. Hærothestî argued that no one had to be harmed to make the mortals respect them. She just needed more time to convince them that no harm would come to them if they stopped immediately and taught the praise of their gods to their followers.

"It is our fate," Ananke said. "If you defy your destiny, you will face your consequences." The subject was laid to rest. Hærothestî's thoughts were not. In the end, she couldn't sit back and let a group of kids die. Men knew what they were doing when they defied their gods; kids were running on impulse and observance. If she let them die, it would fester upon her soul for eternity.

Gathering all of the strength she could muster, Hærothestî seduced her release from Hades, but it wasn't enough. She was too late. The bodies lay waste upon the land in fire and ash. Her tears burned hotter than the flame of Hell, and with them came her resolve. Within each drop came flesh and blood, and in minutes, all of the lives that were taken (including several children who couldn't have been more than ten) were given fresh breath. She sat with them all to explain the reason for their rebirth and the dangers of squandering it with pettiness. They agreed to abide by the rule of the gods. Satisfied, Hærothestî returned to her mother's side, only to witness her compassion come crashing down upon her.

The kids took their resurrection to the people, declaring that they lived because their resolve was true. The gods were there only to destroy them, but life would heal them. They lied to every ear that would listen and built an army so large, not even the Titans could contain it. Hærothestî was a pile of tears as Ananke punished her daughter with the cold hand of shackles. Just as the mortals must be punished, so too did Hærothestî, lest other deities rise up amongst their fathers. Ananke brought together a panel of seven, including deities Chronos and Thanatos, and Titans Prometheus, Themis, Phoebe, and Perses. Together, they would decide her fate. Hærothestî's words were all for naught, as the deafness of her trial was overwhelming. Her sentence was even more so.

It was decreed that Hærothestî would be granted her very own piece of land, carved out in the breast of the three sons of Chronos. She would be blessed a community of followers, for which she could grant her will as she saw fit under the watchful eye of Chronos' daughters (to which they would not interfere). However, every seventeen years the source of life would be eclipsed and remove all souls of those who had already taken witness of the event. The only way to end the cycle would be the sacrifice of the child born with the eclipse, under her own accord, without interference or coercion. The sacrifice must also be pure of regret and fear, or else time would be at an end for all, including that of Hærothestî. The punishment was set forth to teach Hærothestî that only the pure of heart were worthy of rebirth, and that she would be granted hers when a mortal believed that she deserved it, unselfishly exchanging their life for hers.

"I've been praying for someone like you for centuries on end, Zoe," Brittany concluded. "Someone who understands the necessity of all that I believed. If you don't find it in you to do this, I don't know how many more generations I can support. My people are dying, Zoe."

"It was your own fault," Zoe said. "You put this burden on yourself and in turn forced the rest of us to follow in your shoes. What makes you think I'd sacrifice myself for someone who has no regard for the consequences of her actions?"

"I was genuine in my conviction. You have to believe that. I never wanted to hurt anyone or cause them pain. It wasn't I who put you in this position, it was my mother. She used you to punish me."

"Maybe so. But I might have been able to live a full life if it hadn't been for you."

"Zoe, I understand if you don't want to do this. You deserve as long a life as you can get. But look around you. It's not only the eclipse that will destroy my people. This land is dying. You see it in the desert. You saw it at the lottery."

Brittany was right. The lottery proved that their special community had less people than ever before, and it seemed there would be even less in future generations. "Why?" Zoe said.

"It was punishment for my further indiscretions."

"Further indiscretions?"

Brittany lowered her head, regret noticeable across her body. "After the first hundred generations had passed, I was losing my people; I was dying in the wake of their disregard for me and my love for them. And not one child had ever attempted to make the sacrifice, even though the desire to do so was inherent within them. The more I was forgotten, so to was the path. When I realized that the child of the eclipse was no longer able to understand her destiny, I intervened. Not with a hand of might, but with a gesture of romance. I spent several generations seeking a way to break free of my shackles in the ether and bind myself to the child. My first attempts failed. I didn't know how to communicate what needed to be heard. Finally, as I almost gave up hope, a young girl named Ivy fell in love with me. It was not my intention and I never wanted to use her, but it was all I could do to make her listen. When she found out who I was, she felt so betrayed that she killed herself at the dance. From that point on, I knew I couldn't interfere in that way. I could guide them, point them along the path. That's when I wrote the book and planted it into the hands of the nobles. Each new headmaster took it upon themselves to write their own version, each time diluting the story until one day it simply wasn't the truth. It was only what the people wanted to believe. So I hid it. And for generations, my life continued to dwindle, not because my people were forgetting, but because my people were dying. The desert spread and the waters rose. You are the first child I've opened myself up to since Ivy because your heart is the most pure of any other, and I hoped that you would listen to it and do what you feel deep down is right and just."

"I don't see how I can," Zoe said. "Not now. Not after this."

"You can. You just have to feel it."

"But you've been manipulating me this whole time. If I didn't know any better, I'd say it was you that wrote that lumber art on the mill."

Brittany lowered her eyes. The guilt and shame was pure.

"Feather my tail, Brittany. You almost got Kayla killed."

"No," Brittany said, her eyes glossed in moisture. "I would never have done that. Susanna wasn't ever going to let Kayla die, not like that. I simply put into motion a series of events that I hoped would lead you to understand your fate."

"How does that help me? That isn't love; that's not compassion. It's control."

"All of the actions you've taken, all of the decisions you've made were yours and yours alone. I may have provided assistance, but never once did I make you do anything you weren't already willing to do. You've always been able to do as you wish.

You know all that you need." Brittany leaned up and kissed Zoe gently. She waited for her to say something, to keep her close, but there was nothing speaking to her at all. So she turned to walk away. Zoe stood.

"What did you mean when you said that the eclipse would remove all souls who had taken witness of the event?" Zoe said softly. Brittany heard the words clear and loud. She turned back. This was something she was going to have to look Zoe in the eye to say.

"It means that no matter how far you go from here, as long as the eclipse extinguishes the source of life, and you once took witness, your last breath will be with the eclipse."

Zoe stepped back; it was all she could do to keep from falling flat on her back. Her head felt lighter than a balloon scurrying across the sky. She raised her hand and attempted to steady herself. Brittany went to give her support, but before she got close, she was no longer needed.

Henry wrapped his arms up through Zoe's and steadied her enough to sit her back down against the stage. "Careful now," he said. By the time Zoe realized who it was, she was laying her head against his chest. Lenny was standing next to him. Her head was curled slightly downward across the lip of her shoulder blade. "You don't look so well. Perhaps we should take you to the physician."

"I'm fine," Zoe said. She lifted her head. For some reason, he smelled unreasonably foul.

"Are you sure? It might make this a whole lot easier."

"Make what easier?" Zoe no longer felt dizzy. In fact, she was more alert than ever.

"I wish I didn't have to do this, Zoe. Believe me, this is the last thing I want to do." Henry stood with his hands placed firmly upon his hips. Zoe looked at Lenny and caught sight of Brittany standing like a useless statue behind her. "Zoe, you are under arrest."

"For what?" Zoe was on her feet. Lenny tucked her head closer to her body (if that was even possible).

"For harboring a convicted criminal."

"I did no such thing."

"Did I not hear you and your friend speaking of Kayla?"

If any words could have saved Zoe from this accusation, they surely would have found their way to her lips. But as it was, only air could slip through. Henry took that as a plea of guilt and grabbed her arm. Zoe wasn't going to let this happen without a fight.

"Let me go," she screamed. Henry wasn't much taller than Zoe, but he was still twice as strong, the veins in his arms rippling as he forced her against his chest.

"This will only make it worse, Zoe. Tell me where Kayla is and this will all be over."

"Go to Hell," Zoe said. "Kayla's dead and you know it."

"If you say so. Come on."

"Let me go," she screamed again, hoping to attract some attention. Which she did, most of whom were more than willing to help her—until they saw Henry. None of them were willing to go against him, not with the rumors of Zoe's indiscretions still hovering like the trail of the skunk. He curled her around the stage, an act of malice if there ever was one. Henry could have taken her directly to Quorum Circle and avoided the crowd with ease—this was deliberate. He wanted everyone to witness this, most likely to turn them all against her. And she would be right. Henry pushed her to her knees in the center of the dancers and squeezed her shoulder sharply. The pain was excruciating, making her want to throw up, if not pass out.

"Take notice," Henry called out to everyone. "Zoe, ward of Frances and Maisy, has admitted to harboring Kayla, ward of Daniel and Catherine, and refuses to identify her location. Therefore, it is my duty to sentence Zoe to death. Does anyone object to this decision?"

If silence could be measured, there would be no number to quantify the weight of what Zoe heard (or didn't hear, for that matter). "Very well," Henry said. "Zoe, ward of Frances and Maisy, will be hung by the neck, here in the square at the turn of the eclipse."

"I object," Brittany said, exposing herself to the crowd for the first time. Zoe noticed a few shocked breaths from those who knew Brittany long ago, and still others who chattered in confusion about who she was.

"And you are?" Henry said.

"You may call me Snow White."

Henry smiled. "Cute. Okay, Snow White" (you could taste the bile of his words). "What say you?"

"I know for certain that Zoe has no idea of Kayla's whereabouts. But I do, and I shall take you to her if you let Zoe go free."

"Why should I believe you?"

"Because I have defied death myself, and I know the consequences that come with that."

"Is that so?"

"It is," shouted Nestor, who had grown up with Brittany. "I saw her die at the last eclipse." Several others were quick to confirm her death, yet here she stood in front of them all.

"I went against the Fates, and in return caused great pain and anguish for many who did not deserve it. I don't want Kayla's misguided actions to do the same for Zoe, or anyone else here for that matter. Release her, and I will give you what you want."

Henry's grip remained as strong as ever on Zoe's shoulder. He wasn't buying it. What he truly wanted was Zoe's death, not Kayla's. But there was no fighting the will of his people, and as the chants to release Zoe grew (with a taste for vengeance against Kayla, no doubt), Henry had no other real option.

"So be it," he finally said and pushed Zoe forward. She rose quickly and ran to Brittany, wrapping her arms around her, both out of gratitude and a need to find out why.

"Go. Find Kayla," Brittany whispered. "Warn her."

Zoe pulled away. She had so much to say but couldn't find the words. Brittany rested her hand on Zoe's cheek and nodded, acknowledging every one of them. Zoe matched her nods and backed away as Henry forced himself against Brittany.

"Come on then. Lead the way."

"The ward of the eclipse will guide you," Brittany said. Henry's confused ignorance was Zoe's reward. As Brittany led Henry, Reynold and Gavin from the hub, Zoe ran as fast as she could to the fields where Janette was still running about with her friends.

"Janette," Zoe called, needing nothing more to entice the child into her arms. Zoe smiled graciously as Janette urged her to join the fun, but there were far more important things at stake. "Wait, Janette," she said, kneeling and holding her gently across the arms. "I need you to tell me something very important."

Janette nodded and stuck her finger in her mouth (a gesture of innocent confusion, no doubt). "Do you have a secret hiding place, or a spot that you go when you're scared or need to be alone?" Janette bit her finger. It was obvious she did, but didn't want to reveal it. "It's okay, Janette. I won't tell anyone where it is. But I need to know. You have to show it to me."

She was quite reluctant.

"I'll get you a massive cupcake for the eclipse," Zoe said, switching tactics. "One bigger than your whole head. And Gertrude will never know. It'll be our little secret." That brightened Janette up (guess Zoe was wrong about her being sick of them). She gripped Zoe's hand tight and ran to Gertrude's pastry shop. They sprinted inside and went straight to the back, where Janette led her down a set of stairs into the storage room. Toward the back, Janette pushed a tray cart away from a boarded up wall. She pulled a loose board away, revealing a hole underneath. It was hardly big enough for even Janette at her size to fit into, but as Zoe got to her knees to survey the hole, she found there was enough room inside for Janette to stand on herself, and went deeper than she would be able to see if it wasn't for the handful of small rocks that lit the walls.

"Brilliant," Zoe said. "Thank you." She hugged and kissed Janette, who giggled with pleasure. "When I get back, we'll work on that cupcake, yeah?"

Janette nodded and Zoe squeezed her way into the hole (which was no small feat; in fact, it took her several minutes). Once inside, she was able to navigate her way through the tunnels, feeling Brittany's directions as if she were right there with her leading the way. Despite the thick heat and the enormous weight of the dress, Zoe ran as fast as her legs could carry her and didn't stop until she reached the hatch in Pasture Ranch (and even then, she was moving with the momentum of a jet in space). She climbed up and out, and prayed to Heather that she would get to Kayla before Henry.

"Kayla, we have to go," she said as she ripped through the crevice. That's when she came to a halt so abrupt, it was as if she had run into a wall of bricks. JD and Kayla lay together with nothing more than their skin between them. Zoe let out a scream (more of a squeak, really, but enough to wake Kayla up), again ready to fall, this time out of shock and betrayal. Her hand was on her lips in seconds as was her knees on the ground. Her eyes flushed with tears she thought might never end.

Kayla sat up. Her mouth was held agape in wordless guilt. Nothing she could say would make anything better and she knew it. JD simply remained still, pretending to be asleep. Zoe knew better. His shame sowed through the posture in his shoulders and his reluctance to even acknowledge his betrayal. Kayla held her hand out, hoping Zoe would accept it as a sign of apology. It wasn't even close to being enough. Zoe shook her head, her hand glued to her mouth (now dripping in salted water), and turned her back on them. In her mind a gesture that would last forever.

"Zoe," Kayla said finally, but the remorse in her voice wasn't enough. Zoe ran from the cave and into the desert.

"Zoe, wait," Kayla continued to call out. "Please, let me explain." She wanted to run after her, but it was better to leave her be. She turned to JD. It was clear he felt bad about what they had done, but on a deeper level, knew it was meant to be. He took Kayla's hand and brought her into his embrace. "She'll be okay," he said and kissed her forehead.

"I'm not so sure," Kayla said. But whether it was his touch or the slight beat of his heart, Kayla wanted nothing more than to taste his kiss once more.

"So lovely," Henry said.

Kayla was shocked into wrapping her arms across her chest as she turned. JD held her tightly; there was nothing more he could do as Henry leaned against the wall of the cave (Brittany shamed in guilt behind him), his smile a crooked heap of perversion and delight.

28

Finding Empathy

Zoe was a heap of a mess as the winds layered her with sand. By the time she was able to collect herself enough to walk again, her dress was no longer a succulent light blue, but striped with a dusty brown, and her hair was as knotted as a battered bird's nest. But what did it matter? Her world had been torn asunder. What was left, really, but death? Given the eclipse was on the horizon, Zoe felt bad for even thinking such a thing, but it was hard not to. Her best friend and the man she thought loved her had fallen into each other (and had done so behind her back, which hurt most of all) without even a second thought. JD had played her, as far as she was concerned. If he didn't love her, and instead had feelings for Kayla, why would he continue to allow her to act like such a childish pixie with a lust of a crush? It hurt that he couldn't open up to her; that he would lead her on like this. But it hurt even more that Kayla would even do such a thing knowing how much Zoe (thought) she loved him. Then again, it just may have been the betrayal of her soul that pierced her heart the most.

Wandering the desert was all Zoe could do to try and wrap her head around it all. It was remarkably cool and the air almost moisturized her skin, despite the dust particles that whipped about. She thought that she might just walk forever as Susanna was destined to do, but a soft voice stopped her from eventually becoming just another memory among the sweeping sea of the sand. It wasn't clear what it was, and she imagined it was another attempt by Brittany to manipulate her into doing more of her bidding. But her gut told her otherwise—that it was really her own compassionate nature that was telling her she was meant for more, that she needed to reach out to those who harmed her and walk in their shoes before judging them. Why should she? As far as she was concerned, Kayla and JD no longer existed and were no longer worthy of her energy, her forgiveness, or her compassion.

Zoe dropped to her knees and let out a yell that sprinted through the wind, releasing her of her confusion, hate, pain and spite. Her tears warmed and faded upon her cheeks, and though she could see much clearer, it all still seemed to be a jumbled mess. Nothing she believed was real, nothing she trusted existed—at least on the surface. But she was afraid of digging any deeper in fear of what she'd find. Even if it was what she wanted—what she always thought—just knowing that the deepest part of her could have been a false mirror of who she thought she wanted to be was a terrifying realization. How was she going to be able to rectify her sermons when she herself was only pretending?

Something startled her just then.

For a split second, she thought Henry had caught up to her, or even worse, that Kayla had. But neither was true. As Zoe turned up onto her feet, Maisy and Frances walked up to her. Maisy rested softly against Frances' chest, her smile sparkling gloriously. That is until she caught sight of Zoe's distraught, anxious features.

"Zoe?" Maisy asked. It was hard to see much under the soft light of the moon, but the instinct of a mother was beyond reproach. "What's wrong? What happened?"

Zoe's nerves got the better of her. She started shaking and crying uncontrollably. She felt ashamed and embarrassed, and was reluctant to allow Maisy to bring her to her breast like she used to when she was a child. Perhaps feeling like a child again upset her, because being in her caretaker's arms opened the floodgates, unable to lock them back up for several hours. Maisy and Frances all but carried her to a small, rocky cliff (oddly rising from the middle of the desert) where they sat in silence until Zoe was ready. When she was, her first question wasn't anything of importance; it wasn't in regards to her situation. It was an innocent question that led to much more than Zoe could have conceived of.

"Where are we?"

Maisy smiled and brushed Zoe's hair back. Her head lay gently across Maisy's lap. Frances sat next to her, his arms wrapped across her shoulder. "This is the very spot Frances and I were at during the last eclipse."

Zoe sat up, intrigued. "What were you doing all the way out here?"

"My friends and I used to come out here all the time when we wanted to play cowboys and Indians, or whatever other game we felt like," Frances said. "We always said it brought out a more authentic feel than any other part of Heather, and it was a place we could do other things that we might not otherwise be able to do if there was a crowd, if you get my meaning."

The shocked smile felt right at home on Zoe's lips. "Frances."

Maisy's smile matched Zoe's, but was more endearing than anything else. "He was a little bit of a bad boy, I'll give him that," she said. "But it was one of the things that we loved about each other. I was more cautious and straight-laced; he was much more a wanderer by nature."

"You complemented each other," Zoe acknowledged.

"Very well, indeed." Maisy kissed Frances. Zoe's smile faded slightly, as she couldn't help but be reminded of JD... and Kayla.

"We used to come out her often together," Maisy continued. "This became our spot; the place we could go to be alone whenever we wanted, to do as we pleased without anyone knowing. Sometimes I thought some of Frances' friends might have followed us, and probably got a nice show every once in awhile—"

"Maisy," Zoe said, her cheeks flushed red. Maisy played into it with a wide-eyed wink.

"I didn't care as long as I was with him. On the night of the last Parting of the Eclipse dance, we left early to come out here and watch the sunrise. As it cracked over the tip of the mountains, Frances looked at me, took my hand and said..."

"Maisy, ward of Rachel and Samuel," Frances said, "I have fallen head over heels in love with you and there is no breath I wish to take that isn't yours. Will you become my union for the rest of eternity?"

Zoe felt so enamored, her arms tickled with goose flesh. "That's so amazing," she whispered.

"We never came back here after that, but told ourselves that if there was one place we wanted to be when our last breath was taken, it was here, where our life truly began."

Zoe had no words to share; a hug would have to do. Not only because of the magic of the story, but because they never pushed her to talk about why she was such a blubbering mess. She wanted to thank her (thank them both, really) for everything they had ever done for her, and *would* do for her had they the opportunity. When she let go, and caught sight of Maisy's bright, loving eyes, there was only one thing Zoe had on her mind.

"What would you have done if Frances had been with another?"

Maisy understood now why Zoe had been so upset (and Zoe knew she did; she wasn't stupid), but Maisy didn't press it. She answered the question with all the honesty in the world. "In all honesty, I don't know what I would have done. I probably would have wanted to kill him—well, her more than him, I think, but they'd both be on my hit list. Then again, what would be the point of dwelling on all of that hatred? If Frances had done such a thing to me, all that would say is that he wasn't truly meant for me, that there was something much greater out there for me. All I would have to do would be to stay on the lookout so that it didn't accidentally pass me by. If I was to dwell on that betrayal, and spent all of my waking hours thinking about it, and the 'what if' surrounding it, I might have missed the true love that actually did come along."

Zoe felt a bit confused. It sounded almost as if someone *had* hurt Maisy. Could that even be true? Maisy rested her palms against Zoe's chin, telegraphing the importance of what she was about to say. "Forgiveness is a drug you want to partake in, Zoe, no matter how much pain you're in, because it's only when you're able to forgive that you're able to see life for what it is."

"And what's that?" Zoe said.

"Anything you want it to be."

Tears were returning, but no longer out of pain. "How do you know when it's right?"

"You know," Maisy said and rested her hand over Zoe's heart, "when this feels right."

"But why does it have to hurt so much?" Zoe said.

"Our heart is our compass, Zoe. At times it may hurt, at times it may play games, but it will never let you down, so long as you are honest with it, and understand that when things seem like they're spinning out of control, it's only because you're fighting the truth that's inside of you trying to point you in the right direction. So long as you believe that nothing is ever wrong and that the mistakes you make, the disappointments and the failures you incur, are nothing but a road map to your ultimate goal, you'll never be wrong."

Thank you. Zoe could hear the words in her head but couldn't be absolutely certain they actually came out of her mouth. Maisy acknowledged it, though, with an inaudible, *You're welcome*, before they hugged once again.

Zoe stepped away from the rock. She held onto Maisy's hand as long as she could before the tips of her fingers slipped away. She stopped then and held her hands together at her waist.

"I know where my heart is leading me," Zoe said.

"Live it with no regrets," Maisy said.

"I will." Zoe pressed her fingers to her lips. She blew the kiss to Maisy, who collected it quickly and pressed it to her chest. With a light squeak of a childish smile, Zoe turned, storing the last image of Francis and Maisy she would ever have in the depths of her soul.

29

Cell Mates

The holding cell door tore open and Henry walked in. Susanna had been lying in the farthest bunk from the door (which sat nearest the kitchen area) trying to get some sleep. She sat up instantly upon his step into the cell, confused by why he would be coming to see her so late. Terry remained asleep on the cot next to her.

"Shouldn't you be at the dance?" she said.

"It's not all it's cracked up to be," Henry said. "I have some company for you."

Reynold and Gavin pushed Brittany, Kayla and JD through the door. Henry automatically forced each onto a cot. (JD was about ready to punch him for even thinking about touching Kayla, but he thought better of it; this wasn't the time.) "Have a good night."

Henry left with a devilish grin and the coldest of laughs, Reynold and Gavin in step behind him.

"Jackass," Kayla whispered.

"What are you guys doing here?" Susanna said the second the lock sounded.

"The same reason you are," Kayla answered.

"Hey, you're not even supposed to be in Heather. Don't bite my head off."

"You think you might help out a bit?" Kayla turned, revealing the binds on her hands.

Susanna took a second to ponder whether she should (in the end, it was only right) and then untied Kayla's hands. She did the same for JD. "You lied to me."

"Yeah, well, there seems to be a lot of that going around."

"Were you ever going to leave, or was all of it just an act?"

"For your information, I was about to leave before we were ratted out."

"You were—" Susanna couldn't finish. She just didn't see the point. As she sat, Kayla turned around, happy to end the conversation. JD didn't know quite what to do, but his stomach growled, so grabbing something to eat became his best option.

Brittany ignored them all. The moment she saw Terry, she gravitated toward him. She sat at the edge of the cot, just off the touch of his waist, and watched him. When he opened his eyes, the love that was present was unmatched by any other before it. He smiled, gaining hers in return, but to think it would last was foolish. Tears swarmed his eyes as Terry placed his hands over them. "Heather's feathers," he hissed.

Susanna turned to him. "What is it?"

Embarrassed, Terry played it off. "Ah, nothing."

"Terry, what's wrong?"

"I'm just hallucinating," Terry said, clearing his eyes. "I thought I saw—"

When Brittany's face remained in his sight, Terry let out a flash of a yell and backed away as much as the cot would allow. Brittany reached out for him (Kayla surprised she was able to get her hands out of the binds), but was unable to go any further, fearing her touch would send him into hysterics.

Everyone's eyes were now on them.

"It can't be," Terry said.

"Who is that?" Susanna asked.

Terry turned to her. He wasn't sure of anything anymore.

"She's the rat piece of Heather's ass who got us in here," Kayla said, rubbing her wrists.

"I have my reasons," Brittany said, a voice that only caused Terry more pain.

"I may have lied but you betrayed us. How could you do that to us? To Zoe?"

"I may ask you the same question."

That shut Kayla up straightaway. She turned her back, unable to look at her or JD. He went to her, tried to touch her—relax her—but she pushed him away.

"How is this possible?" Terry was finally able to spit out.

Brittany looked back to Terry with a smile. "I'm not who I appear to be."

"I don't understand."

Brittany set her hand on Terry's arm. "Dear, Terry. I've watched you ever so carefully spend your life caring for others, choosing to lead with compassion and heart. For this committed expression of kindness for me and all of my sons and daughters, I thought it only fitting that I should return that love in kind."

Terry (not to mention Susanna) was more confused now than

ever. Brittany had to smile, squeezing Terry's arm affectionately.

"I have a message for you, from Brittany."

Terry's heart stopped. He sat up, not quite sure why, but he needed to get as close to the face of his companion as possible.

"Brittany wanted me to tell you not to worry so much over her. She's been watching over you these past seventeen years, and she's happy with the man you've become and will continue to be. And until that time when you are able to reunite, she'll love you with all of her heart. She will always be with you, no matter how bad things may get. She doesn't ever want you to forget that, and I don't think you ever will."

"This can't be. How…?"

"It can. And it is." Brittany picked up the charcoal bear from underneath the bed and handed it to Terry. His hands shook as he accepted it, tears streaming down his cheeks. "You remember this?"

"I do. But, I buried this with her."

"And now she wants you to have it back. To remember her." Brittany held his arm.

He knew it wasn't really her but he could feel Brittany through her embrace. "Thank you," he said.

"Wait," Kayla said, breaking the tender moment. "If you aren't Brittany, then who are you?"

Brittany walked to Kayla and JD. She took each of their hands and cupped them together. "I am exactly what you needed." She smiled and then walked to the bathroom facilities.

Kayla pulled her hand away from JD. "A nut who belongs in the asylum," she said. She lied down on the cot, making sure to keep JD at least a cot's length away. Susanna went to Terry and lay with him until they fell asleep.

Just before dawn (not like Kayla, or anyone else for that matter, could tell, what with the complete lack of windows in the cell), Kayla woke abruptly. She rubbed her eyes and sat up. Her back pinched a little, but it wasn't anything a little more sleep wouldn't fix. But she needed to take a leak so bad it felt like some was trickling out before she even got to the toilets. It only dawned on her after she was through (and washed her hands like a good little girl) that Brittany was gone. She checked each cot, the bathrooms and the kitchen—nothing. She even went as far as to check the door to make sure it was still locked (it was). Kayla thought of waking JD to tell him, but she figured they would be up soon enough for their sentencing. So she lied back down and couldn't find a wink more of sleep before Henry came to do just that, completely unaware of Brittany's absence (if not complete existence).

30

Forgiveness and Understanding

Zoe didn't want to go back to the Grand Hub (couldn't, really, or else be subject to everyone's displaced anger) and she didn't want to take the chance of running into Kayla or JD if she crossed past the mountains. She knew she had to find it in herself to forgive them, and she was close to finding the heart to do that, but she still needed time. So Zoe trekked cautiously through the fields of Pasture Ranch, picking some vegetables from Gail's garden and grabbing a few quick handfuls of water from Timber's well. When she reached the large oak, she sat at the swing and reminisced about all of the fun she and Kayla had had over the years together. They were the truest and most honest of friends. It was still hard to believe that she would keep such a secret from her, but then again, how did she know that it wasn't just one of those things that happens so rapidly, you can't control the impulse of your own actions? Looking back now, Zoe could see the signs that she was ignorant of (or absolutely refused to see) before. How could she possibly fault them for doing what they did? The two of them had been flirting, no matter how inadvertently, since this whole thing began, and whatever JD did a few hours ago finally sparked the fire that had been between them the entire time. They each loved Zoe, she knew that, but they were completely *in love* with one another and always had been. She had to believe that at some point JD would have told her, but then again, there was still that small lingering hint of doubt. If Kayla were going to die in just a few short hours, he wouldn't have had to choose. He could have coupled with Zoe without her ever being the wiser, but was that really any better? Zoe loved JD, that was certain, but was it true companionship—a fated connection—or was it simply that Zoe had been so smitten with him because he was the first young (hot!) man to give her that type of affection that she kept herself hidden from the truth—that what she believed to be love was in reality a simple infatuation? It was best that she knew that before she made the mistake of living the rest of her life unhappy, hiding behind a mask of love because she was afraid to be alone.

Zoe felt lighter, clearer, and as the sun licked her cheeks with heat, Zoe was ready to find and accept the whole truth. The best way she could think to do that was to look inside of JD with her new outlook in place. It was her best chance at forgiveness.

Her nerves didn't start acting up until she was close to Winter's. She needed to do this, needed to know, but she was worried. What if her love for him was real? What then? How could she forgive Kayla if they both felt the same for JD? Would she be able to give him up for her friend, or would her death at the hands of the eclipse fill her mind? The thought of such a thing was so sordid, it made her sick to her stomach. Who in their right mind would wish their best friend dead (especially if they had the power to stop that death) over the supposed love of some guy? It didn't make a whole lot of sense; then again, as Zoe was slowly finding out, love, in all of its intricate levels, was the most confusing, nonsensical, mystifying and uncontrollable emotion that anyone would ever have to contend with. Trying to control it was like trying to tame a lion—it works until the lion decides he's had enough and devours you. Maisy was onto something; it was better to just let love stay free and wild, allowing her instinctual compass to guide her through the chaos of it all.

Zoe had expected JD (or at the very least, Jack) to answer her knock. When no one did (after a second, louder whack), Zoe opened the door and called out for Winter.

"I'm here," Winter called back from the bedroom. Zoe went to her and was surprised to find absolutely no one with her.

Weird.

"Where is everyone?" Zoe asked.

Winter sucked in a few breaths and clenched her teeth for a few seconds before answering. "You tell me. When JD didn't arrive at sunrise like he was supposed to, Jack had no other choice but to go look for Nestor." She let out a slight scream. Zoe grabbed a hold of her hand. That was a mistake, as Zoe wondered if she would have any unbroken bones when Winter let go.

"Do you need me to do anything?" Zoe said when Winter finally relaxed and she felt the flow of blood return to her hand.

"No, dear. No, you've done enough."

Zoe smiled graciously. Winter sat up slightly and finally took notice of the dirty, torn dress. "Oh, how was the dance?"

Zoe's smile faded. "Not as grand as you might think."

"What happened?"

"I'd rather not speak of it right now," Zoe said. The curl in her brow told Winter not to press the matter, and she was happy to oblige. Though she did feel compelled to make light of whatever might have happened.

"At least the dress had a good time."

Zoe laughed. Part of her felt bad for doing so (covering her mouth to try and hide it) while at the same time, it felt really good to let it out. "I'm really sorry. I never meant to mess the dress up like this."

"Don't you worry about that, sweetie." Winter pressed her hand to Zoe's cheek. It felt just as warm and comforting as Maisy's. "It was yours to do with as you please. Though it would have been nice to see it passed onto her." Winter rubbed her exposed belly as Zoe laughed again.

"Me, too."

Winter clenched her teeth then and crushed Zoe's hand again. She let out a few breaths as Zoe tried to calm her (though she had no idea what she was doing). The contraction ended rather quickly. "That was a little more intense than usual," Winter commented.

"The little guy must be feeling the pinch to get out, huh?" Zoe said.

Winter's smile lit the room. "You bet she is. I can't wait to see her, either." Zoe's silence was plenty to spark Winter's interest. "What's wrong?"

"I don't know." In all honesty, she didn't, but looking at Winter coaxed her to elaborate nonetheless. "I guess it's just that I'm not sure anymore how you, how Maisy—how anyone—can be so ready for what's about to happen."

"It's our fate, our nature. There's nothing we can do, so why fight it?"

"I get that. In fact, a week ago, I would have said the exact same thing."

"What changed?"

Zoe didn't answer. She thought maybe she couldn't, but that wasn't true. Deep down she still didn't want to accept it. She was happy when Winter answered for her. "It's JD, isn't it?"

"It was different before JD," Zoe admitted. "I had people in my life that I loved dearly, who I certainly wasn't ready to let go of, but knew that it was necessary. At least I made myself believe it was necessary. But now, I just can't imagine letting go of someone you love so much without even a second thought, without even a fight."

"That's just it, Zoe. I hate Heather for forcing me to give up my baby. She's a part of me. If I had my way, I'd live forever and raise her to become the woman I know she will be. But at the same time, I've accepted Heather's fate and will trust that my child was meant to be with you, that she will be happy and safe with you looking after her. Everything is as it's meant to be, so to be able to see her at least once is a dream come true for me."

"I guess so," Zoe said, still unconvinced.

"I love my child, Zoe. I love you, and I love Jack. The time I've spent with you all have filled a lifetime of dreams, which is all any of us could ask for. Love doesn't stop with death, Zoe, it continues on in those you loved, no matter how long you've spent with them, no matter how much pain and grief they may have caused; or how many laughs you've had; or intimate moments you've enjoyed. Once you've loved someone in any way, as a friend, a ward or a caretaker, you've planted a seed that will carry through them for their lifetime and beyond. To love is the only way we'll ever live forever."

The words helped solidify what Zoe already felt. "Thank you," she said. "That was exactly what I needed to hear. And trust me when I say that no matter what happens, you will always be right here." Zoe tapped her chest above her heart.

"I know," Winter said, pulling a sweet smile from deep within Zoe—that is until she contracted again and nearly broke Zoe's finger. Zoe took the pain as best she could, fighting her own need to scream in favor of relaxing Winter. As she finally did, letting her breaths come slow and deep, Zoe rested her hand next to Winter's leg and felt cooling moisture just underneath it.

"What happened?" Zoe said.

"I think my water just broke," Winter said, confirming what Zoe suspected already. "The eclipse is starting."

Zoe looked outside. Winter was wrong. The eclipse hadn't yet begun. Something was wrong. "I need to find JD," she said.

"No, Zoe. I need you here. At least until Jack comes back."

Zoe grabbed her hand. This time, Zoe cupped Winter's cheek in her hand. "I know, and believe me, I wish I could stay and help. But there's a lot more to this than you realize. If I don't find JD, everything may be lost."

Winter nodded, seeing the delicate truth in Zoe's eyes.

Zoe kissed Winter gently on the other cheek. "Your dreams will come true. I promise."

Zoe left as fast as she could, hoping to keep from getting pulled back. Winter screamed as she shut the door, but no matter how much she wanted to go back in and help, reconciling her heart was far more important—for everyone's well being.

It didn't take long for her to get back to the cave.

"JD!"

Zoe was surprised to find it empty and eerily cold. She stopped in the middle of the room and looked around (as if that would help them all magically appear). When that failed, she called out for him again and jogged into the back cavern, which was extremely dark due to the sun being as low as it was. When her calls continued to fall to deafness, Zoe turned to leave.

"You know they're not here," Brittany said. Her voice was soft and a bit remorseful, yet Zoe heard it as if she was speaking directly into her ear. She flipped back around. The curvature of Brittany's cheekbones and the hint of her left eye were highlighted by a sliver of light that somehow found its way into the cave, which also swam with the lightest of touches in the water behind her.

"What did Henry do to them?"

"He looks to have them hanged within the next hour."

"How can he do that?" Zoe said. "Kayla's going to be dead soon anyway, and who will take care of our people if JD dies along with Nestor." A tiny dimple formed in Brittany's cheek upon hearing Zoe say *our people*. But she wasn't about to make light of that. She couldn't, not if she wanted to break her curse.

"It doesn't matter to him," Brittany said, keeping the topic on point. "This is a show of his leadership, of his command. He is breeding his presence among the people and without a strong hand, he fears he'll have none."

"That is so ludicrous. There are plenty of ways he can show his authority. He doesn't have to kill people who don't deserve to be killed to prove that." It was then that Zoe finally understood Brittany's (or, more to the point, Hærothesti's) moral dilemma. To be exact, her reasons for doing what she did, and the absolute cruelty she was burdened with at the hands of her mother. It wasn't right; none of this was right. But at least now, Zoe was on Brittany's side.

"I have to stop him," Zoe said. "Come with me."

"I can't."

"Sure you can. Explain to them, let them see the truth."

"Only you have the power to do that now."

"How?"

"Be honest."

"I don't know if I can do that."

"You have it in you, Zoe. It's always been there, you just have to accept it."

"I can't. I can't do this without you."

"Why?"

"Because I'm scared." The echo of that statement lasted longer than all other echoes in the world combined. It radiated so much truth, so much conviction, and so much authenticity that it was impossible for Zoe to ignore. This one reason is what had been keeping her from being able to follow her internal compass. But now that it was out, now that she was able to absorb it and understand it, she felt a weight lift off her shoulders that she didn't even know was there. She felt light, and ready to tackle anything.

The shimmer of a tear rolled across the spotlight on Brittany's cheek. She didn't have to say another word. Zoe stepped back, unable to remove her eyes from that sign of acceptance.

"Fear only hurts you when you let it," Brittany said.

"I forgive you," Zoe said. And then she was gone.

As was Brittany, but not until after she pressed her hand to her lips and lowered it gently in Zoe's wake.

31

The Sacrificial Lamb

By the time Zoe reached the Grand Hub, it seemed the entire community had found a place to witness the unnecessary deaths that were about to happen (and she wasn't just thinking about Kayla and JD). It made her a bit sick to think that so many would forgo their last hours with their loved ones to camp out and watch someone struggle to take their last breath. If this was what Heather had become, she wasn't sure if she wanted to save it. Then again, maybe that was the whole point. At least she had the Heather Biters on her side (even if they would have no problem knocking her lights out had they seen her), chanting their disapproval from the hillside.

Kayla and JD stood on top of a long, thin log, propped up by two thin cross-sticks at either end. Their hands were bound tightly with a shard of thinly laced rope and their heads were covered with dark masks, hiding their eyes from witnessing... what exactly? The faces of all of the people finding enjoyment in their death, or the ones who would turn away, disgusted by what they saw? Susanna and Terry stood off to the side of the stage with Gavin.

Reynold tossed a pair of long ropes over the top of the gallows surrounding the two (which, even with its utter simplicity, was actually an impressive feat to have been built over night; it made her wonder when they had actually been built). He adjusted them until the end of the noose hung just below the base of the victims' necks and tied them off a few feet away. Henry appeared then and lassoed the nooses around both Kayla and JD's necks, tightening them just enough to keep them from choking before the inevitable drop.

Zoe made her way through the crowd as Henry finished off yet another arrogant speech (or, to be more precise, his justification for doing something so demented). When she reached the front of the stage, she bounded up like a jackrabbit and waved her arms in the air to grab everyone's attention.

"Wait," she called out so that even Winter might have had a chance to hear. "You can't do this." Henry was quick to wrap his arms around Zoe's and pull them tightly behind her.

"Well, look what we have here," he said. "The third in our trio of criminals. Glad you could join us."

Zoe wasn't having it. She quickly jammed the heel of her foot into his leg as hard as she could. Feeling his head drop slightly in reaction to the pain, Zoe shoved her head back into his nose. That was enough to back him off, giving her the chance to step away and address the crowd.

"We are not criminals," Zoe said, clear and determined. "I have proof that Kayla is an innocent pawn in this whole mess. She did not write that message on the lumber mill. Kayla isn't a fan of Heather and her rules, that's not in question. But if you knew her, you'd know that she's a respectful young woman with a tremendously big heart. She may have fought at times to convince others to believe what she did, but she wasn't a true-blue Heather Biter because she would never disrespect what others believed. She has far too great a heart for that flavor of cow pie. And because she didn't do what you all blindly accused her of doing, that means JD and I are innocent as well. We were protecting a friend that we knew was wrongly accused. How does that make us guilty?"

"You have proof?" Henry said, finally bringing the flow of blood from his nose to an end. "Then show it to us."

"You have to take my word," Zoe said, knowing full well that would never fly.

"She has no proof," Henry said, addressing the crowd. "She's stalling, a last ditch effort to free her and her friends. She's trying to convince you that they don't deserve what's coming to them. You can't trust her. She's been lying to you this whole time."

"He's right. I don't think we deserve this. We didn't kill anyone; we didn't rape or harm anyone so severely that it warrants the death of an innocent. Even then, I don't think anyone deserves this." Zoe made a point to focus on the noose around Kayla's neck. "But aside from all of that, every single one of you here today should be ashamed of yourselves. Not just for supporting Henry in this sickening act, but for bringing your wards here to witness it, teaching them that even when someone is falsely accused of a crime, it's okay to write them off, simply to make yourselves feel better. We are on the verge of our next eclipse. Half of you won't even be here to see the ramifications of any of this. This is a time that you should be spending with your families. This is a time to enjoy your love for one another, not display your hatred for someone you're never going to see again. That is not a society I want to be a part of. That is not a community I want to support."

"And we don't want you to be a part of it," Henry said.

"*You* don't," Zoe countered quickly. "*You* don't want me here. I know the root behind all of this and it isn't the words that you pretend to detest so fervently. It's your desire to get rid of the eclipse, to end it once and for all. Am I right?"

Henry didn't answer, so Zoe repeated the question, this time with much more zeal. "Am I right?"

"Yeah, I want to end the eclipse." Henry turned to the crowd to gain as much support as possible. "Isn't that what everyone here wants? To live a longer, more flourishing life?" The crowd cheered in ardent agreement. Zoe's grin never wavered as the crowd's cheers died down.

"That's all well and good," Zoe said, ready to hit her point home. "But let me pose this one simple question. If all of you are so adamant about ending the eclipse, isn't that the exact same thing you're accusing all of us for? Yeah, the wording of that message was harsh and uncalled for, but in the end it meant one thing: we want to live. So if you are seeking the deaths of Kayla, JD and I for wanting to see this curse end, then you are all guilty of the exact same thing and should all be punished for your crimes of blasphemy."

That hushed the crowd straightaway. Even Henry was silenced into a stupor.

"I know how badly we all want to remain with those we love. We all accept the eclipse because that's what we know, but in the end, none of us want to die. Henry is manipulating you all into thinking that Kayla is a bad person who deserves a death that is twice as horrendous as the one most of you will encounter in less time than it takes to make a beautiful, delicious cake. What he hasn't told you is that, just like there is only one way to bake a cake, there is only one way to break this curse, and that's with me. He used that message to frame Kayla in order to draw me out. He never wanted to convict her; he needed a way to convict me, and that was the best possible way to do it."

"Is that true?" came a call from the crowd, followed by several more, each one desperate to know the truth. And even though Zoe knew it wasn't Henry who actually wrote the message, she let it play out that way to help get the crowd on her side for what she was about to do next.

"I didn't write that message," Henry said.

"But you used it to get to me. Which one's worse?"

Henry was speechless, as was the crowd.

"You see? None of this is what it seems to be. Henry used Kayla and Susanna's enormous heart, not to mention most of your private lives, to dig his way into a level of authority that would give him the power to finish me off. I'm here to say that if there is one person who deserves to be sent away from Heather, never to return, it's Henry."

Before the crowd could find its voice again, Zoe continued. "But I don't want that. He only did what he did out of fear. He thought he could do something good for all of you; he just did it in the wrong way. So I'm here to make a deal with him, and with all of you, to help us live as we should be able to live." Zoe turned to Henry. She wanted to look him in the eye when she said this. "I'm here, free of any restraint or regret, to offer myself to Heather's grace and end the curse that has plagued us for far too long. In return for this sacrifice, I ask that you release Kayla, JD and Susanna from these dreadful accusations and let them live free, without any further hardships."

Henry took his time to contemplate the offer. He could have just as easily taken Zoe back into custody and strung her up with the others like the criminal that she was, but he knew better than that. If he was going to stay in power, he would need to keep the crowd on his side; Zoe was doing a terrific job of turning them against him. He may have manipulated everyone into getting what he wanted, but Zoe, it turns out, was just as skilled and crafty as he was. He had to respect her for that.

"I accept," he said and urged Reynold to remove the nooses. After, he untied their hands and removed their masks. Kayla couldn't have been happier than when she saw Zoe and wrapped her arms around her. There were no words she could use to convey her appreciation, except, "I'm sorry."

"Don't be sorry," Zoe whispered.

Kayla released Zoe with a face full of tears. Zoe turned to JD and took his hands—this was what she was waiting for. As she looked him directly in the eye, the love, the desire, the burning in her soul that she once had for him was gone. And she was happy. She leaned up to give him a light kiss on the corner of his mouth. "I'm happy for you," she whispered, then let go of his hands, her eyes burning with panic.

"What is it?" JD said.

"You have to hurry. Winter's water broke some time ago. She needs you."

"I can't leave you here," he said.

"Don't worry about me. Just take care of Winter and her baby. Please."

JD wanted to argue, but knew better of it. He nodded, squeezed Zoe's hand in admiration and confirmation of her acceptance, and jumped from the stage.

"I'll go with you," Susanna said. Part of her wanted to make sure Winter was okay (once a leader, always a leader), the other part just wanted to get as far away from Henry as she could possibly get.

"Go with them," Zoe said to Kayla. She didn't want her to have to witness her death either.

"To hell I will. Zoe, you're my best friend. I'm not about to leave you alone."

Zoe saw her determination and knew that nothing would convince her otherwise. She held Kayla's hands until Henry pulled her away. Kayla reached out to stay with her until the bitter end, but Reynold was quick to pull her off the stage and become just another face in the crowd.

None of that was of any concern to Henry. He was focused on Zoe, tying her hands together and positioning her in the center of the log, all the while remaining extremely cautious. It all seemed far too easy. Zoe let him do everything without even the slightest of opposition, almost gracious for what was to come. As he adjusted the knot of the noose around her neck, the tip of the curtain that would soon cover the sun slid into position. Zoe's chest tightened, but relaxed quickly as she felt her freedom.

"Any final words, Zoe, ward of Frances and Maisy?"

Zoe took a breath. She was ready to remain silent, but the sound of her caretaker's names urged her to say one last thing. "There are two people sitting together in the desert right now, wishing no more than to be in each other's arms when the end arrives. There is a woman giving birth to a child she is happy to lay her eyes on if only for a few seconds. They all couldn't care less about what's going on here, and the turmoil that all of you seem so desperate to enjoy. They never once doubted my resolve, or my courage. They respected my decisions, gave me strength when I felt I had lost everything, and trusted that whatever I chose to do was right, and would defend me no matter what. I not only do this for them, in honor of their selflessness, their devotion to each other and to me, but I do this for you, to show you what kindness and honesty and loyalty truly mean. I may not believe in every choice you've made, but I love you. I love you all because of who you are and what you represent. My family."

"That's enough," Henry said, shoving the mask over Zoe's head. Apparently, her speech had gotten to him.

"We can't let this happen," Kayla screamed. "It's not right."

"If we don't, you'll die," Henry said. "If that's what you want, you might as well get back up here and die alongside your friend."

"Maybe I will. At least then I can die with honor." Kayla was climbing back up on stage before she even finished her statement. If that wasn't shocking enough, what happened next left several people speechless.

"No. Stop." The voice was light and airy (a little too adorable for some) but held a command that was oddly stout. Who it came from was unclear, but everyone was incredibly interested in finding out. Except for Henry, who retied Kayla's hands together. It was a lot easier now than it had been earlier when he had to nearly knock her out to get it done.

"What are you doing?" Zoe said quietly.

"The right thing," Kayla said.

Zoe wasn't sure she believed her. If this worked, Kayla was going to be able to live, and she was willing to give that up—for what? But Zoe kept her mouth shut. For what it was worth, she was happy to have her best friend at her side. As Henry wrapped the noose around Kayla's neck for the second time, Lenny steamrolled across the stage like a little mini freight train and rammed her head into Henry's gut. He was down to one knee in a flat second and couldn't seem to catch his breath. "Stop," Lenny said. "Bad man."

Kayla could barely see her through the joyous tears now streaming down her face. And she wasn't the only one enchanted with delight at hearing Lenny's voice—Catherine and Daniel could hardly move, much less speak. Lenny shifted to Kayla and held her hands tightly.

"What's going on?" Zoe said.

"Come here you little brat," Henry said, fiercely pulling Lenny away from Kayla. Lenny screamed uncontrollably, squirming and jerking around, pounding her head with her hands. Gavin grabbed hold of Terry to keep him from stopping Henry as Reynold went to help him (or perhaps went to help Lenny). Jonas, though, stepped in front of Reynold, commanding his retreat.

Kayla would have smiled, if she wasn't screaming her head off. "Get your hands off of her!"

She wasn't the only one. Daniel yelled the same as he tore his way through the scattering crowd to join Christian up on the stage. Kayla would have done it herself, but any movement now would have resulted in hanging herself. Luckily, Jonas was a step ahead of her. He untied the ropes of each of the girl's hands with the speed of a fisher. After ripping the noose from around her neck and tearing off the mask, Zoe got her first glimpse at Henry gripping Lenny to his chest (despite the constant and erratic kicking, screaming and punching) with a knife to her neck.

"Henry," Kayla cried out. Like he was going to pay any attention to her. Zoe grabbed her before she could jump off the log to charge him, causing her screams to match Lenny's almost perfectly. She slapped Kayla to shut her up and looked her directly in the eyes.

"Calm down," Zoe screamed.

A little shocked (and impressed by Zoe's confident poise), Kayla took a breath. "But we have to stop him."

Before Zoe could think, Terry sent an elbow to Gavin's jaw, sending him to the ground. At that same moment, Jonas urged the girls to stay put (which, especially for Kayla, was a lot harder than it might seem). Zoe wasn't sure if she wanted Terry involved—this was her fight, not his. But the fearlessness in his step as he crept around the stage behind Henry made Zoe believe that this was his burden to bear.

"Let him take care of it," Zoe said.

Every one of Terry's steps was silent and calculated. The other men kept their cool, making sure not to give him away. Only when Terry swiped his hand up under Henry's arm, allowing him to push the knife into the air, did they react. Christian slid in and swept his foot in between Henry's. He twisted his body to knock Henry's knee loose and push him sideways. As he did, Daniel wrapped his arms around Lenny, pulled her into his arms, and ran from the stage. With Lenny's weight gone, Henry got the upper hand on Terry, breaking his nose with his fist, and then put Christian down for the count with a punch to the gut that broke at least two ribs. At that point, the majority of Heather Biters had made their way to the stage to join in on the fun. Jonas didn't hesitate to help them.

That was Zoe's cue. "Come on," she said. She grabbed Kayla's hand and pulled her off the stage. Kayla didn't fight her; knowing Lenny was safe and back with Daniel was enough. Keeping a firm, tight grip on each other's hands, the girls weaved through what little crowd was left, only to have Gavin stop them in their tracks. Blood poured from his mouth and his eyes gleamed with hatred. Zoe didn't know what to do. Luckily, she didn't have to do anything. Before she had a chance to blink, Harper laid Gavin out with one hard knuckle pop to his temple.

Zoe held her breath as Harper stepped up to her. "Take care of her," she said and squeezed Zoe's shoulder.

"I will," Zoe said. "Thank you."

"Get. We'll hold them off."

Zoe wasn't about to argue. Kayla slapped Harper on the shoulder as she was pulled past her. Harper watched them sprint down the road for a second before she joined the rest of the Heather Biters to chase Henry in the opposite direction toward the Circle.

Kayla and Zoe were in the clear for now, but with the sun now eclipsed over halfway, she didn't know if she could make it to where she had to be on the surface. So she pulled Kayla into Gertrude's shop.

"What are you doing?"

Zoe didn't say a word until they were in the basement. "If I'm going to end this curse, I have to sacrifice myself at the apex of the eclipse. It doesn't give us much time." Janette hadn't replaced the boards or the tray rack, so sliding back into the hole was a piece of cake. Kayla followed, but not nearly as easily as Zoe. When Kayla was back on her feet, Zoe was waiting with her eyes closed as if she were meditating.

"Wow," Kayla said. "Okay, I get it now. You're going to suffocate yourself in this hole." Kayla bounced her shirt against her chest, attempting to cool herself down.

"That would take too long. There's only one place I know that I can do what needs to be done."

Kayla's eyes went wide. "Death Rock."

Zoe didn't need to say anything more, even though the light from the rocks barely highlighted her features. Kayla nodded. "How do you know this will take us there?"

"I know." She opened her eyes and pulled Kayla through the tunnels with a true foot, as fast as their legs could carry them (and their lungs could handle).

The forest surrounded them as they climbed from the hatch. The cool air against their skin was more refreshing than if a bucket of ice-cold water had spilled over them after sitting under the sun for hours on the hottest day of the year. A mile away was Death

Rock. By the time they reached it, Kayla was spent. Her legs burned like a raging fire and her lungs weren't much better. She dropped to the ground at the edge of the pit.

"You know what this means?" Zoe said.

"Times up?"

"I have to put you out of your misery, you speed demon."

Kayla laughed (or coughed and gagged in an attempt to laugh). "Don't worry, you're off the hook. The eclipse is about ready to do that anyway." She pointed up at the sky. The shroud of darkness was nearing its completion.

"Not if I can help it." Zoe stood at the edge of the pit. She looked down, feeling the pain, fear and misery trying to claw its way out—and she waited.

"Are you sure this is going to work?"

"Not in the slightest."

"It's been a fun ride."

"It sure has."

"Here's to making a difference." Kayla stood up (even though her knees screamed not to) and held Zoe as tight as she could in an embrace that would ignite the darkness of the eclipse. Just then, a bright light shot from the flares of the eclipse, forming a waterfall that dripped to the ground somewhere in the desert. Zoe was shocked and awed by what she saw.

"What is that?" Kayla said.

"It's our answer," Zoe said. She turned to Kayla. "In the light of the eclipse."

"Is that what that meant?"

"It has to be. Kayla, I need to get to that light."

"Yeah, of course. Let's go."

"No," Zoe said, stopping Kayla cold. "You need to stay here. Henry no doubt will use the tunnels just like I did to get here. You need to stop him from coming after me."

Kayla didn't want to, but she nodded.

"Thank you." Zoe hugged her friend for the last time.

"You don't have much time."

Zoe grabbed Kayla's face with both hands. "Take care of him, okay?"

"I promise."

Zoe smiled, knowing that unlike so many others that dripped from her lips, this promise would never be broken.

32

Inside Death Rock

" **W**here is she?" Henry's voice was gruff with antagonism.

Kayla sat up. She had lied down after Zoe left, the burn still coursing her body. She must have slipped off to sleep because she didn't even hear him come up to her. If she had, it wasn't a long nap. The eclipse was still in full bloom and the stream of light showed as bright as ever.

Kayla stepped between him and the light. "None of your business, Henry."

"It is my business, Kayla. I am the quorum headmaster. I demand to know."

"You're going to have to kill me first."

"With pleasure." Henry grabbed a hold of Kayla's neck and forced her to the pit. She screamed and squirmed to get free but it was all for naught. Even with all the damage that had been inflicted on him, Henry was still twice as strong as Kayla ever would be. But before he could reach the pit, he caught sight of Brittany standing at its edge—or was she? He could see her, could feel her, but it didn't seem as if she was really there at all.

"Out of my way," he said. "I've got some unfinished business."

"I'm afraid I can't allow that. You've done enough damage."

Kayla stopped squirming. With Brittany here, she no longer felt she had anything to worry about.

"What do you know about it?"

"I see everything, even that which you believe is unseen."

"What are you talking about? What do you mean unseen?"

"Your heart has lost its way, my dear Henry, and I regret not being able to have done anything to keep it from blackening so."

"I don't know who you are," Henry said, "but if you don't get out of my way, I have no problem sending you down the pit with a Kayla chaser."

"It would be my pleasure. I have failed you, and in that failure, I deserve whatever retribution you feel is worthy. Come, I beg of you."

Henry now suspected what Kayla knew to be true. Brittany wasn't a resident of Heather come back to help stop the eclipse—she was Heather, but how that was possible was way out of his ability to comprehend. He was completely unable to accept it because he was unable to believe it. Brittany was right when she said that Henry's heart had been blackened, and Kayla couldn't help but wonder if it was her fault, in a way. He once loved Heather in all of her glory, just as he once loved Kayla. For rejecting him so frequently, Kayla believed she had, in some small part, caused him to turn against her. So much so that he could no longer see anything clearly. All he could see was hate, and his eyes burned with it as he stared at Brittany.

"One last chance," he said. All Brittany did was raise her arms away from her body and push her chin to the sky.

"So be it." Henry let go of Kayla (who dropped to her knees and could do nothing but watch) and stomped toward Brittany, more than ready to give her a nice hard shove into the pit. But as his hands touched her shoulders, all he received was a shock, showing him lives that Heather had witnessed across every generation. It flooded him so fast that he couldn't ingest it all without releasing a scream full of terror—the culmination of regret, guilt, pain and sorrow. When it was through, Brittany spun around to his side, grabbed the back of his neck and forced him to his knees at the edge of the pit. His tears dropped into the hole and even Kayla could hear them hit the ground.

"Smell that," Brittany said. "That is the stench of innocence lost. Not because anyone has ever been sentenced to death here, but because this is where my soul resides. I have been trapped here, along with every single soul that has ever been taken by the eclipse, waiting and hoping that some day, we could find peace within the light. Death should never be at the hands of violence, for this is what happens when it does. Take it in and know that I will always love you as one of my children, even when you have strayed so far from the goodness of your heart. I will never give up on you. I forgive you all your transgressions and I await your return to my side, however long that might take."

Brittany let go of Henry and stepped back. Henry fell into a giant heap near the edge of the pit and cried for what would turn out to be days.

"Hærothestî," Kayla whispered.

Brittany turned to her. Without warning, she fell to the ground and started convulsing dramatically. She grabbed her chest and dug her fingernails into her skin as if she was trying to pull her heart from it. Kayla slid over to her to help, but any attempt at prying her hand away just made Brittany dig even deeper than before. It wasn't until she realized that this had everything to do with the eclipse that she knew there was absolutely nothing she could do. It was all up to Zoe now.

33

In the Light of the Eclipse

The shock wave that exploded from the base of the light blew Zoe back several feet. She thought at first that it was a reaction to her proximity (as if it had a mind of its own, which initially did seem rather silly), but as she picked herself back up and really listened to the essence of the wave itself, she realized it wasn't a silly idea at all. The wave, in fact, was alive in its own organic way and was laying the foundation to reach out and steal its fresh new bounty of souls. Upon its impression on her, she now knew how much time she had (and it was not at all enough). If she was going to make it in time, Zoe was going to have to run faster than she had ever run before; she was going to have to run until her heart exploded; she was going to have to run until if felt as if she was on a cloud.

And in a miracle of all miracles, she was able to do just that.

The intensity brought about by the stream of light had faded quite a bit when she did finally reach it, but it was still bright enough to blind a blind man. Funnily enough, Zoe could look right into it without the need to squint or shade her eyes and could see it continue to fade with each new generation (though she wondered if it was just her eyes focusing and adjusting). It was now or never, and for whatever the reason, she couldn't have felt more prepared. She stepped right up onto its edge and touched it with the tip of her fingers. There was no way to describe what she felt, but if she were to quantify it, she would have guessed it was pure, untainted love. It was a connection from every little grain of sand to the largest of all philosophical ruminations. Nothing was left untouched inside this light and the urge to absorb it all was intoxicating.

"This is my gift," Zoe whispered and stepped into the light. Immediately, it was as if everything had disappeared. There was no sound; there was no taste; there was no smell, sight or touch. It was everything and nothing, the beginning and the end—and Zoe was its core.

At first, she was unable to comprehend what she was meant to do (her thoughts all but empty). If she didn't know any better, it felt as if the light was drugging her, hindering any progress by leaving her numb, without a care for anyone or anything except the need to continue to feed from it. But as she steadily focused on the rhythmic beat of her heart, she felt the sweet acceptance of a couple who never strayed from one another, the fright of a child praying for more time, a group of kids lost in the dark heat of the land, and the pain of a man so confused and hurt by what he had done (and the desire to end his life), the journey he was bound to follow was still just a figment of his imagination. She heard the soft cry of a child—a newborn baby feeling the light nip of the air for the first time. She felt the joy of a mother, holding her child as her companion kissed her gently in elation. Friends and well-wishers sitting next to her, watching in joy at the union, giving their blessings for a long life, if only in the quiet of their own minds. She felt the pain of a young man, confused by the love he wanted to express, but was only able to hide. Sinking into his mind, she could sense the need to be with her, to feel her and love her in a way that he always wanted, but was afraid to convey. Guiding his actions, Zoe pushed him to his feet and from the house. He didn't know why but his urge to see her grew with the dark of the shadowed light. It was time to make it right.

On the opposite side of Heather sat a girl, crying for a friend who would forever be lost and for a woman she would never get to know. Her heart gripped to the fear of losing everything she'd ever known without the possibility of freeing itself. But it was possible, if she allowed it to be. In that moment—in the tears she shed—she would stand tall and hunt for the answer she desperately wanted. But to get there faster than light, she would need to cross the threshold of a world she still believed to be off-limits. It was only with the trust of Zoe's touch (and in the whisper of her blessing) that she found the courage to step across the boundary. The lightness of her body carried her to her future.

When she arrived at Lover's Pond, unaware of why she was there but knowing it had somehow called to her, she found the man, he himself confused by his step. The moment their eyes locked upon one another, they knew—they wanted and needed the touch of the other. They sprinted together, flying across the land with the lightest of feet, unaware of anything but who they were and that they were meant to be as one. Crossing from either side of the bridge, they fell into one another, embracing their souls as much as their bodies, and kissed with the magnetic fruit of Zoe's heart.

"I love you," Kayla said without thinking.

"I love you, too," JD said as if it was the most natural instinct of mankind.

They kissed again, and in that kiss, every emotion from every person flooded into Zoe and encased her in a shell of vitality and truth. She turned her body until she could feel the community in front of her and collected every thought, every emotion, every small nuance of every resident. It lifted her up above the ground, spinning it all around her until she couldn't move, cocooned in the world she would be a part of for the rest of existence. The burn scratched at her body but she couldn't do any more until she found that one last piece—that one key that would allow her to unlock it all.

That key lay protected in a battle between mind over muscle. As Brittany fought to keep the seizure from completely destroying her nervous system, her will remained strong and diligent. Zoe reached out for her and caressed her soul with the gentle touch of a true love. With that touch, the magnetism of their shared bond of humanity exploded in a flash of light that shot up the funnel and into the heart of the eclipse.

It was a struggle to keep from giving up as the eclipse continued to resist her. But in the rock-solid bond of affection, Zoe found the strength and courage to push on. The dress ripped and fell to her legs, fusing with her skin until they were no longer legs at all, but a fin that gave her the ability to swim up that funnel. Halfway to the apex of the eclipse, she focused all of her attention on the manor and set the attic ablaze, a spark that ignited the shock wave in Quorum Circle. The energy of heat ripped right through the boundary wall, blasting the whole thing to dust particles in seconds. Zoe smiled; there would be no more secrets under her watch.

By the time she reached the center of the darkness, she had just enough energy left to shatter the eclipse into a blaze of sunlight that washed over the land of Heather with a spirit of generosity and kindness like no other before it. And as the sparks of the old flashed away into a bright, new tomorrow, everyone shared in Zoe's whisper.

I am your love.

34

The Aftermath

Kayla and JD, holding each other tightly, shaded their eyes from the bright return of the sun. Upon the whisper of the wind

(*I am your love*)

Kayla settled her head into his chest and cried. JD kissed her and held her, unable to find any words to console her. He didn't need any; his touch was enough to guide her thoughts. She held her hands tightly over her chest, feeling that if she let go, the tenderness she felt might somehow escape, or else Zoe would be forgotten. Neither was true, but she wasn't ready to take that chance. She knew that Zoe had succeeded the way she always hoped (and deep down, knew without a doubt) she would. She was just sorry she had to say goodbye for it to happen. But that was wrong—she didn't have to say goodbye; she just had to remember, and give her heart to the man that gave her his. When she finally felt ready, Kayla stepped away. "There's someone I need to check on," she said lightly.

"I should do the same," JD answered. They kissed and departed.

When Kayla got back to Death Rock, Brittany had stopped convulsing and lay flat on her back. Kayla wondered if she had died. Now that Zoe had all but taken over as the watchful eye of Heather, it seemed most obvious that Hærothestî was able to return home. But inside those thoughts lay a small inkling of what really was. When she sat still and listened—I mean, really listened—she understood that, although her mother had invited her back home with honor and dignity, Hærothestî couldn't accept it because her home was here with her people, with her family; with her new and ever-loving daughter. It brought tears to her eyes as she felt the souls of thousands of men and women rise up from within the pit, free of the darkness that had haunted and pained their existence for far too long.

When it had ended, Kayla dragged the shell of Brittany's body to the edge of the pit. There, she gave her a gentle kiss and whispered a song that no one shall ever know (and that included Henry, who was still lost in his own mind to notice). She then rolled the body into the depths of the pit and pushed the rock over the top of it (which was a lot easier than she had expected; the rock was so light, it was as if she was pushing a balloon across the sky). Once in place, she stood over Henry's debilitating body. She thought for a moment to say something to him, but there was nothing she had to say. In time she would forgive him, as she learned her lesson (and could feel its value coursing her veins), but for now, she would let him be. When they both were ready, she would not hesitate.

It took her until the sun had all but vanished behind the desert to make her way to Winter's home, being constantly stopped and congratulated, or given condolences from the exuberance of the crowd continuing the party from the night before. Explaining what happened to Maisy and Frances was probably the worst stop of all, and not just because she had to deliver such devastating news to one of the most loving couples she knew. She had run through Pasture Ranch earlier, but she never felt like she was in control then. Now that she was, sucking up the courage once again was much harder. In the end, she figured since she didn't combust into flame the first time, it must be safe. She stepped gently into Pasture Ranch (her fingers curled in tight fists that bled white along her skin, her breaths deep and heavy) and with each consecutive step, Kayla became much more relaxed. Maybe it was because of Zoe, or maybe it was because she realized that it was man (not Heather) who made the land sacred for reasons that would never be known. Either way (or in tandem), Kayla felt she was welcomed there, and always would be.

As she walked up the porch of Zoe's house to knock at the door, she wondered what fun her and Zoe might have had if she wouldn't have been so scared in the first place. The pleasantness of those thoughts died quickly as the door opened and Kayla spilled her words with tears. Maisy dropped to her knees to cry, both in pain for losing Zoe and in knowing that she was where she needed to be; that Zoe gave everyone the best gift anyone could bestow. Leaving was hard, but with a hug of thanks, Kayla knew they would be okay in time and would welcome her home whenever she wished.

After that, Kayla sought out Lenny (and in turn, Catherine and Daniel) to let them know she was okay and that she was not angry with them in the least for what they had done to her (or for what they didn't do for her). She loved them and would always love them. In return, they apologized for believing she would do such a thing, even though it wasn't at all necessary.

Before she left, Lenny urged her to kneel down so that she might give her what Kayla suspected was a hug or a kiss. What Kayla received was far better.

Lenny handed her one of her notebooks bookmarked with a flower from the tongue. The page it opened up to had "Little Snow-White" written at the top.

"I love you," Lenny said.

To say there were tears would be underrated. She hugged her little sister with all of her might, knowing that the words weren't only coming from her.

When she knocked at Winter's door, JD and Susanna were both still waiting for her. Winter was in high spirits, breastfeeding her child with Jack asleep at her side.

"What's her name?" Kayla asked politely.

"Angel," Winter said with a glint of admiration.

"There is no better name than that," Kayla said and kissed JD.

Susanna remained to watch Winter over night so that JD and Kayla could be alone. But neither of them wanted to return home; it didn't feel right. So they returned to the cave at triangle point, where Zoe's presence was at its strongest. They lay together again to become one with not just themselves, but with the friend that they had to leave behind.

That night, Kayla woke up in a cold sweat. A dream, one that Kayla couldn't wrap her head around, chilled her body. But as she caught her breath and let her mind settle, she finally understood.

"What's wrong?" JD said, rubbing his hand across the small of her back.

"Just a dream," Kayla said and gently rested her head on JD's chest with an everlasting smile upon her lips.

ABOUT THE AUTHOR

BRYAN CARON is a multi-talented, award-winning artist with works in several mediums, including print, film and design. After acquiring a bachelor's degree in creative writing and an associate's degree in computer graphic design, Bryan studied filmmaking and film editing while working at a performing arts studio in San Diego, California. He took this knowledge to write, direct and edit films under his banner, Divine Trinity Films. Soon after, he would team up with the Fallbrook Film Factory, a non-profit film consortium, to continue his growth in the areas of writing, directing and editing, all the while fleshing out his talents in fiction writing (publishing *Year of the Songbird* and *Jaxxa Rakala: The Search* in 2013), working as a graphic designer, and beginning his first blog: Chaos breeds Chaos.

His works as writer and director include the short films *My Necklace, Myself* (Best Screenplay, Short Film, 2009 Treasure Coast International Film Festival) and *12*, the feature film *Secrets of the Desert Nymph*, and the commercial *Charlie's Ticket,* which ran on dozens of television stations and in movie theaters in San Diego County to advertise the Fallbrook International Film Festival. Works as editor include the short film *Puzzle Box* and *No Books*, the first of several episodes he has edited for the online sketch-series, *Treelore Theatre*.

Bryan currently resides in Riverside County.

www.divinetrinityfilms.com
chaosbreedschaos.com

www.ingramcontent.com/pod-product-compliance
Lightning Source LLC
Chambersburg PA
CBHW061129200626
46817CB00016B/463

* 9 7 8 0 9 8 8 9 4 4 3 2 9 *